It's YOU Every TIME

Also by Charlene Thomas

Seton Girls

Streetlight People

It's YOU Every TIME

CHARLENE THOMAS

SCHOLASTIC INC.

> Content Notice:
> This book is a work of fiction but discusses many real-world topics, including drowning, death, and grief.

If you purchased this book without a cover, you should be aware that this book is stolen property. It was reported as "unsold and destroyed" to the publisher, and neither the author nor the publisher has received any payment for this "stripped book."

Copyright © 2025 by Charlene Thomas

All rights reserved. Published by Scholastic Inc., *Publishers since 1920.* SCHOLASTIC and associated logos are trademarks and/or registered trademarks of Scholastic Inc.

The publisher does not have any control over and does not assume any responsibility for author or third-party websites or their content.

No part of this publication may be reproduced, stored in a retrieval system, or transmitted in any form or by any means, electronic, mechanical, photocopying, recording, or otherwise, or used to train any artificial intelligence technologies, without written permission of the publisher. For information regarding permission, write to Scholastic Inc., Attention: Permissions Department, 557 Broadway, New York, NY 10012.

This book is a work of fiction. Names, characters, places, and incidents are either the product of the author's imagination or are used fictitiously, and any resemblance to actual persons, living or dead, business establishments, events, or locales is entirely coincidental.

ISBN 978-1-5461-1178-8

10 9 8 7 6 5 4 3 2 1   25 26 27 28 29

Printed in the U.S.A.   40

First printing 2025

Book design by Maithili Joshi

For the broken hearts still beating

October 17, Two Years Earlier

Sometimes, the universe gives us exactly who we need, for as long as we need—but rarely is it as long as we would like.

Part One:

Sydney

September 24: 8:17 a.m.

"*Please, please, please, please, please—*" I tap my phone screen over and over, the same woodpecker pace Dad uses when he's pressing his pointer into my temple. *Think, Syd*, he always says, as if that's gonna help. As if I'm just selectively *not thinking*.

I inch forward in this Dunkin' line while the video on my phone stays stuck. I tap the screen harder, right on top of Mr. Wilson's frozen, ecstatic face. He's basically Santa Claus when it comes to talking about precalc. I'd chop off my thumb to have anything on earth make me as happy as logarithmic functions make him.

A man bumps my shoulder as he squeezes past, his coffee in tow as he heads through the crowd and back to the main door. It's an accident—not the kind of thing you post about or shout over. Dunkin' is packed this morning, but people are so unfazed by it that I guess it's always this way. I'm the outlier, really; the one who's not supposed to be here, evidenced by the fact that I keep standing just-enough-in-the-way to get knocked around like a pinball. I know I'm running out of time, that I'm hemorrhaging minutes I don't even have, but I figure if I'm gonna go to school and bomb another precalc test, and devastate Mom and Dad yet again, I might as well do it with Dunkin'.

I step forward in line and go back to tapping my screen. Mr. Wilson's face is at least sputtering along now, his glitching voice fighting to reach me through my earbuds. God, I wish this stream would load. Listening to him reteach yesterday's lesson on his *Math Is Great* YouTube channel has the same calming effect as closing my eyes right before they stick me at the doctor. Like, yeah, this will hurt, but at least I'm trying to do what I can to make it hurt a little less.

The woman in front of me steps aside and the one behind the counter blinks at me under the visor of her pink-and-brown hat. Early twenties probably. Long, black hair. Dark, pretty eyes. "Would you like to try a dozen Munchkins this morning?" she flatly asks.

"Oh . . ." I pull a bud out of my ear. "No, thank you."

"Okay. What can I get you?"

"Um, can I have the sausage, egg, and cheese croissant, please? Just without the sausage. Or egg."

She squints at me, her fingers hovering over her iPad. "Sorry?"

"Uh, yeah." I force a smile. That helps, sometimes. Convinces people I'm not doing some TikTok challenge they haven't seen yet, or that I haven't completely lost it. "Sausage, egg, and cheese croissant, please. Without egg or sausage."

"So just cheese," she concludes. "On a croissant."

"Yes," I agree.

"So, a grilled cheese."

"Yes! Thanks." I pull a five-dollar bill from the pocket of my oversized cardigan and hand it to her. She frowns as she concocts my order on her screen. When she finishes, she hands me two dollars in change, which is nice. Sometimes I get change; sometimes I don't. There's no set price for an order that doesn't actually exist. Honestly, I just imagine them typing onto their iPad, *Some chick wants cheese for breakfast, can we do that?* and sending it to the kitchen to see what happens.

I step aside and slip my earbuds back into my ears.

Cell service is a little bit better by the window, now that I've squeezed into an open space between two men on their phones. I slide my backpack off my shoulder and guard it between my ankles. Mr. Wilson's voice smooths out again and my screen stops buffering.

I sigh, relieved.

"Now," he says excitedly. *"Let's talk about matrices!"*

I sigh, depressed.

Close your eyes. Get through this. It'll just be a pinch . . .

Someone bumps me again. I scoot closer to the window.

The people in here are a mix of everything. Older, younger. Business-suited and delivery guys. Women in heels and others on their way back from some intense early morning workout (or, at least, dressed like they are). There are plenty I'd be willing to trade with. Trade lives, I mean. This dumb game my brother Sebastian and I used to play when we were growing up—where we'd see strangers and imagine their entire lives, where they were going and who they knew, their biggest fears and favorite colors. I Bet, we used to call it.

Like that girl in the middle of the line right now, in boyfriend jeans and a gray sweater, and a canvas tote bag that looks recyclable and has a black sketch of a duck on it. I bet she's nineteen, and I bet she's picking up coffee before she goes back to the apartment on 59th and Lex that her parents used to live in until they moved to Greenwich and gave it to her. I bet she has an easel set up next to her window and draws pictures of the city, and the world, and the people who don't realize she's watching them. I bet she sells her work on Etsy and promotes her shop on Instagram. I bet her name is Lilly, or Riley, or Abbey . . . something that goes *ee* at the end. I bet she's completely ready for the day she's about to have, for the entire *life* she's about to have.

I'd trade with her.

"And do you know what the greatest thing about matrices is . . . ?"

Oops. Right. Matrices.

"Order number two," a voice calls out, I'm pretty sure. I pull my earbuds from one side and listen again. "Number two . . ."

The giant number stares back at me from my receipt. Two.

I slide through the crowd of bodies, Mr. Wilson's voice in one ear and the sounds of Dunkin'-during-the-morning-rush echoing in the other. I excuse myself each time I bump someone, but no one seems to hear me, or they don't think I deserve a reaction.

I reach the counter and grab the paper bag with my receipt stapled on it. "Thanks!" I call to no one in particular and unroll my bag to peek inside. It's a sandwich, for sure. So, I guess I'm out of here. But there's a bowling ball in my stomach now that there's nothing left to do before I get to school. Failing—when you care, and when you really, really try—is a whole different kind of torture.

I know I have to step away from this counter. It's only been three seconds, but arms are reaching around me for their orders like I'm being swallowed by an octopus. I close my eyes, and turn around, and take a breath before this gets extra stupid. I'm not about to cry over math. Again.

"Ouch!" My phone hits the floor. I'm more shocked than hurt. It's the first truly direct hit I've taken since I walked into this combat zone.

"Whoa, are you okay?" the someone-I-collided-with says.

"I'm so sorry." My hot embarrassment creeps up my neck as I bend over to grab my phone.

"No, no, that was all me," he insists. "They called my order and I'm about five minutes away from being so late that I might as well just fake a coma for sympathy, so I was hauling ass. Are you good? Is your phone okay?"

I put Mr. Wilson on pause and shove my phone into my backpack. "It's totally fine. It's OtterBoxed and screen protected. I could throw this thing off the Queensboro and just dust it off." I zip my bag closed.

"Wow, does NASA know about that phone?" he asks.

My laugh stays stuck in the back of my throat. I was fully preparing to avoid eye contact while I rushed out of here as fast as possible, but his joke cools my neck off just enough for me to steal a glance. He's *tall*. Not neckbreaking, but neck bending, for sure. Brown eyes with flecks of hazel in them. Brown skin the shade of my own, but smooth in a way that's godsent.

I bet he never breaks out and his nose never gets oily, for the whole sixteen or seventeen years that I bet he's been alive. I bet he plays basketball wherever he goes to school. I bet it's somewhere private, since he's in dress pants and a collared shirt, tucked away under a black hooded sweatshirt. I bet he takes the C train home and gets off somewhere between 81st and 125th. I bet he'll go to college on scholarship, nearby but not in the city. Like Rutgers. I bet he's good at math and I bet he has a million girls killing themselves just to breathe the same air as him—

The girl with the duck bag slides between us, smiling sweetly at us both. It's giving *Sorry, but you're blocking traffic*. And yeah, we really are.

But he's watching me back, the longest I can ever remember looking at someone who's looking at me, too. Me, in my patterned black tights, black skater dress, ballerina flats, and cream cardigan. If he's guessing about who I am, what I love, what I do—I'm sure he's wrong. People always think I'm something I'm not. Something Ivy-bound, like Sebastian. Something intellectual, like Mom. Something distinguished, like Dad.

Nope, no, and not at all.

"So." He clears his throat. "Order number two?" The receipt on my bag is facing his direction. He shows me the receipt in his hand. "Same."

"Hm . . ." I hold our receipts next to each other, his warm and crinkled from the time it spent in his pocket or maybe in his palm. Wistfully, I marvel, "Inexplicable . . ."

He strokes his chin and turns on this voice like one of those old-school detectives with a monocle. "Every morning I'm at this Dunkin', and this morning my number exists twice. The question is *why* . . ."

I smile and push my backpack farther up on my shoulder. "Well, I'm never here. So, it's probably my fault."

But he shakes his head, frowns a little as he promises me, "If there's a problem, I'm it. Trust me."

He brushes past me to the counter and rests his hands on the surface. No cologne, just a whiff of minty mouthwash and spiced deodorant.

"Ma'am?" he asks. The woman who's been shuffling back and forth, setting orders out as they're ready, stops and raises her eyebrows. "Sorry," he apologizes. "I know it's like playoff tickets just went on sale in here. It's just that we both have the same order number, and we weren't really sure what to do about that."

I set my paper bag on the counter and he sets his receipt next to it. Evidence. She looks at the receipts and then back at us. "And you two aren't together?"

"Nope," he answers as I get bumped by someone else. "Complete strangers."

I nudge him. "Just because I never texted you back doesn't make us *strangers*."

He bites back a smile, his fingers picking at the chipping edge of the countertop. A comment I'm surprised I made and relieved he liked. "That never happened," he explains to the woman, even though she definitely doesn't care.

"What'd you order?" she asks me.

"Oh, um." I step a little closer so she can hear me better. "I got a sausage, egg, and cheese croissant? With no sausage. Or egg."

From the corner of my eye, he smirks.

"And you?" the woman asks him next.

"Sausage, egg, and cheese with no cheese," he answers. "I guess if you put the two of us together, we'd be a normal sandwich."

But half the West Side is crammed in this Dunkin' and she doesn't have time for our dumb jokes or his cute grin. She unwraps the sandwich in my bag and says, "Alright, this one is the sausage and egg." She rewraps the sandwich, shoves it back in the bag, and hands it to him instead of me. "This one might be you." She reaches for another paper bag among the stacks of paper bags piling up on the counter. Stamped with a number two even though I swear they never called that number twice.

She pulls out another sandwich, unwraps it, and confirms. "Yep, just cheese." She stuffs the sandwich back in the bag and pushes it my way. "All set?"

Our voices weave around each other's as we thank her—"You're the best." "Yep, perfect!" "Sorry about that." "Thanks!"—but she's already walking away, calling out the next number. "Nineteen!"

A guy with a soft cooler labeled GRUBHUB holds the door open for us while the bell jingles above our heads. We step onto the overcrowded sidewalk, standing as close as we can to Dunkin' as people rush past and cars fly by.

"Well." I cup my eyes from the sun. "Thanks for preventing the greatest tragedy that might have ever existed."

"Ordering a sandwich with nothing but cheese and biting

into one that's everything *except* cheese?" He shudders. "Wouldn't wish that on my worst enemy." Then he adds, "I'm Marcus, by the way."

Marcus. It's the first time I've ever learned something real about someone I played I Bet with.

"Sydney," I say back. "But my friends call me Syd—*so you shouldn't.*"

"*So I shouldn't.*"

We say it the exact same time.

I laugh and so does he—not the ha-ha kind but the huh-that's-interesting kind. I'm pretty sure I've never said that to anyone before, and we managed to do it together like we were rehearsed.

"You're late," I remind him, even though a part of me doesn't want to.

"Yeah." His mouth twists like he doesn't want to think about it, but he reaches into the big pocket in the front of his sweatshirt and pulls out his phone, anyway. He checks the time. "Late enough to be in that coma now, though."

"I'm sorry." And I mean it. It was our drama that held him up. "I could shove you in front of a bus so you can play the sympathy card?"

He chuckles and glances down as he slides his phone back into his sweatshirt. He's muttering, but I hear him, anyway: "Wow, you'd do that for me and we're not even friends?" He lifts his gaze to look at me.

I look at him, too, even though it's probably weird. There's something about his face—and his smile, and the way that bowling ball

I swallowed inside Dunkin' isn't weighing me down anymore—that makes it feel like I was always supposed to look at him, at least once, at least for a second, at least for a single moment out of all the other moments in my life.

It has to be almost 8:30 a.m. The first bell is at 8:42. I still have six blocks before I'm at my school, and if I'm late for first period, the rules say Mr. Wilson isn't allowed to let me take that test even if I beg. And I can't take a zero. My C minus can't survive a zero.

So, I'm gonna go. I'm gonna leave whatever this is behind, and turn Mr. Wilson's YouTube channel back on, and count my steps as I take them because sometimes that reminds me I'm actually going somewhere. Not just down the block, or to school, but eventually somewhere even farther than that. Somewhere in this city or maybe nowhere close. But still. Somewhere.

I wait for Marcus to say bye first.

He's peering across the street at nothing, I'm pretty sure. When he turns back to me, it's like he's finally made a decision that I never realized he was considering. "You wanna go sit somewhere? Eat?"

His question hangs between us. Mom and Dad—their questions are so much harder. What are they gonna do with me? How am I ever gonna follow Sebastian's footsteps to Corinthia University if I can't even pass on-level math? How am I gonna go into medicine like the rest of them did when numbers might as well be hieroglyphics to me? How am I ever gonna have a future, and a purpose, and my own freaking apartment? How am I ever gonna be anything at all?

God, I hate that question: *How?* Marcus's just seems so much easier.

The thing about being absent instead of being late is that a sick note means Mr. Wilson can still let me take this test tomorrow.

That's why I tell Marcus, "Sure, I have time."

September 24: 9:43 a.m.

I had no idea there's a dog park on 52nd and 11th. It's only a ten-minute walk from school, but I'm never this far west. Almost like he knew it, Marcus led us down 11th instead of the route I would have taken—down to 52nd and then heading this way.

It's different over here. The sidewalks are wider. It's quieter—open parking spots along the curb and everything. I've always wanted to be the kind of girl who can sit on a bench and read outside, swept off to a world a hundred pages away. But the noise always distracts me, the voices and the horns. I could read here, though. I could close my eyes and be anywhere.

"Yo, Dixon, what's going on?" Marcus leans forward on our bench, at home from the moment we got to this park. The fluffy black dog—*Dixon*, I guess—wriggles at his feet. One of those poodles, or doodles, or dogs that end in *poo*. He barely comes up to midcalf while Marcus scratches him all over. "You want to say hey to him? He's nice."

Marcus's smile is addictive up close. Not the one he laughs with—even though that one's really good, too—but the one his lips naturally curve into when he turns to me like he is right now.

"You say all these dogs are nice." I lean on my knees while Dixon runs figure eights around Marcus's feet. This has to be the tenth dog that's been obsessed with him since we sat down, and he's known every one of them by name.

I hold my hand out for Dixon to sniff, palm open while he figures me out with a bunch of nose nudges and licks.

"What's up, Mr. Parker?" Marcus calls after a few seconds.

I peek up to see who he's talking to. A man on the bench on the other side of this small, asphalt lot smiles and waves. Both the gestures a little delayed. Everyone here is pretty old and pretty slow.

Marcus leans in close and whispers, "He's Dixon's dad."

I smile and wave at Mr. Parker, too, while Dixon trots away. I turn back to Marcus as I sit back against the bench. "How many times have you been here?"

"A few," he says. "A few" to him could be "hardly ever" to me. Or, judging by his fan club, the exact opposite. "They have dogs. I like dogs." He shrugs. "It works out."

My phone vibrates against my foot. I kind of want to ignore it, but seeing as how I've blown off my entire life today, it may be something I really need to know. "Sorry," I mutter as I reach into my backpack.

"You're good," he promises.

I pull my phone out of the side pocket. The lock screen is Sebastian and me at the beach ten years ago, and a notification that I have a new text from Jacq stretches across our eyes like we're wearing Viper shades.

She sends me another message as I open the first.

> Ummmm

>

> Whereabouts???

Jacq isn't in precalc with me—she passed it two years ago—but it's after 9:30 so I guess I've been MIA long enough for her to officially determine I'm not where I should be, and she's never not gotten a heads-up if she wasn't the one skipping with me. If Jacq decides I'm potentially abducted or I choked alone on toothpaste in the bathroom this morning, she's one hundred percent calling my parents. She's never done it before, but we watch way too much crime TV to wait the twenty-four-hour missing person window before launching a search party.

> I'm alive. Totally fine. Just scared of precalc. Call you tonight xo

I drop my phone into one of the oversized pockets of my slouchy cardigan.

The sun makes stripes on Marcus's face as it shines through the red-and-orange leaves. I wonder who's texting him, worried about where he is. I bet he has a team full of guys who've noticed he's missing. I bet they have a group chat where they mostly send memes but, to them, it's an entire conversation. I bet his iPhone is three models old, not because it has to be but because he doesn't really care. I bet he's the type to save numbers by first name only, and he probably has ten Mikes and another ten Megans.

"That was Jacq," I tell him. "My best friend. She's just making sure I still exist since I should be busy failing precalc right now."

He winces. "I'm not sure whether to say 'I'm sorry' or 'you're welcome.'"

I'm not sure which one is right, either. "What about you? What are you blowing off today? School? Private school?" I glance down his long, slender-but-not-too-skinny frame. "I'm going off the uniform."

"Oh." He dusts off his dress pants like he forgot he had them on. "No, not a uniform. Picture day. My mom cares." His mouth twists like he hopes I won't judge him for it.

"That's cute," I tell him, but he frowns and I laugh. "What?"

"You said 'cute' like little-kid cute."

"What, you want me to say 'cute' like Michael B. Jordan cute?"

"Michael B. Jordan?" he exclaims, eyebrows shooting halfway up his forehead. A dog we already said hi to runs back over to make sure he's okay. "*Wakanda Forever* Michael B. Jordan," Marcus goes on. He rubs the dog—a beagle-looking thing—behind its ears but he keeps his warm gaze on me. Amused and sort of terrified at the same time. "That's the bar?"

I laugh while this sweet dog dances around my feet, and a breeze blows, and Marcus waits on me with that smile that's so, so good.

"Do you want to play a game?" he finally says now that it's taken me too long to stop giggling, and I can tell by the tone of his voice that he's changing the subject.

"What game?" I swallow my last laugh, but my smile stays.

He bites back his own grin and nods to himself like he's making a note to get me back for that someday, somehow. "It's called Sixty Minutes." He gives the dog at our feet a few final pats and sends him back off to play. "You know the show? They cover so much ground in sixty minutes. Let's see how much we can get done in the same amount of time."

"An hour?"

"An hour." He rests his elbow on the back of our bench and turns so his body is facing me. "We take turns. You get one, then I get one, and back and forth until we don't feel like it anymore. Time starts once we get to where we're going. You wanna go first?"

This could be the part where I get lost forever. This could be what he *does*. Picks up girls getting ready to start their day, gets them all soft and cuddly at a dog park, then proposes this game and uses his hour to lock them in the back of a truck. Maybe the woman at Dunkin' who doesn't smile is in on it. Maybe that's *why* she didn't smile at our dumb jokes. *Can you please just go and get kidnapped already?* was probably what she really wanted to say.

This could be what he does. Or, it could be something even worse. He could give girls like me hope—hope that there are good things and he's actually one of them. And that the tomorrows we've been struggling to get to, where everyone keeps promising that things will be better, have finally shown up today. He could be the kind of monster who plants that seed of possibility and then yanks it from the root without even realizing how much that bleeds. Without even caring.

I've waited so long for tomorrow. Maybe it's here now or maybe it's not. But that same big thing that convinced me to skip my test convinces me again right now.

"Okay," I agree. "Me first."

September 24: 10:32 a.m.

If scent really is the strongest sense tied to memory, I know that I'm forming one now. That these whiffs of spices and deliciousness are wrapping around me and squeezing so tight that they'll leave an imprint forever. It's weird, sometimes, how a hug can be invisible and still feel so good.

"I'm not gonna lie," Marcus says. "This was a pretty specific idea considering I just sprung this game on you thirty minutes ago." He takes another bite of his mini fried-chicken-and-white-gravy biscuit sandwich, balancing his disposable brown food tray in his other hand. He's devoured every bite-size snack we've passed. Three trays and counting.

We're two out of dozens of people packed into the new Pies 'n' Thighs Midtown location, where they're hosting Gigi Goodall for the few days that she's in town. Like, *the* Gigi Goodall. Winner of season twelve of *America's Next Big Chef*, who skipped opening a restaurant and used *her* two-hundred-and-fifty-thousand-dollar check to start doing these supercool food pop-ups around the country instead. She's been in the city for the past four days, but the event is only open from 10 a.m. to 2 p.m., which means I never had a chance to come by. I obsessively refreshed her page instead and lived vicariously through her posts and stories.

If I ever did get a chance to come here, it was gonna be alone. I was gonna wear a hoodie or a baseball cap. I was gonna take pictures for my camera roll and never, ever post them. So no one would ever know the impossible things I dream about when I'm still awake.

"It's this Gigi Goodall pop-up." I slide through the crowd so we can get to the next booth, but also so I don't have to look him in the eye. I want to try making jambalaya with a dash of saffron because I can taste it in hers. I want to get a picture of myself in front of the giant rainbow chalkboard sketch of her face that's hanging on the wall, that I saw on Instagram days ago, and now it's *right there*. In my impossible, wide-awake dreams, I have a restaurant with tables like these—heavy wood with clean lines and white marble tabletops. "She's kind of this big-deal chef."

I glance at him, but he's too busy chewing for me to tell if he's familiar. He's nodding, though. "Yo, I'd bathe in this gravy."

I laugh and lean a little closer to make sure he can hear me over all the other conversations. "The fifty-dollar fee at the door was actually a donation. That's why there are tip jars all over the place, too, and all the signs with the Cash App deets. She's doing these pop-ups across the country to raise money for local charities."

Marcus glances around, easily peering over most people's heads, noticing all the things he hadn't before. "Do you know her?" Marcus asks as we reach the next table. Shrimp and grits. "Ooh." He reaches for another disposable tray to add to his growing stack.

"Like, personally?" I frown. "Absolutely not. People like me know *of* Gigi Goodall. But that's it."

Marcus watches me as he shovels his food onto the tiny wooden fork that was handed to each of us. "So what made you want to come by?"

I hold my tray in one hand and spear a shrimp with the other. It's buttery, and luscious, and topped with chives. Perfectly opaque in the middle and was cooked in . . . bacon fat?

I chew a second longer.

Yes, bacon fat.

Marcus is still waiting on my answer, watching me the way I wish everyone would. Devoid of the frustration, and disappointment, and *What is she going to do with her life?* sad stares that I get so often at home. Marcus watches me like it's easy. Like it's the easiest thing he's ever done.

I say something out loud that I've only whispered once before, to Jacq. "I kind of want to be a chef one day."

He raises his eyebrows, his eyes lighting up like streetlamps. "You had grilled cheese for breakfast."

I bump him on purpose and he's smiling as he stumbles back a couple of steps. I slide my first bite of grits into my mouth and they warm my already-warming-up insides. He doesn't know how hard it was for me to say that, and he's just joking, not being mean—that's what I tell myself so I don't get embarrassed and take it back. "Gigi says food isn't about what's fancy; it's about what's good."

"Oh, I wasn't talking smack." Marcus helps himself to another tray of shrimp and grits. "That was an endorsement. I'd make it my slogan if I were you. You know how quick I'd be to trust a girl who gets down on a cheese-stuffed croissant?" He shovels more food in his mouth and watches me like I'm already the chef I'll never be. "Do you cook a lot?"

"Not exactly . . ." But it feels so good having him believe in me that I don't want to let him down, so I add, "I watch a lot of cooking competitions, though. And I pretty much follow every food account. Sometimes I go to restaurants just to try food I've never had before and ask the waiters a ton of questions about what's in it. I tell them it's because I have a lot of allergies but, really, it's because I'm trying to figure out what new ingredients taste like." I lower my voice when I say it, one of my dirty little secrets, and Marcus smiles like he's down to keep it. "I would love to cook more but my parents don't really know I'm into it. They're doctors and want me to be one, too."

I take his empty trays and toss them into the trash can behind me. When I turn back around, there's a twist on Marcus's lips and a squint in his eyes like he's been thinking. Then he says, "It's kind of the same, deep down. Chefs and doctors, I mean. They both make people feel better."

His words slide into my chest and settle there. It is kind of nice, not being here alone.

I tell him I hear there's a peach cobbler table, that we should find that next, as a hush falls over the room. Not sudden and not even completely, but like this atmospheric *thing* that's snaking through the restaurant, tapping certain ones of us on the shoulder as it passes. A whisper reaches my ear. "It's Gigi!"

My eyes dart until I see her weaving through the crowd. Her signature pink hair is even more fluorescent in real life. All the rings on her fingers shimmer like armor. She's in torn jeans with an apron tied around her waist, and a casual button-down with the sleeves rolled up, her forearms permanently inked with tattoos so lifelike that they could be photographs. One of them she got just a few days ago, at the famous parlor in West Village where Rihanna goes. She posted the picture on Instagram. I can't see it from here, but I know what it says:

You will.

She's only twenty-six. She's pretty, and cool, and knows exactly who she is. I bet her parents love that about her. I bet they love *everything* about her. I bet they didn't even blink at her tattoos or tell her that success only happens one way. I bet they take their phones out at parties to pull up articles and pictures to show to anyone who will let them. I bet they say, *This is our daughter!* and you can hear the exclamation point at the end. And when she told them that she was gonna be a chef, I bet they hugged her tight and told her, *You will.*

She looks even cooler, the closer she gets. Until it hits me. She's getting *too* close.

She's coming *to me*.

My breath lodges in my throat and I swear it could strangle me.

But at the very last second, the pupils in her eyes are close enough to actually decipher, to notice the minor and extremely significant detail about where they're *really* looking.

At Marcus.

She grins with all her teeth and wraps her arms around his shoulders, hugging him like she's missed him for years. "You didn't tell me you were coming! Is your mom here, too?" Then she holds him by the shoulders and peers into his eyes. "How are you doing?" she genuinely asks.

"I'm good, I'm good," Marcus quickly promises her. "Mom's not here. But Sydney is." He holds a hand out to me and they both turn. "She's gonna be a chef one day, too."

I swallow the breath I was holding, choking it down like cough medicine. So, Marcus does know Gigi and Gigi *clearly* knows Marcus. Gigi, with her five million followers and counting.

And Marcus. With his . . . ?

Who the hell is Marcus?

September 24: 12:01 p.m.

Kala Burke's son. *Marcus is Kala Burke's son.*

"It's not a big deal." He wants me to believe it—his voice strains like he *needs* me to, even. It's the way his head is turned now that we've left Pies 'n' Thighs, so he can keep his eyes on me and not on the hordes of people trying to make it down 5th Avenue during the lunch rush.

"Of course, it's not." But it completely is. Not in a bad way. It's the opposite, really. It officially makes Marcus the most casually famous person I've ever hung out with.

The *only* casually famous person I've ever hung out with.

"I would have told you." He shoves his hands into the big pocket at the front of his sweatshirt. "Or maybe I wouldn't have." He admits that part more to himself. "It's weird how it matters, all of a sudden. For most of my life, it never mattered at all."

I bet he's been on a private plane before. I bet Gigi Goodall is at his house for Friendsgiving every year. I bet it's a penthouse on the Upper East Side . . .

"You should be proud that Kala Burke is your mom. That's, like, the coolest thing ever. My mom is an otolaryngologist. Half my friends think that means she does Lasik for a living."

Marcus is still so busy looking at me that he just misses a woman rushing by in pumps, only because she swerved. "What *is* that?"

"It's ears, nose, and throat stuff." I act like I'm making it that simple so that I don't bore him with specifics and doctor-speak. But really, that's pretty much all I know about it, too.

"Hearing, smelling, and tasting?" Marcus argues. "That's huge. That's, like, my whole life."

He either means it or just really hopes I'm willing to believe his world isn't all that different from mine. But Kala Burke is the founder of Sip, this new nitro water brand that is literally *everywhere*. And no, I don't know what makes water "nitro," but I do know that anyone who claims to be even moderately into health and wellness has been guzzling it down like oxygen. I follow Kala, too, and see all the pictures of her and Gigi having lunches together or promoting each other's stuff. She's pretty and looks too young to be so self-made. Like thirtysomething.

"How old are you?" I ask.

"Seventeen," he tells me. "I'm a senior." He waits a second and then asks me the same thing. "How old are you?"

"Seventeen," I echo. "A senior."

And then I snatch his hand—tugging him to a stop because he's still busy watching me, and the light just changed. Cars zoom past, creating a gust of city-trash smells that wraps around us like a gross tornado. But I barely even notice because his hand in mine is doing something that skin isn't supposed to do. A tingling that tickles so much that I want to shake myself free just as badly as I want to never let go.

"You've really got to look where you're going," I tell him as our hands part.

There's a break in the traffic, and even though our light is still red, everyone—including us—waiting on either side of the street trots across it before the Morton Williams delivery truck gets close enough to be a threat.

"My mom had me when she was young," Marcus explains.

Now I'm the one who turns to him. Because I don't want him to think that's why I asked, even though it was. "Marcus, that's not—I wasn't asking because . . ." I hug myself. "I'm sorry. It's none of my business."

He veers to the left, so he's closer to the storefronts than the street, and he isn't blocking foot traffic when he slows down. I follow. He stops in front of an Equinox. The giant glass windows have a bunch of branded gear flanking each side, and I swear to God—where he happens to stop—there's a huge display of his mom's water bottles surrounding him like an aura. The all-white, tubed plastic bottles with cutouts up the sides that spell *Sip*. I know he doesn't realize, so I'm trying hard to act like I don't realize it, either.

"Listen." He leans against the glass and slides his feet out from the wall, so he's short enough to look right at me and I can look right back. "I know it was probably weird talking to me about how much you love Gigi and then for her to come over like that. That's not what I wanted at all. I really didn't think she would be there. I didn't think you'd find out like that." He drops his neck for a second, and maybe it's his turn to say the kind of thing that he doesn't usually say out loud. "The thing is . . . sometimes people start to act different when they find out about my mom. Like they're scared to be real with me or piss me off. Or they think it comes with all these perks and they want in. So, when we got to Gigi's event, and you were talking to me about all that cooking stuff without having any idea of who my mom was . . . that felt really cool. Like we didn't meet today because of what she does but in spite of it. You know what I mean?"

A woman in a ponytail brushes past, sucking from her bottle of Sip on her way out of the gym. I hold my breath until I'm sure he doesn't notice her.

"Marcus . . ." It's hard, looking straight at him, but in a good way. A way that makes me want to try again. "Okay, yes, I know who your mom is. And yes, I'm a huge fan of Gigi. And meeting her today . . . that was like a freaking *dream*. The way she hugged me and took down my handle and told me to stay tuned for her big announcement coming soon? Do you know how much I'm gonna overthink my posts now?" He smiles and shakes his head like I'm such a dork and I smile, too, because I know I am. "But if I'm being totally honest . . . and I'm gonna be, okay?"

He swallows and nods.

"If I'm being honest," I start again. "Even after meeting Gigi, and indirectly meeting Kala . . . you're still the best person I've met today."

You can tell when people aren't regularly told they're the best. People like us, we look away, tell you you're wrong, make the whole thing a whole lot smaller. Jacq takes my face in her hands when she says it. Smashes my cheeks in her palms and threatens to squeeze harder until I quit talking back. To her, I'm the best margherita pizza maker, storyteller, and matcher of mismatching patterns.

Marcus, he's good at existing. I just *know* it. He's good at being charming, and charismatic, and the right kind of sarcastic. So, it's weird, the way he drops his neck and rubs the back like he doesn't know how to hear that he's the best, because he has to hear it all the time.

"It's your hour, isn't it?" I remind him. "To pick what's next?"

It takes him another half a second, like a computer waking back up, to look at me again. But he smiles when he does. "Yeah."

He peels himself off the Equinox wall and glances left and right before he cuts through the sidewalk traffic to the Citi Bike rack next to the bus stop. "But my thing's kind of far, so we're gonna have to ride."

He takes out his phone and starts tapping his thumb, scanning the bike, pulling it from the rack. But I haven't moved.

He raises his eyebrows. "What's up?"

"I . . ." I shake my head, shrug. "Yeah, I can't do that."

"I can rent it for you, don't worry about it," he says.

"No, I—" I push my curls behind my ear when the breeze tries to make them do the opposite. "Not that kind of 'I can't.' Like . . . actually. I can't. Ride. A bike."

I'm not even ashamed of it. But as I imagine pedaling behind him through red lights and following him wherever he wanted us to go—I wish I did ride.

He blinks. "You don't know how to ride a bike?"

I hug myself, my tongue poking the inside of my cheek. "Technically? No. But I can do trains, buses, walk for miles . . . fast, too. I always walk places in half the time they say it'll take me on Google Maps."

He peers down 5th Ave while I talk, while my voice goes up an optimistic octave in the end, because hopefully one of those alternatives will sound just as fun to him.

He turns to me and jerks his neck. "Wanna hop on back?"

Maybe he's kidding. "For real?"

"Accept. Adapt." He shrugs. "So, yeah." And the part he's left off is, *Why not?*

I can't think of any good reason.

I go over to the bike and adjust my backpack on my shoulders as I stand behind the back tire. It hits me for the first time that Marcus doesn't have a backpack. I bet he's one of those guys who leaves all his stuff in his locker and just carries around a mechanical pencil all day. Which is a good thing, because it means I'll have more room on the back of this bike.

"Just hop on the spokes," he tells me, looking down at my feet to make sure I do it right. "Hold on tight, okay?"

Hold on tight. Hold on *where?* My hands naturally land on his shoulders, gripping him through his black sweatshirt. He's not muscly but he has muscles, just the right amount. The kind that tighten when his hands grab the handlebars and relax when he lets go.

He pulls off and I know we can't be going that fast, but it feels like we're flying, the way the wind slaps my cheeks and whips through my hair. The way it's rushing at me so quickly that it's hard to take a deep breath. The way we're zooming past cars as they creep through intersections and passing pedestrians like they aren't even moving. I've been in this city my entire life and I thought I knew exactly what it looked like. But I've never, ever seen it like this.

"You okay?" Marcus asks, turning his head to check on me, sort of yelling to make sure I hear him. The whipping wind is so loud that I just barely do.

I'm fine. I'm infinitely better than fine. But, more importantly, I'm flying downtown on the back of a bike with no protective gear, a million ways to crash, and a boy more interested in looking at me than at the road.

"I told you, you have to start looking where you're going!" I yell back.

He faces forward again and I feel him laughing—the bouncing in his shoulders and the way his back expands. Maybe he really does answer me, or maybe I'm just imagining how he would. With the same unspoken *thing* that's made me trust him all day and a smile on his lips that makes me feel like I'm spinning. And then a deep breath, a promise, and the words:

Don't worry.

And I don't.

September 24: The rest of the afternoon

It's been, in every way, a perfect day. One that I never in a million years believed could happen to me. I'd do this forever, if I could. Over and over. But it's dark and it has been for a while, and that means that it's ending.

Marcus biked us to the Battery and we spent an hour dancing to live music on the lawn and another hour eating fries on a rooftop. I asked him if he could teach me how to ride a bike—which took longer than my designated sixty minutes—but at least now I know that he's strong enough to hold me up, and how his hands felt on my hips every time he did.

He knows we're running out of time, though. I can tell by the way he isn't talking as much anymore. Like neither one of us wants to risk bringing up the most important thing we've ever tried to talk about at the same moment when the other says, *Well, I guess I should get going.*

10:01 p.m., according to my phone. Three missed calls from my parents and two more texts from Jacq.

"Your people starting to look for you?" Marcus understandingly assumes.

"Kind of," I admit, but it feels too soon. He doesn't have my number, or any of my handles, or any means of acknowledging that I exist ever again, and I'm starting to worry he won't ask. That I haven't done enough today to convince him to ask. So maybe I need more time.

"What part of the city are you in?" he asks.

"Upper West," I answer. "You?"

"BK," he says.

I nod. I should have guessed. Kala's not an Upper East kind of woman. "Well, I'm probably gonna take the 1 back uptown."

He nods, too. We're walking so slowly—reluctantly—down this sidewalk now that even an old man with a cane passes us on the right. "I'm probably gonna take the ferry. But the 1 is on the way. I can walk you?"

"Yes, please."

It takes us ten minutes to get there when it should only take five. We reach the corner, where he should go straight and I should cross to reach the uptown tracks, but since his light is green and mine is red, he lingers.

"It was an honor not being murdered by you today." I hope he knows how much I mean it.

He chuckles and glances at the woman who does a double take as she passes. "Yo, you can't say stuff like that too loud."

"I'd clear it all up in court," I promise.

"Yeah?" He laughs.

"Yeah." I'm laughing, too.

"Well, the pleasure was mine. Far better than being in a coma. At least, I assume so."

It's my turn to cross. I know because, from the corner of my eye, a bunch of people start to.

"Well, maybe I could get your number?" Marcus says. *Finally*. "So we can maybe hang out again?"

I reassured myself during the last few minutes of this walk that, even if he didn't ask, I could find him. He's Kala Burke's son. I could go on Instagram and be on his page in three clicks or less, probably. Jacq could help me figure out a not-so-stalker way of reaching out.

But this way is better. *So* much better.

I recite my number and he types it into his phone, and then calls me so I have his number, too. It vibrates in the pocket of my cardigan.

I pat it and tell him, "Got it."

He takes a deep breath. He flashes his flawless smile. "Alright, well."

"Alright, well."

I back away, toward the crosswalk, and flick a quick wave at him before I turn around. I can't freak out, not yet. Not while I'm pretty sure he's still watching me and, even if he's not, he can definitely still *see* me. I have to wait until I'm underground, and it's safe, and then I can text Jacq, and then I can be a complete fool about it. About a day like this. Happening for *me*.

"Sydney, wait—"

His hand catches my elbow as I reach the middle of the crosswalk, and I turn and face him under the shining red lights. The color turns his eyes into something urgent, something hot.

Kiss me. I want him to more than anything. He has to know it—anyone within a ten-foot radius must know it—because it's burning so bright, such a defining attribute of everything I am in this moment, that it's unignorable.

I take a step closer and he wets his lips. He takes a breath. And then he says, "There's something you need to know about me—"

But the words are cut off by screeching tires, so piercing that it's like needles pricking my ears. Before I know what's happening, there's a pain that's worse than anything I've ever felt before, that makes it impossible to think, or breathe. That makes me want to throw up everything that's inside me, not just what I've eaten but my guts and organs, too. Just to get whatever's hurting out.

I think I double over. I think I cry out. All I'm sure of is the whiteness of it all—maybe it's headlights but it seems so much bigger than that. Blinding.

And then I'm being sucked away, yanked so hard that my back snaps. Away from the crosswalk. Away from Marcus. Away from everything.

September 24, Take Two: 7:01 a.m.

Ouch.

Something's beeping, loud and constant, like a mallet to my head every time. I'm . . . in a bed? A hospital bed. With one of those machines that makes that noise once a second to prove you're alive. *Beep, beep, beep.* With the same frequency Dad uses to tap my temple whenever I'm being an idiot again.

Think, Syd.

Wait, no. That noise is way too loud to be a hospital machine. It sucks way too much to be it, either.

That's my alarm.

I peel open my eyes and this isn't a hospital room, it's *my* room. My bed. My pink polka-dotted sheets that I don't even like that much, but I refuse to let Mom change because I hate her rationale that I'm *too old* for them now.

I grab my phone off my nightstand, where it blares like a foghorn the way it does every weekday morning at exactly this time. 7:01 a.m. I turn it off.

I rub my head automatically but then it hits me—it doesn't hurt. None of me hurts. Even though minutes ago—hours ago?—I was for sure being squashed in a crosswalk. Or something. With Marcus.

Marcus.

I bolt upright on my pillows and unlock my phone. I go to my missed calls so I can grab his number and text him, or even call him—no, that's a lot—to make sure he's okay. But when I scroll through my missed call log, and then scroll through again at glacial speed, there's nothing from last night. Or from yesterday at all. No missed calls on September 24th. Or this week, for that matter. No missed calls since Jacq last Sunday.

But he *did* call me. I felt it vibrate. It was like a tiny lightning bolt zinging me through my pocket all the way up and down my right side.

My phone locks from inactivity, and I set it down in my lap as I stare at the cold, black screen.

I tap it again to wake it up, and the picture of Sebastian and me at the beach glows back at me. I hold my phone so close, it's practically attached to my nose.

The date shining back at me, above my and Sebastian's laughing faces, is September 24.

The day of Mr. Wilson's precalc test.

The day I said screw it and went with Marcus instead.

The quintessential day that girls like me don't get to have.

Yesterday.

"What . . ." I whisper.

There's *no way*. There's absolutely zero chance that all that was a dream. Dreams don't last that long, or make that much sense, or burn like fire. That was real. *Marcus* was real.

Right?

I pull myself out of bed really, really slowly, in case more weird stuff is about to happen, like the furniture starts talking or the floor gives out and swallows me whole. But the planked wood is as solid on my feet as it's always been. I wander to my closet and open the door.

The dress I wore yesterday is hanging where it was yesterday morning. The cardigan is where it was, too. And the tights . . .

I step aside and slide open my top drawer, digging through piles of socks and underwear.

. . . are not here. Because they're probably hanging over the dryer. *Like they were yesterday.*

I choose a different outfit because . . . I mean, I don't even know. Because wearing the same one as yesterday is tacky? Unhygienic? Way too accepting of the fact that yesterday didn't exist, even though I know it did, because *what the hell*?

I grab my high-waisted boyfriend jeans instead, the ones with the ripped-up knees. I get a scoop-neck, fitted, white tank top and tuck it into my waistband. I pull my cream-colored, slouchy cropped sweater over my head. Then I go to my dresser and start doing my hair.

I went to the hairdresser last weekend for a wash and straighten, and even though I *know* I curled it yesterday, it's straight. So, I'm standing here in front of my mirror, curling it again. Slow and habitually, I twist one section after another around my straightener and let each piece fall into a soft, beachy wave. Whenever I finish one, I tap my phone and check the time. And time is moving, for sure.

So why doesn't it *feel* like it?

Think, Syd.

I catch my reflection on my way out of my bedroom and it hits me that I don't remember showering last night. But I do every night, so I'm sure I did. The same way I'm sure yesterday happened, and that Marcus is real.

Or I've fully lost my mind.

I don't want to feel like this again. Like there's this world happening but I'm not in it. Like I'm irreparably broken because all the pretty, happy things that everyone else sees go off like railroad warnings to me. *Don't cross. Stay back. It's not safe*. So many people aren't scared. They live their lives and hop across the tracks like they barely even notice them at all, trusting they'll always be warned before the next train. But sometimes, you're not. Sometimes trains come speeding at you with no heads-up at all, and you can't stop them, and they flatten you on those same tracks that no one else even seems to be scared of, and they keep running over you, railcar after railcar, until you forget what it was ever like to be alive at all, and—

I place my hand on Sebastian's door and push.

It's never closed tight so I never have to use the knob. My parents keep it just open enough that my foot can fit in the gap with an inch on either side. So that's the way I always put it back, because I don't need them knowing I sneak in here every day, after they've gone to work and before I go to school. They'll call the therapist again.

I turn on the light on his nightstand, and the room reveals itself to be the exact way it's been for the past two years. Sebastian didn't push back on Mom's determination to adultify *his* room, so it's basically this Pottery Barn cutout with a nautical theme. Random ship pictures on the walls. A giant cream-colored rug with a navy anchor in the middle. A deep blue comforter on his perfectly made bed.

I climb onto it and roll on my side, facing the wall that his four pairs of shoes are still lined up against. Two pairs of snow boots, an extra pair of sneakers, and Timberlands. His apartment at Corinthia was so small that he did shifts based on the seasons. He was supposed to come back for this stuff and drop off his summer stuff. Med school left him barely any time, but he had a fall break that he was gonna use to come back to the city for a couple of days.

The pillows don't smell like him anymore, and I can't convince myself that I feel his imprint on the bed. The comforter is cool to the touch in a way that I hate, in a way that mine never is when I crawl into bed at night. It's cool like it doesn't belong to anyone anymore. No one tosses things on it mindlessly or accidentally spills a soda. It's just clean and perfectly creased and abandoned.

When I talk to Sebastian in the mornings, it's not like . . . this ceremonial speech. Sometimes I barely know what to say. Sometimes it freaks me out how much easier it can feel to talk to him now. Sometimes I cry like it just happened yesterday and I don't even know why, why this bed can make it suddenly feel like my body is caving in on itself.

"Hey, Bas," I say to his empty bedroom. "Something good happened to me yesterday. I think. Maybe." I take a deep breath. "There was this boy . . . I know, you don't want to hear about me and boys.

But there was . . . and he was nice to me, and he looked at me like it didn't make him sad to, and he took me dancing outside and I started to learn how to ride a bike." The skin around my eyes tingles, anticipating tears. Conditioned, now. "That is, if yesterday actually ever happened. Which I think it did . . . most of me really, *really* thinks it did, but . . ." I gnaw my lip, my eyesight blurring as I stare at nothing. "Another part of me thinks that maybe missing you is destroying me."

I wait for him to answer like I always do. I swear, he really does sometimes. Gives me this feeling or something pops into my head that wasn't there before. Like it does right now.

I've got to get to Dunkin'.

🌹🌹🌹

Okay. Here goes nothing.

"Hi." I step up to the same girl behind the counter who was taking orders yesterday. She's in the same pink-and-brown hat. She has the same nonexistent enthusiasm about dealing with this mob scene as she did the day before.

"Would you like to try a dozen Munchkins this morning?" she asks.

"No, thank you. Can I please just have a sausage, egg, and cheese croissant with no sausage and no egg? Like yesterday?"

She blinks like it's the first time. "Sorry?"

My stomach sinks. "Just cheese, basically. On a croissant."

"So, a grilled cheese."

"Yes, please."

She starts typing on her iPad. I pull out a five-dollar bill. She gives me two back. I tongue my teeth as I take the receipt from her.

Number two.

I go to the window and stand between the same suited businessmen on their phones. Just like I did yesterday.

Everything is like yesterday.

Maybe it's not because yesterday never happened. Maybe it's that it's happening *again*.

I scan the scene from where I'm standing, searching for Marcus. It's so packed I don't see him, but my adrenaline is pumping like it's coming from a fire hose because I know it's coming *soon*.

"Number two!" they call.

I slide through the crowd and take my paper bag from the counter. Well, Marcus's paper bag. I hold my breath before I turn around, preparing myself. I can't be all relieved to see him if we've never even met. But *God*, I can't wait to see him.

I turn around and—

Nothing.

What?

I wait for a second. Then more seconds. The Grubhub guy, with the same mini red cooler from yesterday, slides in next to me and needs more space to scoop up all his orders.

I step out of his way.

Everything is the same except for the only thing that matters. I uncrinkle my paper bag and pull out my sandwich, just to be sure.

Wishing to some kind of intergalactic time-genie that this sandwich is gonna be wrong.

But it's not. Just cheese.

I was right all along—girls like me don't get days like that.

I think I'm gonna be sick.

I push my way through the crowd. I need to get out of here, even though I have no idea where I'm going. I can't just act like things are all copacetic and go fail Wilson's test now. I can barely *breathe* now.

I crumple up my receipt so I can throw it into oblivion the second I get outside.

And then I get slammed so hard that I'm on the ground.

Legit, on my ass at the Dunkin' main door, a mixture of my backpack, my hands, and my grilled cheese breaking my fall on the brown-tiled floor.

But standing over me is Marcus, panting and staring like he just accidentally shot me, and it's okay.

I know it now. Whatever this is, whatever's going on.

It's gonna be okay.

September 24, Take Two: 9:39 a.m.

We're in the dog park again.

He looks exactly the same as he did yesterday—dress pants and a collared shirt under a black hoodie, no backpack. While he apologized obsessively and helped me off the floor at Dunkin', I held my breath, hoping that he'd take my cheeks in his hands and whisper, *Sydney, what the hell is going on?* But he just smiled the way you do with someone new and introduced himself.

He insisted on buying me another sandwich along with his and, when he did, his order number was two. We ended up standing next to the girl with the recyclable tote bag with a duck sketched on it while we waited, and when he admitted he was officially too late to be worthy of consciousness, he asked if I would eat with him instead. And I said, *Yes, of course, absolutely.*

Well, in my head that's what I said.

In real life, I just said, *Sure.*

I don't know why I thought that he'd be the one thing today that wasn't the same as it was yesterday, or why I thought he'd remember me. Maybe because I could never forget him. But I guess that's not enough, not always, not even after a day like ours. I just wish I knew where the past goes when you're the only one who knows it.

At least he's here.

We're on this bench again, with these dogs again, and their old people. My mind is finally working its way out of its rut. For the past couple of hours, it was just spinning in place, like a tire stuck in the mud. But now that we've avoided catastrophe—re: Marcus not existing—it's slowly prying itself free again. There's this one thing that I can't stop thinking about. That I barely even remembered, and now it's burned into my brain.

Marcus, in the crosswalk last night, grabbing my elbow. His eyes under the gleam of the red light. And the words he said before everything spun out of control: *There's something you need to know about me.*

Maybe that's the problem. I never found out what I needed to know. Maybe I need to make sure I find out this time.

"Do you have a dog?" I ask while he leans over, rubbing Dixon. It hits me that I never asked him yesterday.

"Nah," he says. He peeks back at me over his shoulder. "Is it obvious?"

"It just seems moderately likely you'll stuff one of these guys in a duffel one day and never come back."

"Man, you found my Facebook group?"

I laugh and lean over to pet Dixon, too. "Why can everything ridiculous be traced back to Facebook?"

Our fingers brush on accident while we tickle Dixon's fur. And, when they do, we pause—hands hovering centimeters from where they bumped. My skin reacts just like it did yesterday when I grabbed his hand. It's wild how something that happens to my fingers can send a shock wave all the way to my toes.

And now that we're hovering and not actually petting, Dixon decides we suck and trots away.

My phone vibrates and I use it as an excuse to sit back up. It's Jacq.

> Ummmm

> ...

> Whereabouts???

I put my phone away.

"People starting to wonder where you're at?" Marcus asks.

"Yeah . . . Jacq. We've been friends forever. I'll hit her back soon."

He's giving Dixon's dad an easy wave across the asphalt. "That's Dixon's dad," he tells me.

I smile and wave at him, too. "But back to the dog thing . . ." I hug myself and face him.

There's something you need to know about me . . .

"Why *don't* you have one?" I go on. "I mean, you obviously love them. They seem to kind of like you, too."

But he doesn't get a chance to answer before another one is at his feet now—about Dixon's size but fluffy and white. One I didn't meet yesterday. "'Sup, Sash?" Marcus rubs her all over. "This is Sasha," he tells me, and then he glances around the park. "That's Sasha's mom," he adds, nodding at the older lady who's smiling at us as she slowly makes her way to an empty bench. She's in a full fur and it's in the low seventies today. I smile back, too.

I'm about to ask Marcus again, partly convinced that maybe I *did* stumble upon something that matters if it's taking this long to get an answer, but he picks back up from where we left off on his own.

"Honestly, I probably could get a dog now. My mom likes them, and our place is bigger than it used to be. But the thing is, Ashe is allergic. Bad. Like the plague just got her, or something." He shrugs and sits up straight again while Sasha follows her nose to a rock. "So, for years, it wasn't even an option."

"Who's Ashe?"

"My bad," he says, like he just remembered he never told me. "She's my mom's best friend." Then he twists his mouth and rocks his head a little. "My mom's . . . *friend*." He amends, but he chuckles like he knows he sounds awkward. "They don't really use titles, honestly. They met when I was a baby at this park on Eighty-Second street when they were both trying to figure out how to be moms—she's my boy Austin's mom. They had us young. So, we all kind of grew up together."

I tuck one leg under me but keep my gaze glued on him. "But why was the dog thing only not an option for a few years if they're still . . . *friends*?"

"Oh," he says, like he just now realized that's something else I don't know. "Mom and I used to live with them."

"Really?"

He nods. "We moved into their place when we couldn't make rent at ours. They were struggling with payments, too, because Ashe had lost her job, so we figured we could help each other out. It was a one-bedroom—so a dog wasn't fitting in that, whether Ashe was allergic or not. *We* were barely fitting in that. The landlord couldn't even know. It was a code violation, but on top of that, dude was real strict and would stop by unannounced all the time—" He stops himself. I think he thinks he's rambling. "So maybe I will go ahead and snatch up one of these dogs on my way home. These old people ain't catching me, anyway."

I laugh but insist, "Keep going. It's a good story."

He glances at me like he isn't sure, like he's scared I'm just being nice or something.

"How long were you guys in Ashe's one-bedroom with the super strict landlord?" I ask, to prove how much I was listening.

He watches me for an extra second, his gaze swallowing mine and, for a moment, I'm in that crosswalk again.

"Two years," he tells me. "It was funny because we all knew it wasn't permanent and we couldn't live like that forever. But we still *liked* it, you know? Mom and me trying not to bust out laughing every time we hid in a closet because the landlord was back. We had traditions and chore charts. Every Thursday night we watched *Grey's Anatomy* together because my mom and Ashe were obsessed, even though it's ridiculous. Have you seen it? I watched an icicle stab a woman through the heart on that show." I laugh and he does, too.

"No cap. But we still watched it every Thursday on our one TV with tuna fish sandwiches. It was stuff like that, you know? Like it can't be forever but it's real nice for a long time."

He grabs his balled-up Dunkin' trash and tosses it from one hand to the other, one hand to the other. Rhythmic and calming, and I almost relax enough to ask why. Why *can't* it be forever? Why can't the good parts be what last? But I keep it to myself because I don't want to undo what's happening right now, the way it feels like this story means something.

"Two years." I fold my legs under me. "That's two seasons of *Grey's*. They probably covered, like, twelve natural disasters in that amount of time."

He chuckles. "You watch, too?"

"No, but I've seen the spoiler accounts. For what it's worth, I think it's really cool you guys all lived together for a while. And figured stuff out together. And had each other."

"Yeah. It was." He kicks at a twig on the ground. "We all used to work because we had to get by. Our moms did all these different jobs around the city—cleaning houses, babysitting, waiting tables. They had to know Aus and I were working, too, because we always had money to contribute when rent came due, and we were way too soft to be selling drugs." He smiles, caught up in a memory. "There was this restaurant in the East Village where we cleaned the kitchen every night after they closed, except Thursdays. Because, you know, *Grey's* and tuna fish. And we weren't old enough to work, but Mr. Felix could see how bad we needed the money. I think you can sort of smell that on people, you know? That it's gonna be real hard for them to take 'no' for an answer.

"So, he'd do this thing with us." Marcus scoots a little closer to me, and I'm not sure if it's on purpose, but I let him lean in, let his breaths tangle with mine. "Where we had to bring our backpacks every day and prove we'd done our homework before he'd let us start cleaning. And then he'd hang around until we finished, and give us twenty bucks, off the books. Mr. Felix changed our lives, man." He shakes his head gratefully. "Almost an extra five hundred a month." We're quiet for a second, and Marcus waves at someone who waves at him first. Then, like he's back from a trance, he admits, "I don't know why it was so easy to tell you all that."

It was just as easy for me to listen, to imagine these people I've never met surviving and probably never once calling it that. "So, you guys were able to move out of Ashe's place?"

"Yeah." He takes a deep breath, his shoulders rising and falling with the weight of the nostalgia. "Yeah, we were. Ashe got her degree online and has a PR job now, and my mom started a business a few years ago that's doing pretty well."

I nod. "Will you show me?" I ask.

He smirks, confused. "Who, my mom?"

"No." I laugh, and it makes him smile for real. "Will you show me the restaurant? The one where you used to work."

September 24, Take Two: 11:21 a.m.

I hop off the back of Marcus's bike and he wheels it into the Citi Bike rack on 12th and 1st. He was just as shocked today that I can't ride as he was yesterday, but even if I can ride a bike one day, I think I'll always prefer being on the back of his.

"Is this it?" I ask. We're lingering, sort of, at this wooden door with a big glass window. NINA'S, the awning says.

"Yeah," he answers, and for a second, I think I see something that matters in his scrunched eyebrows, in the way he swallows. But when he chuckles, it's gone. "It's just been a minute," he explains. "Hopefully the guys don't give me hell about it."

He pulls the door open for both of us and a bell jingles over our heads as we go inside. It's a gourmet sandwich shop with oversized wooden booths. The floor is black-and-white tile and there are floating pots holding green plants that I'm pretty sure are real. It smells like the best deli ever—like something savory, and sweet, and warm at the same time. The menu is carved in cursive on a white slab of wood that hangs over the register.

"Look what the cat drug in!" the guy behind the counter says, with the hint of a Puerto Rican accent.

I stop gazing at this gorgeous room and notice him instead, in a white T-shirt and black apron with NINA'S stitched across the front. Marcus is smiling bigger than I've seen yet—relieved, probably, for the warm welcome. He heads over to the brown-skinned guy with jet-black hair who looks like he's only a couple of years older than we are.

They slap hands over the counter and pull each other in for one-armed hugs.

"I know it's been too long, man," Marcus says.

"Where the hell have you been?" the guy goes on. "We've been thinking about you." He gives Marcus a little shove like he means it. "Felix asks about you all the time."

"I know, I know." Marcus rubs his shoulder where he just got pushed. "I'm sorry. It's been a lot lately. We'll catch up for real, though. I promise. But hey—" Marcus turns to me. "This is Sydney. Sydney, this is Javi."

"Oh, *Sydney*, huh?" Javi smiles the way boys do when they think their friend is getting laid.

"Nah, man, you're gonna chill today," Marcus warns him. "I just want to show her around a little bit."

"Of course, the place is yours," Javi says. "But you know Felix doesn't get in until around four on Thursdays. You guys gonna be around that long?"

"I'll catch him next time." Marcus nods at me so I'll follow him to the back.

"Good to meet you, Javi," I say.

He smiles. "Hey, you, too."

Marcus's hands are in his pockets as we walk down a short

hallway with signs to the bathroom. He takes a big breath and lets it out slow. I glance at him, catching the end of it as we hang a right and leave the bathrooms behind.

"It'll be packed in here by lunchtime," he tells me.

"Oh, I'm sure."

"But before that happens, I can show you the kitchen I used to clean?"

I smile and so does he. "That could hold my attention for a minute or two."

He pushes our way through a swinging metal door and we walk into the epicenter of the scents. Breads and freshly shaved meats. Men in black jeans and white T-shirts and white aprons with black Nina's baseball caps are prepping ingredients on metal workspaces while their loud voices tell stories and laugh together. One of them notices Marcus and then they all do, men closer to Dad's age than ours, asking where the hell he's been. He gets swallowed by their hugs, back slaps, and head rubs. *Of course* they're happy to see him, and the smile on Marcus's face is like a kid who expected to get grounded but got a new video game instead.

I wander while they talk.

It's not a huge kitchen, but it has everything that the kitchens in *America's Next Big Chef* always do. The multi-eye gas stove, a huge refrigerator and freezer, a deep fryer, and a giant rotisserie. I peek in the fridge and find all the cheeses, condiments, spreads. I look around a corner and find the oven where all the bread is baking.

I wonder how many people it takes for a kitchen like this to be considered fully staffed. I wonder if one person is responsible for a whole order or if they divvy it up like an assembly line. I wonder how long it took for them to memorize what goes on each sandwich, or if there's a cheat sheet somewhere. I wonder if these men always wanted to make food or if it's something that just sort of happened—

"Hey," Marcus says, and I turn around like I've been caught. He's leaning against the fridge. "Just a heads-up, if you poison the turkey, I'm not sure I can get you off. Good news is they still like me, but I don't know if they twenty-years-to-life kind of like me."

Skeptically, I ask, "Who poisons turkey?"

"Oh, *that's* the part that sounded off to you?"

I probably look like I'm browsing a museum, the way my fingertips are grazing anything that's not edible. "How long did it used to take you guys to clean this place?"

"We'd sweep, and mop, and wipe down the surfaces. Make sure everything was where it belonged before the cooks came back in the next day." He gnaws the inside of his bottom lip, peering at the kitchen like he can see them cleaning now. "A little over an hour?" he eventually answers.

"Twenty dollars an hour is a good rate," I say, impressed, and start opening the cabinets where they keep the spices.

"Yeah, especially for a couple fourteen-year-olds." He waits a beat, then adds, "Don't take this the wrong way, but I kind of feel like you're up to something."

Probably because I've just discovered the recipe card for the spiced ham and I'm studying it like I'm about to go drop it on WikiLeaks.

That's when I remember that he doesn't know anything about me wanting to be a chef one day. He doesn't know I'm a huge fan of Gigi Goodall; he's never seen me at her pop-up event. To him, I'm just a girl who orders grilled cheese croissants at Dunkin'.

I put the recipe card where I found it and turn back around to face him. "Sorry. Not plotting, just absorbing. I've never been in a commercial kitchen before. And it's really cool because I'm kind of obsessed with food and have this ridiculous dream of being a chef one day, or something." It's still so hard to say out loud. Even the second time.

He starts to smile. "You had American cheese for breakfast."

"Well, don't you think a chef's greatest responsibility is knowing what tastes good?"

"For sure. American cheese is the GOAT. I'd vote it into the White House," he says. "You know, I bet Mr. Felix would let you come by here sometimes, if you want. Maybe even help out in the kitchen. Especially if he knows why."

My heart skips at the possibility but I take a breath so it slows back down. "Maybe."

I think he knows I'm just scared. He's looking at me like I'm probably one of those girls who's supposed to have a different path—as if an Ivy League future emanates from me like an aura. "You'd be great in this place," he tells me, and it's the last thing I expected him to say.

But it's pretty cool that he thinks so.

"I'm not even hungry and I'm gonna eat this whole thing." I take another bite of my sandwich.

"You don't have to eat the whole thing," Marcus tells me from the other side of our booth.

"It's like . . . four pounds." I swallow and stare at the half that I'm holding.

"You can stop," Marcus reminds me.

"I *can't* stop. It's too good to stop." I take another bite. "You stop."

He licks a dripping drop of pesto from his crust. "Oh, I ain't stoppin'."

It was his idea to order sandwiches at Nina's so I could taste one. Once he found out that food is my secret passion, he swore that Nina's has the best sandwiches in the city. They've even gotten awards for it, which he pointed out lining the walls when we got back to the register. We placed our orders with Javi and when Marcus reached for his wallet, Javi told him not to worry about it. But Marcus insisted and paid in cash.

It's getting busier in here by the minute, people placing lunch orders and delivery guys grabbing paper bags off the counter to go. Almost all the booths are taken.

"So." A piece of turkey falls from my sandwich to the wrapper and I pop it into my mouth.

"So," Marcus echoes.

"Why haven't you been back here in a while?"

When it takes him a second to answer, I figure he must be chewing, and when it takes him another second, I look up to make sure.

But he isn't chewing, he's watching me. I realize I've gotten way too comfortable *way* too fast, that I need to stop acting like I'm alone on the couch streaming *Love Is Blind*, when I'm actually facing this very cute, tingles-inducing boy instead.

I set my sandwich down and pretend like it's because I need a sip of my water.

But he has these little creases in the outside corners of his eyes, and they don't go away even now. Maybe he wasn't watching me inhale food. Maybe I was just a safe enough place for his gaze to settle.

And maybe whatever this answer is, it matters.

There's something you need to know about me.

"Things changed," he says, and shrugs like it's nothing. But then he leans back on his side of the booth and brings his glass of Sprite with him. "Isn't it wild how things just . . . change?"

"What changed?"

He chomps on the ice that slipped into his mouth when he swigged and sets his glass back on the table. He doesn't answer until he's swallowed. "Priorities. Money. Our lives, I guess." Before I can figure out a noncreepy way to ask if he's talking about Sip, he gives me a half smile and adds, "Anyway, can it be your turn now? I feel like we've been on my turf all day. Tell me something about you."

The fact that he feels like we've been on his turf all day is both good and bad. Good, because it means Operation Dig Deep is working so far, and bad, because I feel like Marcus is too self-aware to just be interviewed all day and believe that's fun for me.

This is my turn to balance things out so we can get back to him.

So that I can keep trying to figure out what I never got the chance to hear last night.

He takes another bite of his sandwich and waits on me to answer. But I don't know what I want to say, or why I have this urge to try to say something *real*. Maybe it's because of everything he told me this morning about Ashe, and his mom, and Austin. How quick he was to let me know his world simply because I was willing to ask.

Or maybe it's because of this in-between I've been in for the past two years. Where I've met these people—cool people, *great* people—who could, theoretically, exist without ever knowing about Sebastian. Without ever knowing about the single most life-destroying event I've ever experienced, unless I go out of my way to make sure that they do.

I'm pretty sure that's it, actually. The reason why I have this urge to say something real, and why that real thing only makes me think about Bas. Because if I'm gonna have staticky skin, kiss-me-please feelings about this boy, I want him to *know* me.

"So." I gnaw my lip and fold my arms on the table, leaning a little closer. "My brother Sebastian and I used to play this game that we called I Bet. Basically, you pick a stranger and decide everything about them. We called it I Bet because that's what all your predictions should start with." He's listening but he's also squinting like he's trying to follow, so I glance around the restaurant and pick someone. "Okay, so you see that guy in line right now in the business suit and the REI backpack? Well, I bet he's twenty-seven. I bet he's working some banking job to pay the bills, but, really, he's a creative at heart. I bet he heads to the Catskills on weekends and brings that backpack with him up a mountain. I bet he likes to cook dinner outside and isn't scared of bugs. I bet he's found his people—like his real, soulmate kind of people—and I bet he loves them so easily that he barely realizes he's doing it."

A silence sits between us. Marcus watches the guy I was talking about as he steps forward in line, with his non-Apple earbuds, rocking from heel to toe. "Wow," Marcus says. And then he turns to me. "How old's your brother?"

Here we go.

No one's asked me that in the time since I stopped knowing how to answer it. When the aneurysm came in the middle of the night and he never woke up again, he was twenty-four. My parents would argue that's the answer, then. Past tense. He was twenty-four. Their science-y minds would insist that aging requires time, and time requires a physical entity to experience its passage, and since Sebastian is gone, so is his time, and so is his age.

One of the many reasons we don't talk about Sebastian.

"He's twenty-four," I tell Marcus, something like a hiccup catching in my throat. "He was twenty-four. When he died. Two years ago."

Oh my God, the way his face drops. The way he stares at me like he swallowed his tongue and truly may never speak again. I shouldn't have said anything. No one ever knows what to do, how to respond—and now Marcus, of all people, who's known me for, like, three hours (as far as he's aware), is stuck here trying to digest his sandwich and my buzzkill story at the same time.

His gaze doesn't leave me, even when I break eye contact to pretend like I'm more interested in my sandwich. I glance at him and he's still there, with me, processing.

Finally, a robot low on batteries, he manages to tell me, "Sydney . . . I. I'm—" He clears his throat. "I'm so sorry."

It's barely any words, and maybe I'm just reaching, but he's done a good job. He's done enough. He's still sitting here. He isn't forcing the conversation to be something else. He isn't scared to look at me like knowing a dead person makes me Medusa. Maybe that seems like the very bare minimum that anyone can do, but it's not. Sometimes all it takes to be there for someone is to . . . be there.

"Hey, Romeo," Javi calls in our direction, past the line and through the growing crowd. I nod in Javi's direction so that Marcus knows he's being summoned, and Marcus turns around. "Felix just called. He had to come into the city early today. Says he'll be here in fifteen!"

"Damn," Marcus says, sliding out of our booth. "We're about to dip, man. Tell him I say hey, though, okay? And that I'll see him next time."

Javi frowns as Marcus wraps up his sandwich, so I start wrapping mine, too. "Alright, well, make it soon, okay? We still have to catch up. And he's been wanting to see you."

"Soon," Marcus promises, and then he turns to me. "They're gonna need this table for lunch. Eat while we walk?"

Eat while we walk. As in, *not* while he runs away from me.

"Yes," I agree.

September 24, Take Two: The rest of the afternoon

We head back uptown and stay there.

The rest of the day, we walk around, talking and stuffed full of sandwiches. They're the easiest conversations I've ever had with someone. Anything could come up right now and it would be okay. Including Sebastian, even though we haven't talked any more about that since we left Nina's.

When I check my phone tonight, I'm sure it'll say that I've done at least twenty thousand steps. But it feels like it's only been minutes. I can't even remember what streets we took or turns we made. It was just us, and our stories, and the city noises that we both grew up around, and that's what makes it so easy to shut them out.

I find out that he doesn't have a favorite color and that his biggest fear is rats with red eyes. He's an INFJ according to that Myers-Briggs test, which he only slightly pays attention to because Ashe is big into personality types. On his own, he admits that his mom is Kala Burke, and I'm sure that something happens between us when he tells me this time. Yesterday, when he told me the same thing, his back was—literally—against the wall. If I'd asked about it at Nina's, his hand would have been forced, yet again. But today, it's something that comes because he wants me to know it, because he doesn't want his mom to be a secret the same way I don't want Sebastian to be a secret. And now, neither of them is.

I'm not sure if I've done it—if I've figured out what it is that I need to know about him, but I'm sure I've done *something*. I'm sure this day matters more than the one that happened before it. I'm sure my immediate crush on Marcus wasn't just a fluke. I was supposed to meet him at Dunkin', and walk all over this city with him today, and tell him all the things I have.

And now it's just after ten p.m., and we're on the opposite end of the city from where the accident happened last night. It's time for us to start getting ready for tomorrow.

"I can probably still catch the ferry," Marcus says, glancing at his phone.

"No!" I blurt, because that's way too close to where everything got weird. But I act like it's because that idea is absurd. "We're all the way on Ninety-First and Broadway. Why would you go a hundred blocks back downtown to catch the ferry?"

"Yeah," he allows, like it's hitting him that it'd be nice to just get home without all the extra commuting. "Wanna split a cab?"

He hails one heading south and we both hop inside. I don't have very far to go—74th and Amsterdam—but I still want to pay half. I insist that he tell me how much it ends up costing, and I'm pretty sure he's just placating me when he says "okay," but at least it seems to conveniently remind him, "Do you think I can maybe have your number? You know, so I can let you know how much it costs."

I recite it and squeeze my phone in my hand, waiting for it to vibrate. The number I don't recognize illuminates my screen. For sure. There's not a doubt in my mind, and I just know that things are right this time. I'm not loopy over this boy I've just met, but I'm grounded. I really know him now. And he's amazing.

As our driver slows down in front of my building, Marcus peers out the window to see where we are. A twenty-two-floor co-op with a doorman and modest balconies in every unit.

I could get out on my side, but Marcus's side is on the curb, so he opens his door before I can and tells our driver, "I'll be right back. Just letting her out."

Our driver nods, disinterested.

I climb out of the back seat behind Marcus and we leave the door open so no one gets their hopes up about grabbing our cab.

"Well." He nervously wets his lips. "I guess I'll let you know how much the cab costs."

I smile. "Okay."

He smiles back. "What?"

I shrug. "You're just weird sometimes."

"No chance," he declares, like there have been dozens of Cool People polls conducted and he makes top ten every time.

"Okay," I say again.

He hangs his head for a moment and I look down, too. The tips of our shoes could be touching if one of us would just close the gap.

He peeks back up at me, the same eyes that I saw in the crosswalk last night but also *so* different. Calm. Warm. "Can I . . ."

I nod, and he leans in so I don't have to. His palms on my cheeks send a spark through every bit of me. I can't believe that maybe, finally, the good part is here—the first really good thing since I lost Bas. The good thing that I kept telling myself could happen eventually because Jacq and the therapist always told me that, eventually, it'd come. I didn't believe it, but I said it because it made me look okay on the outside. Because it made everyone else less sad.

He bends his neck to press his lips against my own.

But before he can—

No.

Screeching tires.

Please no.

Headlights. Pain that sucks my lungs empty. A blinding white light. And then I'm being yanked backward into the sky, into the night, away from everything.

Again.

September 24, Take Three: 7:01 a.m.

No.

I grab my blaring phone off my nightstand and mute it without even opening eyes. I don't have to look to know where I am. Again.

Okay, fine, maybe a peek.

I barely open my right eye, just enough so my vision isn't like peering underwater, and my lock screen stares back at me. Sebastian and me at the beach. No missed calls. And the date.

September 24. Yesterday. Or two days ago now. I don't know.

I don't know, I don't know, I don't know.

I close my eye again and slam my phone down on the mattress.

This is bad.

Maybe I didn't find out what it was that Marcus needed to tell me, but we talked about *so much*. We talked longer than I've ever talked to anybody, and this time he didn't grab me right before I left, he didn't insist, *There's something you need to know about me.* Because I must've already known it. I must've already fixed it.

Unless that wasn't the problem to begin with.

I pull myself off my pillows and sit up. My room is lit by daylight only, the sun shining through my cracked blinds.

Think, Syd.

Okay, we were in the crosswalk when it happened the first time. He grabbed my elbow. *There's something you need to know about me.* Skidding tires. Headlights. This sensation like I was being stabbed by a thousand knives-on-fire at once. Until I was yanked like someone had a string around my waist and everything went white.

This time, we were outside my apartment. He'd just gotten my number. I swore he was gonna kiss me and everything stopped, a city full of a million people went silent, and—for a second—I was the only girl alive.

Then skidding tires. Headlights. Blah, blah.

I lean back against my headboard and hug my knees to my chest, blinking at this furniture that I've had forever, at the pale pink walls, at the drawers I never fully close—like they're puzzle pieces that will magically slide together into a picture that might actually make sense.

The first time it happened, we'd just exchanged numbers, too. I thought he was gonna kiss me, too . . .

Maybe we need to finish the moment—before the tires and the headlights and all hell breaks loose.

Maybe we just need to . . . kiss.

In fairy tales, the kiss always fixes it. I'm not trying to say I'm some princess or anything, but maybe there's an ounce of truth in that. Maybe we grow up loving those stories because there's this survival instinct deep inside us that says we're gonna need them one day.

I roll out of bed and jog to my closet, faster than I did yesterday morning or the yesterday before that.

Because, this morning, I need enough time to stop for mints.

September 24, Take Three: 9:42 a.m.

I went back to Dunkin'. I ordered my cheese sandwich. I waited for it between the same two men in business suits and grabbed it when number two was called. I lurked in a corner when I realized Marcus wasn't there yet, and watched the door for exactly two minutes before he walked in. He was in the same dress pants and collared shirt under his black hoodie, and I pretty much linebackered him as soon as he walked in. He stumbled into the girl with the recyclable tote with the duck sketched on it, and she spilled her iced coffee so he bought her another. He said he was so late he might as well be in a coma, I offered to shove him in front of a bus, he thanked me for my commitment to his lies, and invited me to the dog park to eat.

I force my knees to stay still the whole time he's introducing me to dogs that I already know and saying hey to old people I've already met. I ignore how dry my mouth gets, watching his lips as he speaks, remembering how close they've been to meeting mine. I chew through the adrenaline, and swallow past the nerves, and brush my pocket a million times to make sure my Tic Tacs are still there.

"You okay?" Marcus asks with a half smile, the sun glinting in his hazel-brown eyes. It's only been three days but I swear I've known his gaze my entire life.

I quit brushing my pocket. "Sorry, what?"

"Dixon's dad." Marcus nods his way. "He's saying hey."

Mr. Parker is on the same bench he's been on the past two mornings, smiling and waving in slow motion. I bet he's there every day, though. I bet he has toast and jam every morning for breakfast, and almost always beats the *New York Times* crossword puzzle, and then kisses his wife goodbye on his way to come here with Dixon. I bet, whether it's a year ago or a year from now, that's his bench, and that's where he'll be.

I smile and wave back. Now that I have, he stops.

"Didn't want him breaking his arm trying to get your attention." Marcus sort of chuckles and I do, too, and then we fall into a silence that's weird for us. Not one of the easy ones like yesterday, where the words weren't there but we still were. This one is awkward and feels like a countdown. The first time since we've met when someone really might say, *Well, bye.*

My palms are sticky with sweat and Dunkin' crumbs, and I reach for a napkin stuffed into my paper bag. This sucks. *I* suck. And I don't want to risk losing him because I can't get out of my own head.

That's when it hits me. I don't have to *make* us kiss. Every day we almost kiss. It just needs to happen before the bad part does. That's all.

That's all, Syd.

I take a breath as my phone vibrates next to me. Jacq, I'm sure. *Ummmm . . . Whereabouts???* I'll look and write back in a little bit.

"You wanna know something weird?" I tuck my knee under me so I'm facing him instead.

He smirks like he's a little bit intrigued, and a little bit preparing to hear me say I poisoned his croissant. "Maybe."

"Sometimes, when I get really quiet—like, too quiet to notice an old man ignoring all arthritic symptoms just to say hi to me—it's because I'm having this completely unrealistic, embarrassingly aspirational daydream about being a chef one day."

He smiles, glad to not be poisoned and like that's really, really cool. "Yeah? With cheese-stuffed croissants as your signature dish?"

"Breakfast of champions."

"Oh, I can see it." Marcus holds out his hand like he's painting the picture in the space between us. "A bakery with a couple tables. Bagels, and rolls, and cheese-stuffed croissants. Sold out every day by nine a.m." He drops his hand and asks, "What's unrealistic about that?"

I rest my shoulder against the back of the bench, and I tell him how it wouldn't be a bakery, it'd be a food cart. We'd have a new menu all the time, full of modernized comfort food and everything that makes you lick your fingers. We'd be in a new location every day, unannounced, all over the country, with brick-and-mortar restaurants, too.

He doesn't stop listening and I don't stop talking. It's the most I've said all morning, the most I've ever said about any of this. It warms me from the inside out that he's so into my pointless rambling, like—to him—it isn't pointless at all.

Just like that . . . *just that fast* . . . we're the people I knew us to be yesterday.

September 24, Take Three: 1:47 p.m.

We end up at Bounce House, this new indoor playground in Midtown East for big kids and adults. There's bowling, and mini golf, and arcade games. And a bounce house, obviously, that's as big as my entire apartment.

No one's really here at this time on a Thursday, and Marcus and I have the bounce house to ourselves. It's all neon lighting that makes our teeth glow and our eyes shine, and we jump so long and laugh so hard that there are times I can barely catch my breath. I haven't been in one of these in over a decade, but the feeling rushes back and squeezes me tight the moment they zip us inside. Bounce houses are for secrets and made-up quests. They're forts impenetrable by the outside world. And while we're in ours, with our alien glow, we say even more things we've never said before. He used to play basketball until he decided to take a break from it this year. Jacq and I aspired to be the next Venus and Serena for a solid three days before we discovered that tennis is hard. He tells people he's allergic to oranges because he just doesn't like how they taste. I can bend my pinkie all the way back.

We've hopped, and talked, and laughed so long that we're starving, so it's time to leave in favor of sustenance. I rub my eyes. The normal lighting by the main doors burns.

"You like burgers?" Marcus asks.

"What was that?" I cup my ear like I didn't hear. "Sorry, I thought you just asked me if I'm a human being."

He laughs. "My bad for trying to give a voice to vegetarians."

"You know I'm—" But I catch myself. *You know I'm not a vegetarian because you watched me devour a turkey sandwich the size of my torso at Nina's yesterday.* "—actually kind of craving a burger now."

"There's a place not too far that's pretty good if you want to go there? They probably don't get too busy until dinnertime—"

"Sydney?"

The voice catches us as Marcus grabs the handle of the glass main doors. I'm never in this neighborhood—no one knows me here.

I turn around and my stomach flips.

He's in jeans and a long-sleeved black shirt. His arms look stronger than they did back then, and he's grown a beard that he couldn't when I knew him.

"Max," I manage to say. He's just standing there behind the front desk like he used to just stand there in my living room.

I want to run away but also get closer. I want to tell him I'm sorry but I'm not sure for what. I haven't seen him since the funeral—the only funeral either of us has ever been to. Well, at least, it was the only one at the time. I hope for him that it still is.

He takes big steps to close the space between us and he hugs me like we're friends. We're not, but that's probably the simplest way to put it. "How've you been?"

"I'm good." But the words are hardly real, swallowed by his shoulder while my mouth stays pressed against it. He lets me go and, for a moment, we just look at each other.

"I'm Max," he says, offering Marcus his hand.

"Marcus," Marcus says.

They shake and it shakes something in me, too. This grounding reminder of how people act. You know, like they're normal.

"What're you doing here?" I ask Max, and manage to finally smile when I do.

"I'm one of the managers." He laughs like it still surprises him. "I know, I know—finally got my life together." He slides his hands into his pockets and pushes his shoulders up toward his ears. He takes a breath. "Are you guys still on the Upper West Side?"

I nod, and suddenly I can't stop picturing him and Bas in our bathroom at home when they were thirteen years old, stuffing themselves with Pop Rocks to see who would explode first.

Sebastian, I guess.

"Are you?" I ask.

"No, moved out to Jersey City about a year ago, actually." He rubs his head with his palm. "Treason, I know. But me and Leah just had a little girl, so we needed the space."

It's been too long for me to punch him so instead I say, "Shut up."

"Yeah, I know." He chuckles and pulls out his phone, starts thumbing through some pictures. Babies always look a little bit like earthworms to me, but not this one. She has Max's smirky grin and Leah's big, dark eyes, and she's happy.

"She's perfect." I'm thrilled about it, and I hate it, all at the same time. "We have to go."

"Oh." Max jumps a little, like he'd drifted to la-la land and I just him woke up. "Yeah. Of course." He locks his phone and slides it back into his pocket. "Well, it was really good to see you, Sydney. Come by anytime, okay? Games on me, just let me know. You have me on Instagram, right?"

I muted him and all his friends two years ago. I couldn't stand looking at the lives they still had. "Yep! Well . . . bye."

"Good to meet you," Marcus says, shaking Max's hand a final time.

"Yeah, you, too," Max answers, and I know there's more he wants to say, words he's probably practiced but never thought he'd have to use. I don't wait for them, though. I don't want them.

Marcus holds the door open and we walk outside.

The weather is the same as it's been the past three days, but now it's not warm enough, or cold enough, or anything enough.

"Who was that?" Marcus asks, like I'm gonna say something easy. He waters our plants when we're on vacation, or goes to my dentist, or used to deliver the newspaper.

"He was Sebastian's best friend in high school." I don't want to tell him again, but I have to. Today, and maybe the next day, and maybe every day for the rest of forever as long as the days stay still. "My brother. Who died."

When we got the call from Sebastian's roommate at Corinthia, my insides shattered. It was like every structural component of my body went to dust and I was nothing but floating bones held together by melting skin. The shattered part—it never built itself back, not really. Not the way that TV always promises that it will. It stayed fragmented and every other part of me just learned to compensate. Like losing one sense so the others ramp up.

But once I'd compensated—once I was walking around looking like a human again—there was still something inside me that never came back. That stayed hollow and dark. Like a candle that used to burn until it got crushed by all the rubble.

You get comfortable with the darkness, with the warmth that's not there, and I'm used to it. Really, I am. But I wasn't ready to see Max today, just like I wasn't ready that time a year ago when the guy behind the counter at Insomnia Cookies had a name tag that said SEBASTIAN, or a few months ago when I got served an ad for the Northface Bas always used to wear. Sometimes, I'm just not ready.

I try to slow my thudding heart, vacuum back the tears, get it together so we can get on with this day. It's fine. Nothing's happened, nothing's changed.

"I'm so sorry," Marcus says, just like he did yesterday. But *I'm* not who I was yesterday. Yesterday, stuff came up because I wanted it to. Today, I'm trapped. Maybe that's why he adds, "Are you okay?"

I'm one of those people standing in the middle of the sidewalk, the kind of people who people like us can't stand. But he's watching me and I'm watching him back, and for now, it's nice to be still.

"Sometimes," I admit.

He nods. "When did it happen?"

"Two years ago. October seventeenth."

He almost winces, like when something hurts but you don't want to show it. "It's still hard?"

That's when I can't hold the tears back. I'm not crying, but they flow. Back when I was seeing the therapist, he said tears need a place to go—otherwise, you drown. Maybe he was right—I do cry way more easily now. But he also said that I could be sucking at math because my brother died, and I've been bombing math long before that ever happened, so maybe he had no idea what he was talking about.

"Sorry." I wipe my cheeks with the back of my hand, but Marcus stays put like I'm perfect. "Yeah, it's still hard."

I sink onto the window ledge next to him, and the sidewalk traffic keeps rushing by.

"It's just weird, you know?" I stare across the street. "I mean, Max and Bas used to do *everything* together. I watched them microwave a bag of marshmallows and almost burn the apartment down twice. And then my brother . . . he got into Corinthia for undergrad but Max was never that great at school and that's when they started growing apart. Then Bas went to med school and . . . yeah." My fidgety fingers scratch at the brick that we're sitting on. "It's just weird how Max has a job and a kid. How he's old enough and changed enough and . . ."

"It's not right," Marcus says.

"It's wrong."

"Yeah," he agrees. "It's really, really wrong."

I take a deep breath. My chest isn't so tight anymore. For a little bit—or maybe a really long time—we just sit.

"We can do something, if you want. On October seventeenth?" Marcus says. "Or maybe you don't want to. Then we don't have to. But if you do, to sort of, you know . . . remember stuff. Or forget stuff. We can."

That's the funny thing about those movies where the kiss fixes it all. The girl thinks about it and thinks about it and as soon as she stops, there it is.

Here it is. A moment that happens so fast that there's no time for mints. And I'm not sure if I do it, or he does, or it's an equal mix of both, but I'm sure that it's more than just a kiss. It sends something prickly down my spine that slowly flows through the rest of me. Until that candle in my center—the one that I thought went dark the moment we got that call two years ago—proves it's not out yet. Not completely.

It's just a spark, but a spark can light the world on fire.

September 24, Take Three: The rest of the afternoon

I get home as the sun is setting, a little after seven p.m., and the apartment is as empty as it was when I left this morning. I like it this way, though.

I'm full after our lunch at a place four blocks from Bounce House that had a bunch of open tables for Marcus and me to choose from. I ordered a burger with bacon and extra cheese and ate it all, and all my fries, and half a chocolate sundae. I wasn't even hungry enough for all that. Just empty—in a good way—now that the tears were gone.

Marcus walked me back here. He got my number and my phone vibrated in my pocket. We didn't kiss again, but he glowed beneath the setting sun and took my hand and squeezed it. I can feel it still—my fingertips tingling like they've been dipped in magic.

I walk down the hall to my bedroom, and the only sounds come from the honking cars and accelerating trucks sixteen stories down on the street below. I want to put on sweatpants, and lie down, and wait. For nothing, hopefully.

Sebastian's door is just as open as it always is. I start to pass it, but I poke my head inside instead. I didn't this morning—too busy deciding which bodega would have the shortest line so I wouldn't be late for my daily head-on collision at Dunkin'.

The bed is the same; the shoes lined up in the corner are the same; the notebook that's just barely hanging off the nightstand is still there. This room is the exact place it's been for the past two years, and that it'll be for the next two years, seven years, a million years, too. Not a single thing in here proves that I'm stuck, that it's been the same day for the past three days. Or maybe *everything* in here proves it. I just never really noticed that before now, before everything else started staying stuck, too. Maybe this room has been stuck for years. Maybe that's what grief is. Just a series of yesterdays forever.

I pull the door back to where it was, measuring the openness with the width of my foot. I'm too full and too tired to talk right now, even to Bas. I'll tell him about Max and Leah tomorrow.

Tomorrow.

I go into my room and shut the door. I grab a hoodie and sweatpants from my drawer and crawl on top of my bed. I'm not sure what time Mom and Dad get home tonight because I've never been back home on this day before. But they have late patients, and meetings, and dinners sometimes. They'll check my room whenever they get back.

I lie down, with Marcus in my head probably a little too much. But I like him there, how I'm not alone even when I'm by myself. If there's any kiss in the history of the world that could right the universe, it was ours.

I roll onto my side. I swear, it's like I blink and when I open my eyes, it's dark out and I'm still here. I wasn't yanked anywhere—I know it, because pain like that would snap me awake from the deepest sleep.

So maybe I did it and I'm that kind of girl. The main character kind of girl. The kind that the universe chooses for Something Amazing.

It's a fantasy, and as I nod back off, it's all mine.

Something's happening outside. An accident or an almost-accident.

I open my eyes, but no.

It's not happening outside. It's happening in here.

Tires. *Screeching tires*.

Again.

September 24, Take Four: 7:01 a.m.

WHY.

I turn off my phone alarm and check the date for no reason. I already know what it says, what this means, where I am. Back in yesterday. Again.

I pull my pillow from under my head so I can smother myself. Marcus and I talked about *everything*. Our kiss was freaking cinematic. I actually almost believed—

I drop my pillow onto the bed next to me and stare at the ceiling, tears tugging behind my eyes. I have no more hunches, no energy left to convince myself that maybe this isn't happening. It *is* happening—whatever the hell it is. And I have no idea how to make it stop.

Except maybe . . .

No.

Just maybe . . .

Ugh.

Maybe I can't get yanked away from someone I've never met in the first place. Maybe Marcus isn't here in spite of me being stuck, but maybe he's the entire reason why I am. I mean, that's when all this started, right?

But no. *No.* He's supposed to be the good thing. He makes my insides feel like they're functioning again. I don't want to lose that, not yet. *It's not fair.*

But what's the point if, every night, I get yanked away? What's the point of only having as much of him as he's willing to give me in his first day of ever knowing me? While I... what? Fall harder and harder for him based on days and days of interaction that he doesn't even know exist?

I'd be alone, anyway. After a couple of weeks, or even months, that'd be so lonely that my chest is tight just thinking about it.

I want to go to Dunkin' so bad, but it's pointless. I'd just be prolonging a kind of purgatory that I didn't even know was possible. So it's better this way, to just feel it now. Before I care even more.

My throat starts to burn and I squeeze a pillow to ignore it. This sucks, but at least I know how to deal when life starts sucking. This has to be the answer. If the universe wanted us together, why would it keep ripping us apart?

I'm listening, okay, Universe? I hear you. You win. You give me tomorrow, and I'll stay in this bed until it gets here.

Just, please, make it stop hurting?

Part Two:

Marcus

September 24, Take Four: 7:01 a.m.

. . . Anddddd we're back.

Nice.

Four days and counting. It's funny, you know? How fast you can get used to nonsense. I really think our bodies are made to adapt, always looking to call something "typical" so we can feel comfortable again. Adjust to a new normal, or whatever this is. A new forever, I guess.

What I mean is, my heart is still pounding out of my chest—like it was that first morning when I woke up. I've never sweat this much in my life—the sheets are wet and I wouldn't be surprised if the mattress is damp, too. But by now I expect to feel like I'm just about to die and then wake up mid–anxiety attack. Don't get me wrong, it's trash. But I've just got to accept that this hurts like hell, that every day it does and every day it will.

I roll over and hop out of bed. Literally. The first three mornings, I wiped out, tripping over the sneakers I left next to my bed. But today I know what's up. I'm accepting. I'm adapting.

I hop over the sneakers and then kick them aside.

Mom and I don't believe in hiring a house cleaner, no matter how little time there is or how much bigger our apartment gets. Nothing against anyone who hires the help they need, we just refuse to need it. To need any of those kinds of luxuries, really. Surviving has been our thing for so long that we're always resisting getting too far from that. Maybe it's pride, maybe it's fear that if we ever forget how to do things for ourselves, we won't know how to do them when everything comes crashing down.

When. It's imminent. Stuff falls down. Call it gravity, or call it the curse of knowing me.

Accept. Adapt.

I start to make my bed. I know it's pointless in a world where I'll never actually *go* to bed again—because that's the best part of a made bed: climbing back into it—but I do it, anyway. It's a habit, and if Mom comes home looking for me, I want her to come home to a made bed. I know it's the last thing that matters right now, and that "tomorrow"—when this day repeats itself yet again—she'll forget it ever happened. But I still want to give her a moment, at least, of the happiness she feels over tucked-in sheets.

Oh! Before I forget . . . let me set this alarm right now. I was paying attention this time—I was walking down Grand Street just so I didn't have to be at home and it was 10:15 p.m. on the dot when all that screeching, and bright lights, and knock-me-off-my-ass pain stuff started happening. I'm almost positive that's when it happened the day before, too. It was for sure after ten o'clock.

I figure if I give myself a heads-up at 10:14 p.m., I'll at least be ready this time.

Alarm set. I drop my phone back onto my bed.

Shower time.

I take a long one this morning. I'm sticky from all that sweat, and even more than that—I have the time. I run into Sydney around 8:30 a.m. I can be in Midtown in thirty minutes. I've never taken a whole hour to get ready for anything. I barely studied that long for my SATs.

I stand in the shower, letting the water start out hot and then twisting the knob to make it a little hotter every time my skin gets used to the new temperature. It's wild how unhot hot can feel when you ease your way into it. You think someone could inch their way all the way up to boiling? I guess I could try it one day. Worst thing that could happen is I melt my skin off until tomorrow.

The only bad thing about hot showers is the way they make your mind wander. You can start off mumbling Chance the Rapper lyrics and end up wondering where Albert Einstein's kids are. I really don't need that right now, all these thoughts popping up that I can't control.

Let's think about Sydney. Yeah, that's a good choice.

I don't want to sound like I'm buggin', but I never knew a girl could look like that. There's always been girls that are so pretty it's hard not to look at them. But I never saw a girl for the first time, and every time after that felt like the first time all over again.

Alright, so I *am* buggin'.

That's why I need to tell her the truth. Trying to say it on day one doesn't count. She needs to know what she doesn't know yet, even if I have to tell her again every day. She needs to know so I can be sure that she really wants to be around me. So that she can make that choice, too. It's just that, saying it out loud . . .

Saying it to her . . .

Alright. Shower done.

I wrap a towel around my waist and walk back into my room, open my closet door, and stare. For the past three days, I've picked the same outfit, the one I needed to wear when tomorrow existed. Now that it doesn't, I can pick anything, but I don't. Something inside me feels like *I can't* yet. I guess a part of me wants to act like that day is still coming, and it still matters, and I should dress like it. Maybe one day I'll shake all that, after I've done this a million times. But not yet.

I grab the same pants, the same button-down, the same shoes. I grab my black hoodie from the drawer and slide it on.

I walk out to the front of the apartment and flip on the main light. This room is the reason Mom decided to buy this spot in the first place. Black wood floors and the whole back wall facing Manhattan is just one big window. We're on the fourteenth floor, so you can see everything from here. The day before the days stopped moving, we had this huge storm. It came out of nowhere, and I was here by myself when it happened. I just stood there and watched, stared out at the East River through the raindrops on the glass. It's wild how fast the water changed. How, all of a sudden, it was two shades darker and crashing into itself. And all I could do was imagine myself inside of it, pointlessly trying to swim my way out. How fast I'd lose and be gone forever. I didn't even notice when the rain stopped. Eventually, I just realized I was staring at the sun instead.

There's gonna be a note on the kitchen island this morning. It's gonna be from Mom, written on a pink Post-it so I don't miss it on the white marble. It'll say: *I'm sorry I had to leave so early this morning but I'll see you soon. We're gonna be ok. M&M forever* ♡

M&M. It stands for "Mom and Marcus." She's been saying it my whole life.

I grab the note and skim it just because. This is the fourth day she thought she'd see me soon and the fourth time that she won't. I miss her, but I also don't know what to say. It's not her—she's perfect. She's the greatest woman on this planet, bar none. It's me.

I slide her note into my pocket and take out my phone. I put it on silent so it's easier to ignore it when she starts calling. Then I peep the time.

7:59. Time to go.

September 24, Take Four: 8:29 a.m.

"Hey! How's it going, Jenessa?" I step to the front of the Dunkin' line.

But the girl who's working behind the counter is giving the same *Why are you playing like we're friends?* look as always. It's not just because she doesn't remember the past three days. I've been coming to this Dunkin' almost every morning since freshman year because my charter school is right up the block. She takes my order almost three times a week. I know her name is Jenessa because I've read her name tag so many times.

It's pretty much my life's mission to get her to admit she knows me. It's time. We oughta be like those bartender-cowboy duos in Westerns by now, where we're asking about each other's weekends while she hands me my "usual" and I hand her perfect change with a two-dollar tip. At the very least, I want to make her smile *once*.

"Would you like to try a dozen Munchkins this morning?" she asks.

"Nah, I'm good, but thanks." She swipes at something on her iPad while I keep going. "You know, for so long I wondered why you all call them Munchkins. Most places call them donut holes but it finally hit me that maybe it's because you munch on them, and they're from Dunkin'. Munchkins. Am I right?" I smile. "If that's some kind of trade secret, I get it. You don't have to tell me."

Anything? An answer? A smirk?

She barely looks up from the iPad. "What can I get you?"

Oh, well. There's always tomorrow.

"Just a sausage, egg, and cheese croissant. No cheese. Thanks." I hand her cash and she hands me change along with my receipt. Order number two. I bring it with me to my waiting spot at the back of the restaurant.

The room is thick with bodies that have been here for the past four days, just like me. Day two was the only one when I almost didn't show up in time, because I was busy, you know, trying to figure out what the hell was going on. But at the last minute I decided to get here, anyway. To see if Sydney might be here again, too, and she was. That was really the moment when I decided, whatever this is, it's not so bad.

I guess the truth is, aside from her, this has been the worst month of my life. The kind of bad that makes it feel like I'm not even awake. But I almost started to forget all that when we hung out that first day. Being with her is almost enough to make me forget that anything bad was ever real in the first place.

"*Number two!*" the same voice as usual calls out.

I smile. It's like a string of Christmas lights is decorating me from the inside and they all flip on at once. I wonder what Sydney and I will get into today. If we'll start repeating stuff eventually or if we'll always have a new idea. A new idea forever sounds kind of wild, but so does being stuck where we are, so we'll see.

I grab my paper bag and glance around to see if she's grabbed hers yet, but she isn't here. I hang by the counter and keep an eye out so I don't miss her.

"Sorry, excuse me," she says as she tries to squeeze by.

I step back on purpose so that I bang into her. Even though, I guess I could try meeting her some other way. It doesn't always have to be a head-on collision. Maybe next time I could just try saying, *Hey*.

I spin around to help. *"Oh—"*

It's not her. It's the girl with the tote bag. The one I banged into yesterday when *Sydney* bumped into *me*. But at least her iced coffee didn't go all over the floor this time. It's just sloshing around her see-through cup while she freezes in the aftermath of almost getting squashed by me. Twice.

So glad she doesn't realize it's been twice.

"I'm so sorry," I tell her. "Are you good?" Some of her napkins drifted to the floor and I bend over to pick them up. I hand them back. "Really, my bad."

"It's okay," she tells me. "All good. My brother is tall. I know it's hard to see people all the way down here sometimes."

I chuckle and she reaches past me for a straw before she disappears into the crowd on her way back to the main door.

I glance around some more, but still no Sydney. I'll get out of the way, at least. Stand by the door. That way I'll see her when she walks in or catch her before she leaves.

I wait.

And wait.

Now it's almost nine o'clock.

Those Christmas tree lights strung up inside me are starting to burn too hot. This place is still packed but I rush my way to the front of the line, anyway. Back to the woman who calls the orders.

"Hey, I'm sorry," I say, slipping my way to the counter behind a guy who just grabbed his coffee. The woman raises her eyebrows at me as she sets two more paper bags on the counter. "There's supposed to be another order number two. Do you have that order yet?" I show her my receipt.

"Number fifty-nine . . . Number sixty-three . . ." she calls off to the side, and then she studies the piece of paper in my hand. "You're number two."

"I know—" I start, more urgently than what's fair. I take a deep breath and rein it in. "I know. But there's supposed to be another one."

"We don't give two orders the same number."

"Today you do. I mean—" My hand closes around the receipt, crumpling it when I didn't even want to. "Do you mind checking? Just real quick?"

She eyes me like I'm some fool, but I'm sure she's gotten used to fools in this job, so her glare is more suspicion and mild interest than anything else. She walks back to a computer screen mounted against the wall. She reads it for a second, then shakes her head. "Nope. One order number two. Sausage, egg, no cheese. Are you missing something?"

"Jenessa." I slide over to the register and the woman who's been calling orders goes back to it like I don't even exist.

"Number sixty-one and sixty-two . . ."

There's a guy in a suit who was just about to order and I tell him,

"Sorry, man. Real quick. Two seconds. I promise." I don't wait for him to say it's cool before I turn back to her and plead, "Jenessa."

She blinks at me like I'm some dude she tried to ghost. "Why do you know my name?"

"Jenessa . . ." I lean on the counter, resting my elbows on the surface. I clasp my hands in front of my mouth like a fist, like I'm about to stand here praying to the Dunkin' gods. "We've seen each other almost *every morning* for over *three years*. I get the same thing *every time*. A sausage, egg, and cheese croissant with no cheese. Then I make some joke. We should be ride or dies by now. We should have a secret handshake."

She blinks and folds her arms. Nothing.

I drop my neck before I peer at her again. "I'm looking for someone. She ordered a sausage, egg, and cheese croissant with no sausage and no egg."

"That's just cheese."

"Yes."

"On a croissant."

"Yes."

She frowns. "Why would anyone order that?"

"I don't know, but she did. She does, and I bet it's lit because this girl . . ." I shake my head, just thinking about her. "She's incredible. And she's gonna be a chef one day, so she knows what tastes good—"

"No one's ordered that," Jenessa dryly cuts me off.

"Can you check? You've got to be sure. This is really important."

"I can assure you, no one has ordered that. I would remember."

I want to tell her no offense, but trusting her memory while she's blacking out about the past THREE YEARS isn't exactly reassuring. But this guy behind me is starting to mutter about how I need to hurry it up, and he looks like he lifts weights and chugs protein shakes for fun, and the line behind him has gotten even longer since the last time I looked. I can't keep all these people from their caffeine much longer and live to tell about it.

I back away. All of a sudden, this Dunkin' isn't the same place I've been to all those times before, it's not the thing I have to look forward to. It's changed, somehow. I thought I had accepted and adapted. But here life goes again doing exactly what I wasn't ready for.

I keep backing away, watching Jenessa take orders, the other woman call numbers, and people grab their drinks and food while they barely even glance up from their phones. This terrifying normalcy and I'm the only one who's not in it.

People step out of my way so I don't have to step out of theirs, and finally I make it to the door. That's when I turn around, and push it open, and go outside. Where I'm surrounded by even more "normal." The bikes and the cabs and the people walking by. The honks and metallic bangs of truck trailers slamming shut. The city keeps going, always, no matter what. No matter how still you stand, or how scared you are, or how lost you get.

You know how with those Christmas lights, when one goes out, they all do? Well, that's how it happens inside me as I start walking down the block. First, it's one bulb, then another, and then it's all of them, all at once.

September 24, Take Four: 9:22 a.m.

What now?

This dog park used to be the only place that made it feel like I was somewhere else. It's still far enough from the tunnel that 11th Avenue doesn't get all congested, and there are all these trees that sort of block everything else out, so it's quieter here than it is most other places, and it's not full of a bunch of joggers, and sunbathers, and softball games like a lot of the other parks. Which is why it always felt pretty lucky that I'd found it at all.

I could only eat half this sandwich this morning, so the rest is wrapped in the paper and sitting next to me on this bench. Every dog knows it, too. They run over like normal, acting like we're gucci and all they want is some back rubs, all the while inching closer and closer to my leftovers. I don't want to send any of these dogs back home with the runs, though.

"Dixon, nah, man." I pull his nose back toward me. "I promise, it's not gonna be worth it."

He trots off. I get it. If I'm gonna be like that, why hang around? I sit back and cross one ankle over the other.

Sydney gave me her number twice, but I can't remember it. I think it ended in 3-4-9. Or maybe it was 3-9-4. Or maybe it wasn't anywhere close to either of those. Besides. If I did remember her number, what would I even do with it? Call her up with some kind of *You don't know me but I know you* speech? It's the same reason why I know it's out of pocket to go by her apartment, even though I remember exactly where we were when the cabbie dropped her off two nights ago.

"Oh, hey, Mr. Parker." I try to smile when I notice Dixon's dad waving at me from the bench on the other side of the blacktop.

Mr. Parker smiles. He kind of reminds me of the old guy in *Up*, with a way better attitude. It was his birthday last month. He turned eighty-two. It's wild to me that some people get to be eighty-two and others don't even get half that time. "You here by yourself today?"

He says it like he's surprised. Like he's gotten used to seeing me here with someone else. Does he remember Sydney somehow? Has he seen her? Has he seen her *today*?

"You thought I'd be with someone else?" I hopefully ask.

"Your friend," he calls back, trying to remember. "The one who's tall, like you."

I sink lower into this bench. He means Austin. "No, Mr. Parker, I'm alone."

"What's that?" he calls back, cupping his ear and turning it in my direction.

"I'm alone." I say it louder. Loud enough that it seeps into my chest.

"*Oh.*" He nods and smiles again. "As long as it's alone and not lonely."

There's something about that—the same way there's been something about a lot of things lately—that makes me feel like every part of me is seizing up like some slug that got salted. This shrinking, crushing, withering feeling that I don't always want to survive, but every time, I do.

Mr. Parker's been at this for eighty-two years. He's doing something right. It almost makes me want to say back to him, *It is lonely. It's lonelier than I ever knew that anything could be. How do you live in a city like this, and have people like mine, and it's still so lonely?* I want him to tell me how to fix it. Or even if he can't tell me how, promise me that it at least *can* be fixed. That's called hope, and that's the part Mom keeps insisting we have to hold on to.

Hope, hope, hope.

How do you hope, Mr. Parker? is what I want to ask. *How do you hope for eighty-two years?*

But I know I can't say all that out loud, even if it erases tomorrow and I don't have to worry about him remembering a thing. It's the fact that I *physically can't*. I'll break down trying.

So, instead, I call back, "Alone. Not lonely."

Mr. Parker smiles. "Very good!"

On my way out the park, I toss my sandwich to the birds.

September 24, Take Four: 12:01 p.m.

"Hey, man!" Javi smiles from behind the register at Nina's. "What are you doing here?"

I have no clue. But I left the dog park and started walking south, until I looked up and here I was. I almost kept walking, but something told me to go inside.

I'm glad I did because it always feels nice in here. The right temperature, the right amount of daylight, smells good enough to lick the floors.

Javi's still cheesing at me, waiting for an answer while I linger in the doorway.

"Missed you guys," I tell him, and I walk over to the counter and slap his hand before we give each other a hug.

"Man, we missed you, too," Javi says as we let each other go. "Felix has been asking everyone if we've heard from you. Looks like his heart breaks a little every time we tell him no."

Now mine kind of breaks, too. "I know. There's just been a lot going on. I'm sorry."

"Don't apologize." He says it like, if I do it again, he'll knock me out. "We just worry about you, man. You need to come by more."

"I will. For sure." And even though it's been a while, I mean it this time. "Mr. Felix coming in today?" He should be, soon, unless Sydney isn't the only thing that's different.

"Yeah, he'll be here," Javi tells me. "Probably not 'til four, though. Can you stick around?"

"Yeah, I'm gonna stick around. Let me go say hey to the guys in the kitchen and I'll be back."

"Bet," Javi says, and I step out of the way just in time for a customer to walk in.

I stay in the kitchen for a few minutes, catching up with Pedro, Alex, Chet, and Mike. More than I did when I stopped by here with Sydney, just because I didn't want her to feel on her own, like I forgot about her. They're all good, and I'm glad to hear it. Alex and his girl are having another baby so they've been looking at new spots in Queens. Mike's band did a gig in Jersey last weekend and now the bar is talking about making them regulars. They want to know how I've been, too, but there's nothing to say that they don't already know. Besides the whole days-don't-move-forward-anymore thing. But that's not worth getting into. They'd think I was just messing around, anyway.

I mean, who wouldn't?

I go back out front and stand off to the side, catching up with Javi until the lunch rush gets too heavy for him to talk to me and add up orders at the same time. That's when I go to a booth instead and tell him not to worry about it, that we'll talk more in a little bit. I sit and wait, checking the time on my phone every few minutes. Ignoring all my missed notifications.

"Hey, Marcus!" Javi shouts from behind the counter. "Felix just called. Says he'll be here early today—in the next fifteen."

"Nice," I answer, as he goes back to taking orders. I check the time on my phone. 12:42 p.m. That sounds about right.

My heart is already thudding. Here we go. Me and Mr. Don't-You-Ever-Try-To-Lie-To-Me Felix. It's not the rest of these guys, but it's him—*he's* the one I've been avoiding for the past month. The one I'm too chicken to look in the eye, to see all that disappointment. I'm disappointed in me, too. More than disappointed. I don't even like myself anymore. You know what? Maybe he doesn't like me, either. If he doesn't, I deserve it. I deserve everything he's about to say to me, everything he's about to call me, every ban he's about to put on me. *Stay out of my restaurant. Stay off my block.* I'd do it, too. If any of that would make this even one bit easier on him—on anyone—I'd do it in a heartbeat.

Somehow, I know without even turning around that when the bell jingles over the door this time, it's him. The air kind of changes, too, into something that's harder to breathe. He walks to the front of the line, smiling and patting the backs of the regulars he passes (see, that should be us, Jenessa!), until he gets to Javi. Javi says something and nods in my direction.

Mr. Felix is Dominican with a perfect shape-up, always. He's in a tucked-in polo with jeans, every day, even when it's snowing out. He's in his forties and he has two daughters, both in middle school. They, with his wife, are the background on his phone. His wife, Nina—who he's been with since he was my age—is who this place is named after.

I'm not sure why all that makes me think about that game that Sydney said she used to play, I Bet. Maybe because we were sitting here when she told me about it. Or maybe because I wonder how close her guesses would have gotten to who Mr. Felix really is.

Anyway, that thought—and literally everything else—is completely swiped from my brain now that he's walking over.

I swallow hard and feel the trickle of sweat sliding from the base of my hairline, down my neck, down my spine, into my boxers. I've never known my dad, so this man is the closest thing I've ever had to that. I didn't really realize that before now.

There's not even a trace of a smile on his mouth as he reaches my booth, and he hasn't taken his eyes off me since Javi pointed out where I was. I'm not sure if I try to smile at him, either. I can't feel my face.

"Hey, Mr. Felix," I manage to say as he stands over me.

"Come to the back with me," he says, and has me lead the way. Probably so he can keep an eye on me, make sure I don't chicken out and run away. That glare behind me pricks the backs of my eyeballs like laser beams. I can't cry. Not in front of him. He deserves for me to face him like a man. But by the time I reach the back room, where he keeps a small desk and prints the paystubs, the hot tears are already running down my cheeks.

My jaw is gonna stay straight, though. Watch. I'm not about to be some blubbering baby. Not in front of Mr. Felix.

He closes the door behind us and turns around to face me. His eyebrows slide together and he folds his arms across his chest. "How are you?"

"I'm alright." I nod to prove it to him and to me. "What about you?"

His stare won't break, so I won't break it on my end, either. "Devastated."

The breath spurts out my nostrils like I just got the wind knocked out of me. "Okay" is all I can say.

"Aren't you?" Mr. Felix asks.

I shake my head. "Can't be."

"Why not?"

"Don't deserve the sympathy, sir." I sniff, my tears blurring my vision. But my jaw is stone. "It's my fault. Can't be devastated over something I did to myself."

"You didn't do this, son." He says it like I ought to be old enough to know better than that by now. But he wasn't there, he didn't see it, and I don't want to get into all that now.

"Respectfully, Mr. Felix, I did."

He walks around to his chair and takes a seat. There's this crack on the door that was right next to his head when he was standing in front of me, that I was focusing on instead because it was easier to pretend like I was looking at him than to actually look at him. So, if I can swing it, I'd really like to keep focusing on that crack.

Mr. Felix's gaze makes the side of my face hot. "Maybe you were there," he slowly starts. "Maybe there are plenty of things you could have done instead of what you did. Maybe you're thinking about that all the time. But you didn't do this, Marcus. God did this. You hear me? That's just how it works—"

"Why?" It bursts from my mouth like a firework, straight ahead until it splats into that crack. "Why would God do this?"

"We're not gonna know why. And even if you did know why, it's not gonna feel good enough. It never does with stuff like this."

There it is. You never know why. Now I'm glad I didn't ask Mr. Parker about hope, because I bet it's the same answer when it comes to that, too. I bet you don't hope for eighty-two years, you just get used to what it is. What it feels like when all your Christmas lights blow out and stay that way. The way your eyes adjust to the dark eventually. It's not easy. But you'll survive. You'll adapt.

The tears are soundless and I squeeze my eyes shut to try and lock them in, but it just pushes them out faster. *No.* I want to get out of this room more than anything, so Mr. Felix doesn't see me like this, but my feet are stuck, just like the days are.

My eyes are closed so I don't see him get up, but I feel his arms wrap around my shoulders. Trying their best to keep me still. I don't deserve a hug, or his help, or anything. But I can't pull away right now.

I bury my head into his shoulder and he claps a strong hand against the back of my neck.

I gotta stop. *Get it together, man. You gotta stop.*

"You're gonna be okay." His voice breaks. "You hear me? You're gonna come out the other side of this and you're not ever gonna give up. Alright? You hear me?" He jolts me in his arms a little bit to try and make it sink in. "You're gonna do it for Austin, and your mom, and for his mom, and for me. But more important than any of that, you're gonna do it for yourself."

The last part catches in his throat, and even though I can't see him, I know this is as close to crying as I'm ever gonna witness from Mr. Felix. I hate myself for doing this to him. I hate myself for what I've done to all of us. And how they're good to me, anyway. How these guys are still happy to see me. How Mr. Felix is still hugging me and Mom keeps telling me every day that she's gonna love me forever. Like we really are gonna be okay one day.

How?

How does anyone get to being okay after they've killed their best friend?

September 24, Take Four: 10:07 p.m.

I wanted to tell Sydney before we said bye on day one.

I stopped her in that crosswalk and everything, because I couldn't keep knowing this girl without telling her the truth. It wouldn't be fair, and I had to give her a chance to decide on me for herself—before I started falling for her even more. Because I kind of think that's how it is when you meet someone like her. You start falling, just in reverse. Getting farther away from the ground and closer to the clouds.

I wanted her to know the truth about me before tomorrow got here. But then the screeching tires came, and the headlights, and this pain like I'd been dinner for a T-Rex, and we were gone. I didn't know if it was an accident, or a mental breakdown, or what. I didn't know if it was a sign that she didn't need to know about Austin, or a sign that I didn't deserve to know her at all, because of what I'd already done. All I could think was that I hope I didn't kill her, too. If I had, I would leave. I wouldn't tell Mom, or Ashe, or anyone where I was going, and just disappear so that they would be safe. I couldn't keep doing this to the people I love.

Not that I love Sydney or anything. That'd be too much, I know. But you get what I'm saying.

When I saw her again at Dunkin' the next day, I didn't know what was happening, but I decided I'd take it. It was better than hurting her or worse. Those three days with her were the best days I've had since Austin died. They were the kind of good days I didn't think I could ever have again. I felt guilty about it, honestly. To be smiling and laughing. I shouldn't be doing either. What the hell was funny about any of this?

But with Sydney, I smiled. And I laughed.

So maybe it's good that she's gone.

The dog park is closed this time of night, but that doesn't mean much. Just a four-foot iron gate that's shut now instead of open, with a metal sign screwed into it that says this place closes at sundown and opens at seven a.m. It's easy to jump—too easy—so I do. I'm surprised I'm the only one in here considering nothing's really keeping anyone out, but I guess Mr. Parker isn't hopping any fences these days, no matter how short they are.

I lean back on my bench and stare at a bunch of nothing. Just sitting here, waiting for time to pass. I ended up staying at Nina's for hours, in that back room with Mr. Felix. He asked me how I've been doing and I told him I didn't know, because I don't. He asked about Mom and Ashe, and I just shook my head because trying to talk about them—especially Ashe—is way too hard. He told me whatever we need, seriously anything, he's here. I believe that, I really do.

So, I'm glad I went today. But I don't think I'll be back tomorrow.

Oh, man, that's my alarm. I pull my phone from my pocket and scroll past all my unacknowledged notifications so I can turn it off. And then it's way too quiet.

It's 10:14. If I've got this figured out, I should have about sixty seconds before I'm pulverized. Damn. Being this aware of the countdown makes me feel like I should do one last thing.

So, I yell. The way you do when you're a little kid because someone dared you to. Except my lungs are bigger now, and my voice travels so far that some people probably hear it in their apartments. It's the kind of loud that cops and Good Samaritans investigate. Doesn't matter, though.

Thirty seconds left, maybe less.

My throat pulses when I finish, like my vocal cords have a heartbeat. I have to catch my breath now that I've just used it all. The night Austin died, I screamed that loud. But it was different that time, too much rain for it to reach anybody. I had to go to them.

That was the hardest decision I've ever made. Whether to leave him because I could get help faster, or carry him back so he wasn't alone. They don't teach you how to make choices like that, how to pick one or the other when they're both bad. They don't tell you how, no matter what you choose, the choice you didn't make will stick with you—

It's happening. I glance at my phone before I can't. 10:15 p.m., and screeching tires from a car that's nowhere around flood my ears. The pain is almost instant and, don't get me wrong, it hurts like hell.

But tonight, it's kind of nice.

September 24, Take Five: 7:01 a.m.

Alright.

So.

Yeah.

I open my eyes, ignore the sweat, stare at the ceiling. There's nothing up there. Just cream-colored paint and a light that isn't on. Maybe today I'll lie here while the sun comes up. Lie here while Mom rips me a new one for staying home once she gets back. Lie here while it starts all over again.

Might as well.

But two minutes after deciding that I'll stay, I decide that I have to go.

I set my alarm to 10:14 p.m. I make my bed. I take a shower. I grab the same clothes and accept that I still want my sausage, egg, and cheese croissant with no cheese. I wander out to the front of our apartment, grab Mom's note and slip it in my pocket, put my phone on silent.

And I still leave at 7:59 a.m. on the dot. Old habits die hard, I guess.

September 24, Take Five: 8:28 a.m.

I'm listening to music through my AirPods when it's my turn to order.

I pull one bud out and the other keeps playing, so I'm halfway in this Dunkin' line and halfway somewhere else. I don't even have the fight in me to try and get Jenessa on my side today.

She blinks at me from behind the register. "Would you like to try a dozen Munchkins this morning?"

"No, I'm good. Can I just get a sausage, egg, and cheese croissant without the cheese? Thanks."

I slide my bud back in and give her cash. She makes change and hands it to me with my receipt, and I step aside like we've never met a day in our lives.

Number two.

I head to the back of the restaurant and turn my music down enough that I'll be able to hear them call my order. I wait with my hands in my pockets while the Dunkin' crowd cycles in and out. I was thinking that maybe I'd go to the Bronx Zoo today. I haven't been since I was a kid. Apparently, we've got some panda visiting right now, or on loan, or something, and people have been saying it won't be here forever.

I chuckle at the irony.

Someone bumps me as they walk in the door, and I scoot over some so that maybe that won't happen a second time.

But wait, hold on.

I glance back over my shoulder. And I know there's no way that it is, but *it is*.

It's Sydney.

What . . . in the actual . . .

Her phone is on the floor and I guess she dropped it when she bumped me. She's bending over to pick it up and I bend over, too, like something magnetic is going on. She moves and I move with her.

She has this one curl that's falling in her eyes and it's too short to push behind her ears as she grabs her phone and peeks up at me.

I pull out one AirPod and I know I shouldn't be gaping but I'm pretty sure I am. I don't want to creep her out—like, *why is this freaky dude staring at me?*—but I just can't believe that I *am* staring at her.

"Sorry," I manage to say. I have to push it out of my mouth like I haven't spoken in a hundred years.

But she smiles, and shakes her head, and tells me, "Don't be sorry."

🌹🌹🌹

I'm lucky she was willing to come here with me at all.

We're different today. The words aren't coming together like someone already wrote them for us. It's probably me. I'm probably thinking too much, trying to come up with a good reason why she wasn't here yesterday but she's here now. Of course, there's no good reason. There hasn't been a good reason for any of this.

I awkwardly asked her outside Dunkin' if she would eat with me, even though I knew I hadn't given her much of a reason to want to. But she said yes, anyway. I got lucky.

Dixon lays his whole fifteen pounds of body weight against my shins, and I scratch him while Sydney and I sit on this bench in the dog park like we did the days before. Mr. Parker's on the bench on the other side of the blacktop. Our Dunkin' trash is balled up next to us. There's a breeze and it pushes Sydney's hair toward me. I catch a whiff of her signature nothingness; the soap she uses isn't even strong enough to smell. It was the first thing I noticed about her when we banged into each other in Dunkin' the first time—that she doesn't have a scent. I've never liked it when girls smell like something besides themselves. Makes my nose itch.

"Do you think dogs understand words or just sounds?" she asks.

She's leaning over now, too, rubbing Dixon with one hand. He shoves his butt toward me so he can be closer to her. Traitor.

"Isn't it scientific fact that dogs can understand words?" I ask. She pushes her hair behind her ear as I go on. "Einstein created the lightbulb, then built the Great Wall of China, then started kicking it with dogs because they're the smartest species on earth, right?"

She smiles but she's still looking at Dixon. "Yeah, I think so. According to some dude on crack."

I laugh.

"I just feel like . . ." She leans back on the bench again and I do, too. Dixon gives us a chance to change our minds, but when more than a second passes and we don't go back to scratching him, he goes off to find better people. "The words they know—*sit, down, treat*—is it the word, or the way we always sound when we use the word? Like if someone said *fish* in the same tone they use for *sit*, would a dog sit, anyway?"

"No way," I say.

She laughs. "How do you know?"

In defense of dogs everywhere, I insist, "Because *fish* is a whole different word—"

"That's the point! The point is they don't know words, they know how we sound when we say certain words, so they've just learned the pattern but not the actual language."

"Impossible."

"Yeah?" She folds her arms and faintly smiles as she watches some dogs wrestling in the grass. "Alright. Well, I'll let you ask the next one that comes over."

We go quiet again. Mr. Parker waves and I wave back. I can't believe I had so much I wanted to ask him yesterday and now we're here again like that never even happened. I really could do anything. I could say anything. I could feel anything. None of it matters. It just erases at the end of every day. I'm living in a real-life Snapchat.

But that doesn't change the fact that I can't keep hanging out with this girl and not falling for her. If another day comes when she's not at Dunkin', and then she's never there again, I don't want to wonder what it would have felt like to talk to her about this stuff. So maybe talking to her for real doesn't have to be about her and what she's gonna remember. Maybe it's about me. Maybe it's about telling her just because I want her to know.

"I'm stuck," I say.

She turns, glancing at my feet first, then my hands. Like she's expecting to see gum somewhere. When she doesn't, she smiles. "What?"

"I'm stuck." I take a deep breath. I can't look at her while I'm talking. "I'm stuck in this day. It keeps happening for me and I have no clue why. But you and I have met before, and if I'm lucky, we'll meet again tomorrow, and I know that sounds wild. But if you hang around for another thirty seconds, I promise I can prove it."

Even though I still can't face her, I give her a second to opt out. But she doesn't get up and she doesn't start to back away.

"You want to be a chef," I tell her. "And I think that's hella cool. Your mom is a doctor but not the kind that does Lasik. She does ear, nose, and throat stuff. Which I'm still ready to argue is pretty much our whole lives. And I know how to play I Bet. Well, not like you—your imagination beats mine any day—but I know what it is, at least, because you told me. When we did all this before."

Alright, it's time to man up and look her in the eyes.

She's blinking, her face gone slack, and my heartbeat is thudding in my ears while I wait for her to do anything at all. That speech could have been way longer. I could have told her how her eyes change a tiny bit right before she makes a joke, like she's focusing in on a shot she's gonna make. I could have told her how she scratches her left cheek when she's trying not to smile. I could tell her she lives on Amsterdam between 74th and 75th and that there are toddlers who ride two-wheelers better than she does. I could tell her that kissing her was the first time in a month that I felt anything that I wanted to feel again.

But I'm glad I didn't say all that because she's already frozen like the Wi-Fi cut out.

"Look, I know this sounds ridiculous," I tell her. "And impossible. But for some reason it's not, and—"

"You don't have a dog."

"Huh?"

Her breaths are heavy, like she has to remind herself to take them. "And you used to clean the kitchen at Nina's every night except Thursday. And you have stank face when you dance. And I'm stuck, too."

Hold up. *"What?!"*

"I'm stuck, too." Her voice is low, like we're telling secrets. "It's been five days for me. Yesterday I stayed home. The whole time. Because I thought maybe you were the problem. Not you, but us. Like maybe we weren't supposed to know each other and that if I stayed away, the days would start moving again. But they didn't."

Thank God they didn't. Thank God that wasn't the answer.

"What's it like for you?" I ask. "When it happens? Is it always at night? After ten?"

She nods. "Yeah. And it sort of feels like getting your eyebrows threaded. Except every hair on your entire body, no matter how small it is, at once. Like this one huge yank, you know?"

"Relatable."

It breaks the tension and she laughs a little as her eyes shift to my eyebrows. It's quick but I notice it. I almost reach up and make sure they're smooth, but I don't want to call more attention to them if they're not.

"I'm pretty sure it's happening at 10:15 every night. Last night I set an alarm for 10:14 so it wouldn't catch me off guard. A minute later, it started."

"Really?" Something about it weighs her down—makes her shoulders sink and her neck drop. She pulls her knees to her chest. "Like we're trapped, or something."

Trapped? I wrap my hands behind each of her calves. It's not so weird now—at least, I hope it's not—to do the little things I've been wanting to for days. The little ways people touch each other, you know what I mean. I couldn't do it while she'd still only known me for a couple of hours. "Hey," I tell her. "We're not trapped."

"Then what exactly would you call this predicament?"

I'm not sure. I'm not sure what's happening and I'm not sure why. But I've felt that way for weeks now—I'm not sure about anything anymore. Except that her eyes are so pretty, man. Shiny black if you're lazy, but really this deep brown color if you look closely enough. They change in the sun, and when she laughs. If this is forever, it's not so bad.

"I think we're just . . . together. A little stuck, yeah, but . . ." I nod this time. "We're together."

She smiles, then slowly looks me up and down. "Didn't you notice my outfits were changing?"

I noticed everything else about her. I do a quick glance so I know what she's wearing now. Ripped-up jeans and a sweater. ". . . Yes?"

"You're such a boy," she mutters, but at least she giggles when she does. We sit there, letting our new reality sink in.

"If you're stuck, too," she finally says, while my hands are still behind her legs. "Does that mean you remember what happened that first night? When all this started? When you stopped me in the crosswalk and said there was something I need to know about you?"

Oh man. "Yeah."

"Did you ever end up telling me?" she asks.

Nope.

But here we go.

The thing that happened on August 24

My and Austin's moms start a dance party pretty much anytime they're drunk. That's their tell. Not like they're going to the club; they pull out the old-school stuff. Boy bands from twenty years ago. They prove that they still know every dance move, for the most part. Mom's made me watch enough music videos to know.

That night, it was that "Bye Bye Bye" song by NSYNC. Mom and a bunch of her friends were punching the air and snaking their bodies left and right like Howie Mandel asked if they had talent and their whole answer was WATCH THIS. It was good, though. Not so much the performance, just how everything felt. It wasn't just like nothing was wrong, but it was like everything was right. That little difference between when ice is cold and when it burns, you know? The same thing but not.

Ashe was there. Gigi was there. More people, too. A ton of them. Mom got a rental on Long Island for the night so she could host this big party. It was sort of an end-of-summer thing, but sort of a celebratory thing and a thank-you thing, too. Sip had just inked the Orangetheory deal. They'll be the exclusive water brand in gyms across the country, which is even bigger than the Equinox deal.

That one's just regional. But the news isn't public yet. It was supposed to be announced in November.

That's why Mom was going big that night—she was so happy about what they were building, and grateful for everyone who'd been killing themselves alongside her to get it done. All twenty people who worked for Sip were there that night, all the people in our lives who cared about Sip, anyone who'd ever listened to her cry late at night or loaned her a couple hundred bucks when she needed it—everyone came. But the house wasn't even too packed. It had, like, eight bedrooms. Skylights everywhere. Tucked away in this fancy neighborhood with woods all around it. There was a private beach at the end of the road.

Aus and I were out front with beers. I lost count of how many we'd already had. They told us *don't drink* but then looked the other way on purpose. Not because they didn't care, but because they trusted us. That's the worst part. Well, not actually. But it sucks. They trusted us that night the same way they had a hundred nights before. Trusted us to act right and come back home.

"You think the neighbors can hear us?" I stared out at that ritzy neighborhood. It was dark but they had lights all over.

Behind us, the windows rattled while everyone inside sang. Aus shook his head, more times than he needed to because he was feeling his drinks. "Nah. Rich people's houses are too insulated for noise pollution."

He was probably right. Plus, they were all so far apart from each other. A city block, easy.

Then he swigged from his beer bottle and cheesed as he nodded back at the rattling windows. "Yo, you think in another life they would have pimped us out to Hollywood?"

He was always talking about other lives, like all of us had hundreds of them. I never thought about it much back then. But now . . . I don't know. Maybe some of us do and some of us don't. Maybe some people end up with a hundred lives and some just end up with the same day a hundred times.

Something hopped across my feet, from the lawn on one side to the lawn on the other. It was fast and my drinks had me too slowed down to really see it. A cricket or something. Maybe a small frog. "You mean forced us to be a singing group or something?"

"Yeah, man. That's why they geek about it now. They used to love our hits. The Uptown Boys didn't come to play."

I laughed and so did he. Harder than anyone else probably would have. Snickering into our knees like we oughta have a stand-up show.

"Uptown, yeah?" I asked. "We had it like that?"

"Definitely. Multiplatinum and everything. We didn't get famous just to mess around with it."

"I don't know, man." I glanced over my shoulder. The blinds were open. Half of them had their fists to their mouths like they were holding fake mics. "Maybe they're the ones who had a group. Since they're the ones always singing and dancing."

"Nah," Aus said, like he'd read up on our past lives on Wikipedia. "You remember the Temptations movie. Being famous is trash. Anyone who ever did it in one life wouldn't love it so much in the next."

He took another swig of his beer and I nodded. Aus is, hands down, the smartest kid there ever was. Teachers didn't see it because he was smarter than them, too. You know how it is—they care about what's on the test, how much Shakespeare you can quote. While Aus sat there reading a book a week. Played CNN on his headphones while the rest of us listened to Spotify. Devoured documentaries. He never shoved it in your face, but he could sit there killing you in NBA 2K while he quoted Amanda Gorman, and all of a sudden you loved poetry, too.

So, if Aus said famous people in one life don't crave fame in the next? I'm believing that all day.

"How come in all these other lives, you always make it sound like we all still knew each other?" I asked.

He shrugged. "Just seems like that's how it would be. Souls stick together and just the bodies change."

It would be nice if it went that way, huh? If your people always show up somehow, at some point, no matter which one of your lives you're living. Your job is just to notice them.

"You think we made it in this one?" I asked. And when I said it, it wasn't about the Orangetheory deal, or all Mom's followers, or this Max-series-looking house behind us. It was about . . . the stars, and how we could get this far out from the city and actually see them. It was about our Thursday nights with *Grey's* and tuna sandwiches, the way Mom and Ashe loved each other, and the difference between ice cold and ice hot.

He chuckled and held his beer out to me. "Yeah. Yeah, we did."

I tapped my bottle against his, and when he didn't stop swigging, I didn't, either. I polished off the last half of my bottle and left it empty on the step next to me.

We sat there for a minute—maybe two, maybe five—until something wet fell on my shoulder. Bird crap and I was too messed up to care.

Then it fell on my head. Then on my arm.

Nope, not crap. Rain.

The sky opened up and it poured. One of those summertime storms that come in wild and then they're gone. Aus stood up and started heading toward the door. I should have let him. I'm gonna hate myself forever all because I didn't let him.

"What, you're too pretty to get wet these days?" I almost had to yell because the rain was so loud.

He turned around. At some point, I guess I stood up, too.

"I'm waterproof. Just my phone's not."

"Ditch the phone, then." I reached into my pocket and handed him mine. "Put them inside and then come back."

Aus smiled, ready. For what? It didn't matter. We didn't make plans when it was time to mess around, we just did it. Like when it was his idea to ride the L all night, or my idea to shoot fireworks at Morningside Park and haul ass out of there before we got caught, or when we would play chicken in the crosswalk outside our old apartment.

He opened the front door and a few seconds later he was back without either of our phones in his hand. It was raining so hard, I could barely see him standing in front of me.

"Alright, we're invincible now," he said.

"Everything changes after tonight," I told him, and I didn't know where it came from. I didn't know I was thinking about it. I didn't know that was even how I felt. But more than that, I didn't know if I was ready. If I wanted it. "With that Orangetheory stuff," I yelled over the rain. "Stuff's just gonna change."

Aus shrugged. "We're not gonna change," he yelled back.

"I know, but you know what I mean."

So maybe that's why I wanted to be in the rain, why it felt better outside that house instead of inside it. In there, stuff was changing, and out here, it wasn't.

"You know what I think?" He shoved me and I stumbled backward farther than I should have, the drinks mixed with the slick from the rain on this stone patio. "I think you want to be out here in this monsoon so no one sees you crying. You scared, man? You can say it. Come on."

We were laughing again, hard for no reason, and he moved first so he was quick enough to get me in a headlock. One I would have been able to break out of easy if it wasn't for all the drinks and all the rain. But we covered that already, I know.

"Oh, you know I'm not scared—" I said, working to yank myself out from under his arm.

"I know that? I didn't know I knew that."

"Get outta here, man."

"Prove it." He let me go and we both stumbled backward, breathing hard. My shirt weighed five pounds more than it did dry.

And this is another part that sucked. Because I wish I'd just been like, *You know what, man? I am kind of scared. I don't know if I like what this turns into. I don't know if I want Mom to have some kind of empire, and all these people in our lives who are maybe only there because they want something from her. I don't know if I want her to maybe be the same kind of famous that you just said no one ever likes. The kind of famous no one wants in a second lifetime after they survived it in the first.*

If I had said it, he would have sat down and listened. But I didn't. Instead, I yelled back, "Let's go to the beach."

It wasn't far. There were three more houses before the end of the road, and the beach started after the last one. But the road sloped, it got higher on our end and lower the closer you were to the sand, and the rain from the storm flowed down the street like a black river in the nighttime.

We flowed with it, yelling back and forth at each other just to be heard, laughing so hard. I don't remember what was funny but I remember how it felt. My abs burning while the sheets of warm rain ran off me like a waterfall. That ice-hot feeling burning through me like a wildfire.

A long flight of wooden steps led down to the sand, which stretched from the woods on the right to a bunch of rocks on the left.

The sand was so drenched that it was like wet cement. The rain was so heavy, the sky and the water basically existed as one thing. I stared at it. I could have stared at it until it stopped.

"This is unreal," Aus yelled. He was staring at the water, too.

I wanted this to be another one of those stories we'd tell, like our night on the train, and our fireworks, and dodging cars because we knew we were fast enough. It was supposed to be just another wild night, and in a few weeks we'd have another one, and then another one after that, and some Orangetheory deal wouldn't stop us. Nothing would stop us.

"Let's get in," I yelled.

He turned to me. Eyebrows raised. "You think I won't?"

"You think *I* won't?"

"Well, come on, then!"

We jogged into the water until it was up to our knees. Even that close to shore, the waves were strong. But we stayed up. We were stronger.

Then Aus took a few steps farther out and dove forward. I had to squint to find him, but after a few seconds, I did—bobbing in the water too many yards away. He yelled something, but he was so far that I'm still not sure what. It sounded like, "We're kings tonight!"

If he said it, he was right. But I cupped my mouth anyway and called, "Alright, man, come back."

I don't know if he tried to. I knew he wasn't getting closer, and every second he didn't, those waves got bigger. Crashing feet in the air. And then the one that . . . yeah. I just have this feeling that that was the one. This feeling that makes me wanna throw up. That wave knocked me over and I was still only up to my knees. Like that water said, *Yeah, right. You're not strong. You're not kings.*

I tried to get to him. On everything I have, I tried. But every time I tried to force my way out into that water, a wave came and pushed me back. So much that it didn't even feel like I was getting pushed but like I was being pulled. Like I was on some tether that just wasn't long enough.

Then the rain turned into a drizzle, as fast as it'd become a downpour. I tasted blood—I could have bit myself one of those times I fell back down, or maybe my throat was bleeding from how hard I was yelling. But the blood, even though it was mine, just proved that this was real. Blood makes everything real.

He wasn't coming back.

Which was impossible.

But it also wasn't.

I screamed his name and ran into the water now that I really could. I kept my eyes open under the surface, in all that grit and grime, just to try and see him. I really don't know how long I was swimming around in circles. It could have been the same day a thousand times.

I'd swam down to the rocks when I saw something floating in the darkness. Something . . .

Yeah.

I pulled him to the shore, that's all I know for sure. I looked at him with—with nothing left inside him. Like there was a body but there was nothing in it. That fast. That *impossibly fast*.

Ice hot to frostbite cold.

From scared for tomorrow to convinced time wasn't even moving.

I begged to start the day over. That was the only thing I wanted. I cried and begged for it a million times.

September 24, Take Five: 9:27 a.m.

I've never told that story, not like that, with every little memory I could wring out of myself. Not in a way where I had to remember to breathe or I probably wouldn't. Not even when Mom, and Ashe, and the cops wanted to know it.

"I can't believe Austin is gone." She says it like she knew him, too.

I turn to her. I knew she was there but I'm not sure the last time I looked at her. Too scared to, I guess, because I know she should walk away. It'd just be a little easier if I don't have to watch her go.

Her eyes are wet. Man, I don't want to make another person cry. Seeing it on her is how I realize my cheeks are damp, too. I wipe my forearm across my face.

"I didn't want to make you sad. I just wanted you to know."

"I'm not sad." She shakes her head. "I'm just sorry."

That's worse, somehow.

"Look, Sydney... what I did that night... it's complicated. People will say how sorry they are that this awful thing happened, but they don't know. They don't know how sure I was that Aus was gonna stay outside with me when I told him to, and that he was gonna go down to that beach when I said we should, and that he was gonna jump in that water when I brought it up. We didn't tell each other no. Never once. Not in our whole lives. He died because I pretty much told him to die that night." I clear my throat but that doesn't help it get any less tight. "That's pretty much how it is."

I glance at her again, but all she does is nod. Not like she doesn't know what to say, but like she wants to let me finish. It's a relief, because I'm not done yet.

"I don't know why we're stuck, but why should I get to move on? I just get to be all good one day while my best friend stays dead? It's not right. To be honest with you, I don't even *want* things to be right. I mean, does it suck that it's always gonna be exactly one month since Austin died? Yeah. But is that better than watching the days stack up until it's so far away that I haven't known him longer than I have? *Absolutely.* That's a million times better." I chew on my lip. "I guess what I'm saying is . . . what I want you to know is"—I take a deep breath so I have the momentum to push the words out—"you can walk away. From me. I mean, of course you can. But maybe you actually should."

Okay. It's out there. If she wasn't thinking about it before, she is now, and it's for the better. Doing these days without her is gonna be straight trash every time the sun comes back up, but I'll get used to it. Accept. Adapt.

She scrunches her eyebrows. "Stop being weird. I'm not going anywhere."

Just that fast. Just that easy.

Then she bends over and starts scratching the Jack Russell at her ankles.

Part Three:

Us

September 24, Takes Six through Seventeen

Sydney

I basically exist in a world with no precalc now.

Okay, I take that back. I'm sure precalc exists somewhere because the planes are still flying, and the cars are still running, and Mom and Dad are still at their doctor jobs every morning before my 7:01 alarm goes off. So, someone is still doing math. Just not me.

I'm eating Dunkin' grilled cheeses and cuddling with dogs at the park. I'm playing I Bet and Sixty Minutes a hundred different times. I'm running around this city like I've never seen it before because, in a way, I guess I haven't. Not like this. Not with Marcus.

That's our new reality. One where numbers are real but not for us. One where days don't matter because they're indefinitely ours. One where I'm *so free*, all the time, until the sun starts to set and I know what's coming. And then his alarm goes off at 10:14, and we stop whatever we're doing, and we hold hands, and we look into each other's eyes, and we wait for the pain. The moment that always reminds me that something is still undeniably wrong, because good stuff doesn't feel like this. It doesn't wipe you out like

Sydney

someone just let a sparkler off inside your chest—and not in some metaphorical, *I love you* way, but in a very literal, *what happens if a bomb detonates in your heart?* kind of way. And while it happens, while the tires screech and the headlights come, we hold on to each other until we can't anymore. Until the world vacuum-sucks us apart.

We spent an entire morning memorizing each other's phone numbers. We bought Sharpies and wrote them on the other's arm and, for the rest of the day, would randomly tell each other, *Say it*, to see if we still remembered. I still do it every now and then. I pretend like I'm joking but I'm really not. Because sometimes, when he's looking at me at the end of the night, and the butterflies in my stomach start knocking into each other, I can't stop thinking about how he's the only person I have in this world. The only one who remembers, the only one who's also stuck. And if I lose him—because he doesn't remember my number, or worse, remember me—I just.

I can't lose him.

So I make him tell me my number. And he always laughs.

You're stalling, I'll say.

He'll insist, *No, I'm not*.

Then say it.

And every time, like it's his address, or his birthday, or any other number we have to know in this life, he does.

Sydney

I did look Austin up, but only once. @aubaileybailey.

It was right after Marcus and I got yanked apart, and I was back in bed with my alarm going off. We'd just memorized each other's numbers the day before, and I jabbed his into my phone like I had five seconds left before my brain wiped itself clean. Then I stared at it for a minute, his name—Marcus Burke—glowing back at me. And next thing I knew, I was opening Instagram.

I went to Kala's page first. She smiles the same way Marcus does, like one of those people who doesn't have to be reminded to do it in pictures because she never stopped. She hadn't posted since August 22, on a rooftop somewhere in New York, cheersing a group of people with Sip bottles. Up until then, she'd posted every couple of days. Then it just stopped. It made my stomach feel almost too empty to think about why.

I slow-scrolled through her feed. A lot of Sip stuff. Pretty pictures of pretty things with easy and unbothered captions like *Yum* and *Twice as nice*. She did cool things. Went cool places. Had a very cute son who tolerated her tendency to document life.

I tapped a picture with Marcus in it and followed the tag.

The page was so him, mainly because there was basically nothing on it. But considering I'd seen him touch his phone, like, twice—four pics on his entire grid felt very on brand.

1. Some huge hamburger.

2. Dixon in the park.

3. One of those pictures that schools take of their athletes while they're in uniform. His was on an indoor court with a basketball under his arm.

4. Him and another guy sitting on the curb outside Nina's.

I held my breath and tapped the fourth one. The other guy was tagged. His handle was @aubaileybailey. I clicked it.

And there he was. Austin Bailey, according to his bio. Brown hair cut short on the sides and curly on top. Cream-colored skin . . . mixed, maybe, between Black and white. Freckles on his nose that stretched out to his cheeks. A smile as big as Marcus's, with a thin gap between his front teeth.

He barely had any pictures on his page, either. And the ones that were there weren't good. They were the kind of pics that normally just rot on your camera roll. But all the pictures he did have were with Marcus. Them at the movies. Them on the subway. Them in basketball uniforms. And that bench . . . was that . . .

I tapped the picture and made it full screen. I zoomed in so the street sign in the background was clearer.

Yeah, it was. It was them at the dog park.

But then my phone vibrated and the notification popped up at the top of the screen: Marcus Burke. And it was like getting caught digging through his underwear drawer. I cleared my search history and killed the app and opened his message.

It said:

Sydney

> If I've got the wrong number, you should know there's some girl at Dunkin' who's knocking people over and claiming to be you

I didn't know exactly what I was worried he was gonna say instead. *Surprise! I put a tracker on your phone and know you've been stalking my people for the past ten minutes so deuces, weirdo, take your creepy self somewhere else!*

But regardless, it was a relief to not be caught.

I texted him back:

> Anyone who'd tell on her like that probably deserves to be knocked around a little bit.

That was the day he taught me to ride a bike for real. We rented one of the Citi ones and we took it back down to the Battery. This time, he decided the best way for me to learn was to not realize I was learning. That he'd hold me up, and we'd just talk, until my body got used to defying gravity. So that was what we did, we did it for hours, and I hoped so hard that the sun wouldn't set. Because I didn't want to stop laughing, or hearing his voice that close to my ear, and feeling the way his breath would come out in a huff when I said something funny back. I didn't want that feeling to ever go away—that confidence that he was right there to catch me no matter what I did wrong.

Sydney

That was when I knew for sure—I thought I'd known it days ago, but not like this—that the only parts I ever needed to know about the night he lost Austin were the parts he wanted to tell me. That it didn't matter that he was convinced he was somehow at fault—he was wrong. There was no way he wasn't just as ready to catch his best friend as he was to catch me. There was no way that this boy didn't do everything he could to save him. It wasn't fair, it was utterly and absolutely wrong . . . but it wasn't his fault.

"I smell peanut butter again. How can you not smell that?" I insisted, as the bike tires rolled along the route we'd taken over a dozen times now.

But he didn't answer me. And then I realized that was because he wasn't there.

I glanced over my shoulder, just fast enough to see him at the end of the long block, smirking with his arms folded. If I looked any longer than that I for sure would have fallen on my teeth, so I turned back around and kept on my way.

I had no idea when he let me go. I had no idea how he knew that he could. But I was riding. By myself. Somehow.

When I lapped the block and ended up back where we'd started, he was sitting on the corner, waiting right where I'd left him.

🌹🌹🌹

We spent a day in Kala's brand-new used (is that a thing?) convertible, riding up West Side Highway with the top down. Neither of us has a license, but Marcus drove, because he's had practice. Kala decided as soon as he was tall enough to reach the pedals that he should at least know how to make a car move for safety purposes. Which means he's been practicing with her since he was eleven. And he's good at it. He checks over his shoulder when he changes lanes and everything.

We spent a day trying to play tennis because I convinced myself, in this universe, maybe I could be good at it (breaking: in all universes, I suck at it), and we spent a day riding bikes. Not in the street because Marcus, albeit supportively, pretty much told me I'd break myself in half if I tried that right now. We rode in Brooklyn, where the sidewalks are less busy and the parks have more room.

We took a cooking class one day because he said we should try it. It cost two hundred dollars on the Upper East Side, but spending the cash doesn't matter when we'll get it all back tomorrow. They gave us aprons and our own stations with mini kitchen islands. Everyone was twice our age, at least. Our teacher had an accent—Scottish, I think—that Marcus practiced for the rest of the day. They taught us how to hold a knife so we don't cut off all our fingers, and we did a meat loaf recipe as a class. Which was pretty much one of the last things I'd ever want to make, down there with pot roast and other too-mushy meats. But even though I'd never want to eat it, I'd cook it again and again, all because of how it felt to create something that someone else could love, that could make this whole room smell edible. And to trust myself—maybe that was the biggest thing. Every time I wanted to try something that wasn't explicitly written in the recipe—like adding an extra pinch of brown sugar or another dash of salt—Marcus nudged me and told me to do it, that he knew it was

Sydney

gonna be great. And when he tried what I made, his eyes rolled back in his head and he swore it was the best thing he ever tasted.

It wasn't, obviously. But that's the difference, I guess—between food recipes and math equations. They both have steps, but recipes leave room to make them your own. To try things without being wrong.

Marcus said we should come back a different time, when they're cooking something I would actually eat. I'm still not sure if he really believed there would be a different time, or if he just forgot for a moment what it means to be stuck, but that was when it happened again—this pang deep inside me for a future I don't have. One where we come back one day when they're making crab cakes, or lasagna, or deviled eggs. A future where we're scrolling YouTube for the next recipe we're gonna make. Where, one day, I surprise him with a dish that I didn't use a recipe for at all, and it's his favorite one yet.

I can't stop thinking about it—how amazing we'd be at tomorrow if we're already so good at today.

🌹 🌹 🌹

We've brought up Austin and Sebastian, but we also haven't. We've talked about them but we also don't *only* talk about them. I don't know why it's gotten so easy so quickly, why I can be talking about Food Network, and then how weird I think spicy drinks are, and then Sebastian, like it's all just one of the many intertwined parts of me. But I can, and it seems like he can, too, and maybe it was always that way for him but it was never that way for me, not for two years.

Sydney

One day, we were eating ice cream at this gourmet shop in Greenwich Village. It has five hundred thousand followers on Instagram and they have this one flavor with gold in it. It's a fifty-dollar scoop. We got three for each of us.

No, it didn't taste like gold—not that I know what gold tastes like, I'm just pretty sure it doesn't taste like vanilla—but it was better the way everything is better with him. While we were rambling about everything else, I brought up that thing that people say when someone dies. How you should be happy because they'd want you to be.

"But what if they wouldn't want you to be?" I asked that day, sucking down a spoonful of gold (vanilla) ice cream. "I mean, I'm sure Bas doesn't want me to be miserable, but I don't feel like he'd want me to just move on, either. Just . . . forget about him? If I died, I wouldn't want people to forget about me."

That was the kind of stuff we brought up. The stuff that's wrong to say. The stuff I used to be ashamed to think. But this death thing . . . it's not always some super brave and admirable display of emotion. Sometimes it's messy and you look like an asshole. It doesn't mean you are. It doesn't mean you're wrong.

I was never wrong according to Marcus.

He just nodded, scraped the sides of his bowl with his spoon, and agreed like I was the most valid person in the world. "Who wants to be forgotten?"

September 24, Take Eighteen: 7:01 a.m.

Sydney

I grab my phone from my nightstand and turn off the alarm.

I wanted to ask him something this time, before we got ripped apart, but we were sitting on the steps of a brownstone on the East Side when his alarm went off, eating burgers from Shake Shack and playing this game we'd both seen on TikTok. Where you stare into each other's eyes and try to say the same word at the same time. We'd been sucking at it for twenty minutes, laughing so hard we were hyperventilating, until we finally did it. *Splinter*—that was the word. It didn't mean anything but it felt like everything. This victory over something impossible. Success, just because we kept going.

When it happened, my breath caught and all I could do was stare at his perfect face, at the way he smiled like it wasn't what we'd done that made him happy, but the way it made me feel. Then his phone started blaring, and he turned it off, and he took my hands, and asked me, "Are you ready?" but really he was telling me that I am. That the pain is coming but I can take it, I'll beat it—just like I do every night.

I never ended up asking him what I wanted to.

Sydney

I go to my contacts and save the number I've memorized, that I still recite to the same jingle that I used over a week ago when I was trying to make sure it stuck. It's that song that Kit Kat uses. The "Give Me a Break" one. I hum it to myself as I type his number and cuddle into my pillows while it starts to ring.

"Thanks for calling Pizza Hut," he says.

It's always something like that. No matter who calls or texts first, we can never just say *Hey, what's up?* like normal people.

I love being a freaking weirdo with him.

"Thin crust with olives and extra green peppers, please. Can you make sure that cute Michael B. Jordan–looking guy delivers it this time?"

"What?" he screeches, and at first I think it's the Michael B. Jordan comment, but then he says, "Is that for real your order? Olives and extra green peppers? You know I said 'Pizza Hut,' right? Not 'Sweetgreen,' right? Not 'That Salad Bar at Whole Foods,' right?"

"Okay, then what do you get?"

"Uh . . ." he starts, like my question is ridiculous. "Pepperoni? Because I respect my ancestors? And maybe throw some sausage on there if I really deserve it. Like I low-key changed the world earlier that day, nothing less."

"Okay, well that's why they have half-and-half pizzas. You order for your side, I'll order for my side, rock/paper/scissors for that slice in between the halves that always gets some of everything on it."

"Syd, I'm sorry, I'm not ordering that," he says. "I'm not embarrassing myself like that. I'm from Brooklyn. I'll do anything else,

Sydney

I'll take you anywhere, but I'm not about to disrespect pizza like that."

I roll onto my side and pull my comforter to my mouth so he can't hear me laughing at all his pizza-slinging hate speech.

"Does Pizza Hut have a complaint line? I didn't call to experience all this discrimination this morning."

"Olives and extra green peppers," he mumbles, like he still can't believe it. "Do corner spots even have that slice? Do you call ahead and let them know you'll be there Friday, or something?"

"I'm gonna report this Pizza Hut to that lady on channel nine who does the exposés on the five o'clock news if you don't stop."

He laughs, and I'm pretty sure he's still in bed, too. There's a little bit of rustling on his side of the phone, like he's messing with the sheets. "So," he says.

"So," I echo.

So, what should we do today? is the lingering question. Sometimes we have an idea in seconds, sometimes it takes longer. Sometimes one of us already knows exactly what we want to do, but we wait and let the other pitch something first. This is that kind of morning for me.

I wait for him to say he has some great plan, that he was thinking about getting a face tattoo or streaking across the Brooklyn Bridge, but he's quiet.

I speak up instead. "I wanted to see if it was okay if maybe we didn't hang out today." I feel like a traitor, even though there's nothing wrong—not with us, at least. "It's just that . . . well, you know my friend, Jacq? My best friend, Jacq. We go to the street fair on Broadway

Sydney

between Ninety-Fifth and Ninety-Sixth every Sunday. Actually, I guess it's not really a street fair—it's not massive enough—but you know what I mean. It's a bunch of tables set up along the sidewalk selling produce and costume jewelry and paintings—nothing fancy, like watercolors and stuff. And we always buy one thing, and then we go to the Gap across the street, usually just to look but sometimes we buy stuff there, too, because how can you not when everything is always forty percent off? Anyway . . . we take the one thing that we bought at the street fair—not a street fair, but whatever—back to Jacq's and put it in this box that we keep in her closet and the whole idea is that one day, when we don't live with our parents anymore, we'll each take half the things in that box with us wherever we go so our new places don't feel so new. And now it's been three missed street fairs—not street fair, but whatever. And I just . . . I know we can't actually go to the street fair, but . . . I miss her. So, I was thinking that maybe today, I'd see if she wants to hang out."

There. I said it. I'm glad I did, even though it isn't making me feel any lighter yet. It's not like I'm scared to ask for a day off from Marcus. I don't think he's gonna go off on me and instantly morph into one of those people in the #AITA posts on Reddit. The thing that really matters—that made it feel like I was choking down ice chips while I was trying to talk—is the reason *why* I want a day off. How messed up it is. That here I am, telling him, of all people, how much I miss my best friend. It makes my stomach feel like it's eating itself. That's why I almost lied.

But I didn't because I don't want a forever that isn't the truth.

Sydney

I squeeze my eyes shut while I wait for him to answer. It's been ten minutes. (Okay, it's probably been four seconds.)

"Syd, of course you should hang with Jacq."

I can breathe again. "Are you sure?"

"What do you mean? Of course I'm sure."

He isn't crying. He doesn't sound sad. He just seems like he means it—really, truly means it.

Ugh. He's honestly the greatest person on the planet.

"I'll text you today, okay?" I tell him. "Keep your phone on. And I—not to make this into some huge thing that it's not, but . . ." I take a deep breath. Maybe I'm being too much. But the words are out before I can stop them. "I'm gonna miss you."

He chuckles. "Syd, we've got so much time. Have fun. Don't worry about me."

So much time. I start to chew my bottom lip. "Okay."

"Okay."

"Hey—" I blurt before he can hang up. I wait for him to prove he's still here.

"You've reached Pizza Hut," he quips.

"Say my number."

"You know I know it. Besides, it's on my phone right now. You called me, remember?"

But he could lose his phone. Or drop it in a toilet. Lose all his numbers. "Can you just say it?"

So he does. He recites it like it's imprinted on his brain.

"Okay," I say.

Sydney

"Okay," he says.

"Bye."

I hang up. And I lie there for a second, tangled in my covers, until I unlock my phone and send Jacq a text.

> **Hey! I feel like a skip day. Meet at Genevieve's?**

Sydney

September 24, Take Eighteen: 9:47 a.m.

Sydney

"I'm pretty sure I don't even believe in asparagus," Jacq declares in her maroon corduroy jumper.

I laugh so hard that I almost spill my mug of hot chocolate. I was about to take a sip but huffed into it instead, and now an eruption of droplets falls onto the floor and onto me, like some mini, hot-chocolate-spewing volcano.

"You can't just not believe in something that's real," I tell her, pointlessly wiping my jeans with my free hand, but the cocoa has already sunk in. "That's like not believing in the sun, or in Tom Hanks, or something."

Jacq and I are sitting on opposite sides of the tiled floor in the young adult section of Genevieve's. This has been our favorite bookstore for as long as I can remember, ever since we were old enough for our parents to let us start going places on our own. By the way my parents forced me to turn location tracking on in my phone, I'm sure they thought I'd use the ounce of freedom to sneak around with boys and hit up a bunch of parties. But no, just Jacq and me sitting on the floor, huddling against walls of books. Take note, Bad Girls Club.

Sydney

"Okay, definitely intrigued by the fact that we chose Tom Hanks as our best possible example right there," Jacq says, her 4A curls blossoming around her head as she leans back on the shelves behind her. "But I appreciate the stance you're taking." She sips from her mug and holds it in both hands. "I know asparagus is *real*. I'm just not convinced that it needs to be. I mean, if we actually needed asparagus, wouldn't it exist more? Like, Mom wouldn't have to be trying so hard to make it a thing right now if it was actually a thing to begin with."

Her mom has always been obsessed with trying new foods, which is why I love having dinner at Jacq's place instead of mine. Not to mention, I can actually *talk* about how much I love food without it being some kind of taboo, without Mrs. Baxter looking at me like it's not possible to enjoy eating and pass precalc at the same time.

She deemed the past month Asparagus September, which she quickly shorthanded to 'Sparagus September, which Jacq and her dad quickly shorthanded to Spare Us September. They've been grinning and bearing some new asparagus-based concoction every night this month. Asparagus fritters. Asparagus soup. Asparagus salad topped with fried asparagus. For weeks, it was the first update I demanded when I saw her—*What kind of asparagus last night?* It was my favorite thing. It was freaking *mesmerizing*. As far as I was concerned, it was like the kind of breaking news they interrupt scheduled broadcasting for. Until, all of a sudden, time stopped. And it wasn't anymore.

"I agree," I decide, resting my back against the shelves, too. "Darwinism says this is completely unnecessary. There would be approximately a trillion less people if asparagus was, indeed, fundamental to a sustainable human life."

Jacq smiles. *"Darwinism?* Your parents would be crying tears of joy to hear you casually referencing Darwinism in conversation."

I flip my hair like an Instagram model.

Jacq laughs. "Speaking of your parents' tears." She traces her finger along her mug to catch a dripping drop of cocoa, then pops her finger into her mouth and sucks it off. "What's the deal with you blowing off your test this morning?"

On the other side of our aisle, the frothing machine goes off, this gusty sound like someone's pressure-washing a brick wall. Genevieve's is kind of like Starbucks and a bookstore had a baby. It's just as much people with lattes at tables with laptops as it is people browsing for something to read next.

"Honestly?" The milky swirls in my drink stare back at me. "I kind of just woke up and realized there'd be plenty more days to do precalc."

Jacq raises her eyebrows, like she doesn't know who I am but she likes what she sees. Being all Zen and wise has always been way more her thing. The bigger picture. The Whole Point of It All. She's so good at what she does because her parents let her do what she's good at. In her case, writing, directing our school plays, and reading fast enough to be able to see all the credits when a movie ends. She wants to make stories for the big screen one day, and she's gonna be phenomenal at it.

"I love that, Syd," she tells me. "Precalc is just a class. A *stupid* class.

Sydney

My uncle says he hasn't faced a math problem that his phone app couldn't solve in fifteen years, and he just bought a Maserati. I'm sorry, but if precalc can't make you happy, and you can still own a Maserati, then what's even the point?" She goes to sip more of her hot chocolate and then stops herself when the realization hits. "You know what? I don't believe in precalc, either. I don't believe in asparagus and I don't believe in precalc. I believe in sunshine, and Tom Hanks, and you."

It tugs at something deep inside, this little string attached to my heart that's connected to my eyes, and I quickly blink away the tears. This is just Jacq, and I know that. She's talked to me, and about me, like this my entire life. And no, she doesn't suck at precalc. She's great at precalc. She's in AP math now like she's a freaking astronaut. But I still know how much she means it when she says she doesn't believe in it, that she doesn't believe in anything that makes me feel small, or like I'm not good enough, or like my parents will never forgive me for being the dumb kid they have left.

I smile. "Are we a cult?"

She laughs. "Yes! I'll a hundred percent be a cult with you. Except let's not make human sacrifices because you know I'm kind of too queasy for that."

"Yeah, we're not murdering people." I dismiss it like she suggested running a marathon. "We can't even kill a roach. Just bad vegetables and math homework. Our only sacrificial lambs."

"Powerful," she agrees, impressed. "Can we go ahead and perform our first ritual tonight? You know, so I have all the right vibes going into tomorrow?"

Sydney

She has another sip of her hot chocolate and watches a woman pass between us in the aisle. I use the second she's distracted to rack my mind.

"I forget what tomorrow is," I admit, now that the woman is gone.

Jacq shakes her head. "It's probably better that way. I should forget, too. But, you know, it's only been my entire purpose for existing for the past three years."

Film Academy of Manhattan early decision.

"FAM early decision," she tells me, the moment after I remember.

"Oh, yeah! Wow, I can't believe that's . . ." My voice trails off. "Tomorrow."

"Me neither," she says, and I know she thinks we mean it the same way, but we don't. She means it like it's somehow been over three years since her dad took her on that college tour of the best film schools and they stopped at FAM before flying out West to see more. She means it like all the good grades, and hard work, and photo taking, and video making are finally in the hands of someone at FAM who's about to hand her a decision about the rest of her life. She means it like there *is* a rest of her life.

And I mean it like there's not.

"You deserve FAM more than anyone," I tell her. "I'd do endless rituals to make it happen."

She takes a deep, nervous breath but smiles. "And maybe some resuscitation if the news tomorrow is bad."

"There won't be bad news tomorrow."

Sydney

An old man starts scooting his way down our aisle, wheeling a cart in front of him with a fuzzy dog inside that sort of looks like Dixon.

Jacq watches him pass and then says to me, "Okay." And I can tell we're done talking about FAM for now.

I slide my fingers up and down the warm outsides of my mug. "I met a guy."

Her head whips back in my direction, curls bouncing, brown eyes sparkling. *"What?"* She smiles like I just told her that asparagus has been constitutionally banned. *"When?"*

"A few weeks ago."

Her mouth goes sideways. Half smile, half frown. "Why didn't you say anything?"

"Well." I lick my dry lips. "It's just that . . . at first, I didn't really know what was going on? I guess I was just trying to figure it out. But the thing is . . . Jacq, he's like . . . he's like the kind of guy that doesn't even exist, you know? Like those stories on TikTok about guys who do the most romantic thing ever, and then say the most romantic thing right after, and then they can also sing and play the guitar, and you're like, *Okay, liar.* I mean, he doesn't sing and play the guitar, I don't think. And he isn't even romantic—not in like some cheesy way. But it's just like . . . I guess what I'm saying is . . . I think he's ridiculously incredible *for me*. Like, if I'm this weird, food-loving, math-hating, olives-and-extra-green-peppers-ordering, one-of-a-kind shape, he's the other shape. That fits that."

I want to tell her the rest of it, too. That I haven't felt this good since Sebastian died. And specify—because specifying feels important in this instance—that it's not that I feel the same as I did when he was still here. But I feel good again, in a different way.

I don't say that part, though, because there's this thing that happens when somebody dies. This societal rule that everybody follows, that I've been determined to follow, too. It basically enforces that there's an allotted period of time when good people are expected to ask you how you're doing and listen to you talk about how you're not doing okay. It's a few weeks, or a couple of months if you're lucky, but then it has to be done. They have to be permitted to go forth as the lucky ones, the ones who don't feel hollow anytime they reference their still-whole families. And me? I have to be okay.

Jacq already did this whole thing with me. The grief thing. Her dues are way overpaid and her time is beyond up. But if I could bring it all up again—without being a bad friend, an eternally broken friend, a friend who's way too sad—I'd tell her how Marcus doesn't sing (I don't think), or play the guitar (I'm pretty sure), or make cute TikToks (judging by the four pictures on his entire Instagram), but he knows my grief completely. It wraps itself around his and instead of knots, it creates bows. Something easy to untangle. Something that makes me feel pretty. Something that's ours, that we could only make because we have each other.

"Syd . . ." Jacq frowns the happiest frown. "I *love* that. Do you have a picture? I wanna be obsessed with this guy."

I pull up his Instagram and hand her my phone. She smiles as soon as she sees his page and it makes me smile, too. "Oh my God,

Sydney

boys . . ." she mumbles to herself, and I know what she means is, *Oh my God, boys . . . have no idea how to do social media.*

Her fingers start working—tapping and zooming in and zooming out—and after a few seconds, she unilaterally declares, "He's so cute."

"He's *tall*, Jacq. Like six feet, I'm pretty sure. Maybe even a couple inches taller."

"*Really?*" She goes back to the few pictures that I have, leaning into the screen like maybe a closer look will prove it.

"Yeah. I—I really want you to meet him."

"Of course I'm gonna meet him," she insists, and sets my phone down on the floor right next to her hot chocolate. "How about tomorrow?"

I would love for her to meet him tomorrow. For real. Not on a repeat of today that Marcus and I just call "tomorrow" because there's no other good enough alternative. I want her to meet him on Friday, September 25. I want it to be after she's gotten the news of her entire lifetime from FAM. I want us to squeeze each other while we anticipate what's next.

I just have no idea how to get us there.

"Tomorrow," I agree, because maybe the first step is just believing I can.

September 24, Take Eighteen: 2:37 p.m.

Sydney

Jacq and I take all the asparagus from her refrigerator, and all the notes from math class that we grabbed from my apartment on our way here, and throw them into the bathtub. We blast the *Renaissance* album and dance around her bathroom. Mrs. Baxter is gonna be devastated when she realizes we torched 'Sparagus September, and making her sad is among one of the worst things I may ever do, but this is worth it.

Maybe that's all it really takes. Maybe that's all we ever really need to do—is *know*. Be sure. Not complacent but positive. Not taking all the biggest things in life for granted, like menu variety and the way time works.

So, Jacq wants FAM. And I want FAM for her. And I want her to know Marcus. And I want her to make it to October so she can emerge victorious into next month's dinner theme.

I want tomorrow.

You hear that, Stars? Moon? Universe? God?

It's time for tomorrow.

I light the match and drop it on our sacrifice.

September 24, Take Eighteen: 10:13 p.m.

Marcus

Note to self: Don't be here anymore when Mom gets home.

She's so pissed that I ghosted all day. Hulk-like. She called and texted and I didn't answer any of it. She got home at six, after checking all the spots where she thought I might be, and then found me still in bed like a bum. She was yelling and crying at the same time. She screamed, *I THOUGHT YOU DIED!* and then stood there shaking like she didn't know whether to take it back or say it again.

She chose neither, by the way. She slammed my door shut behind her and hasn't come back since.

Of course she thought I died. If Aus died, anyone can die.

Look, I know it's messed up, okay? It's *bad*, real bad, how I do this to her every single day. How I'm off with Syd and she's terrified all the time. I deserve for her to be mad at me. I'm mad at me, too.

I didn't mean to stay in bed all day. It wasn't a plan, just the default. Didn't feel like school. Didn't feel like trying to catch up with the boys. So, I just stayed where I was and now it's about to be over.

My alarm goes off and I mute it. Is it messed up that I'm kind of excited for the pain to come tonight? I guess it's not just tonight,

Marcus

though. I'm always kind of ready for it, and not just because it goes hand in hand with starting the day over.

But it's kind of like, when it hurts like that on the outside—like there's no way I'm ever gonna survive it—for a little bit, a minute, maybe, it doesn't hurt so bad on the inside.

That's why, tonight, I just sigh and settle in when the tires start to screech.

September 24, Take Nineteen: 2:07 p.m.

Sydney

I lie on this floating lounge chair in the rooftop pool at the Jonathan Hotel. In a black cutout one-piece that I bought on our way here, and this short, cream-colored, stringy wrap-skirt that sort of looks like fishing net. Sunglasses, too. A five-hundred-dollar outfit that I put on my debit card like I'm Anna Delvey's mini me.

Marcus booked us a room here (four hundred twenty-five dollars a night) just to get us access to the pool. We figured why not. There's nothing else to do.

It's only us and a girl who's definitely an influencer, with her friend who's very ride or die. I've never seen her page or anything, but she's posing like she's not posing all over this oasis while her friend bends like a straw to get the perfect picture.

Marcus is lying on a nonfloating beach chair, one that's on the patio a few feet away. He didn't buy himself a wardrobe for today like I did—he's still in the same-old dress pants and button-down with his sweatshirt in a pile beneath him that he's worn every single day we've been stuck. But he does have an Arnold Palmer and loaded potato skins from room service, with a burger and buffalo wings on the way.

Sydney

That pang has gotten worse—the one I've been having about the future. It's been like a siren in my brain since yesterday. On my walk home from Jacq's, I put in my earbuds without turning on a song, just to drown out the city and make it quiet enough to think. To figure out this twisting inside me that felt like I knew how to fix this, once upon a time. Like a thought I almost remembered until I lost it. I know that's impossible—I can hardly even spell *physics*, so why the hell would I know how to fix it? *But everything that's happening right now is impossible, too.* So, I made the world quiet and tried to listen to the whispers inside me.

When I made it back to my building, I told myself I'd crawl into bed later and turn off the lights and lie awake. I'd cuddle under my favorite blanket and gaze at the apartment building on the other side of Amsterdam Avenue. I'd let my mind drift on the waves of street noise and eventually think of something. I've always had my best ideas at night.

Then I remembered I don't get to go to bed anymore.

So I hoped instead that maybe my and Jacq's ritual fixed everything, jump-started the universe like a dead car battery, and that was all it took. But the ritual did nothing. It erased at 10:15 just like the hot chocolate stains on my jeans, and when I opened my eyes at 7:01, and Marcus messaged me, *Your Verizon Wireless plan is out of texts—send money or a selfie to this number immediately*, it was the first time since we started our new routine that I didn't fully smile.

"How're the potato skins?" I ask, running my fingertips across the surface of the water. Room temperature. Like water straight from the refrigerator door.

Sydney

He's just taken a bite of one but he raises his eyebrows and the plate, too. He chews, swallows, and says, "Have some."

I shake my head. "I don't want any."

He smirks before he has another bite. "Then why do you keep asking about them?"

I frown. "I don't."

He shrugs the way I've gotten used to, the way that makes me want to push him away in the hopes that he'll pull me back in. "I mean . . . you asked if they have chives. They do. I think." He studies the one in his hand. "Something green's on here . . . you'd know better than me." He has another bite. "You also asked if the bacon is hickory smoked and I have no idea."

Okay, so I've been over-asking about the potato skins. "Well, the first two questions didn't count since you were incapable of answering them."

He squints at me. He's facing the sun. "Didn't know that was the prereq for what made a question a question."

"Well, yeah, like in baseball," I tell him. "If you're at bat but you don't swing, that doesn't count as a strike."

He stays squinting, nose scrunched. "It does if it's a strike."

I have yet to name a sport this boy can't talk about.

"I feel like you want to ask me something else," he says.

I push my sunglasses onto my forehead. "What do you mean?"

"I mean, I know you're the next Bobby Flay and all, but I just can't believe you're that interested in some potato skins."

He has this way of looking at me, this way of trying to *get* me, no matter what it is I'm struggling to say. And he's doing it right now. Trying.

It makes me want to tell him how sure I am that being stuck isn't right. It doesn't feel safe, or stable, or sustainable. Yeah, there are the good parts—no responsibilities, or repercussions, or math. But there's also nothing new—no new cooking classes, or TV shows, or street fairs. No bedtime. No naps on rainy days. There's no us, not really. Not an us with a life ahead and things to look forward to.

"These skins really are good, Syd," he says now that I've taken so much time to answer that he probably assumes I'm not gonna. "You should try them."

He holds up the plate again, and this time I roll off my floating lounge chair. I splash into the water and it goes up past my shoulders. I doggy paddle over to the edge of the pool and fold my arms on the side while I float. Marcus leans over and hands me a potato skin.

"Scallions, not chives," I tell him as I take a bite.

"See? I knew you'd know."

They are good. Salty and chewy and cheesy. Velvety sour cream. Crispy bits of bacon that might actually be maple glazed instead of hickory. There's a hint of sweetness about them.

"Have another one," he says. But I shake my head.

"Do you like what we're doing?" I ask.

He shrugs. "I've never been a big pool guy but I'm cool with it."

"I don't mean what we're doing right now, I mean what we've *been* doing. With the days and everything. How we're stuck."

"Oh." He frowns. "I mean, I wasn't planning for it but what can you do? Accept. Adapt."

I press my hands on the rim of the pool and push myself up out of the water. I sit on the edge. "Do you ever think about tomorrow?"

He rests his arms on his knees and I tuck my leg under me so we're facing each other. My heart kicks a little, like when a song skips. How have we never talked about this? Busy talking about yesterdays, I guess—but he has to have been thinking about it, too. What the hell we're doing. How the hell we stop.

"What part of tomorrow do you think about?" he asks.

I don't even know where to start. Summertime? Snow? Pumpkin-spice season?

"Jacq is supposed to be hearing back from FAM." I watch my fingers draw circles in the puddle of pool water next to me. "Film Academy of Manhattan. She's been waiting our entire lives to get in. And the thing is, *she will*. Because she's a complete visionary. Like, her TikToks are freaking cinematic. But she's one day away. *One day.*" I press my palm into the puddle and watch it spread. "Don't you wanna meet her? And have her actually remember you? You guys will love each other, I know it. And then we can all run around this city together like idiots. There's other stuff, too. Like don't you wanna go to Coney Island over spring break? Or try the next Crumbl mystery flavor? Or see the new *Fast & Furious*? Or find out what announcement Gigi said she was gonna be posting soon—that day we met her at the pop-up? We'll never even get to go to prom together—" But I catch myself. "Not that I'm saying we're gonna . . . or that you and I are gonna . . . but I mean." Breathe. "Aren't you gonna miss any of that stuff?"

I stop because I'm teetering dangerously close to the ever-growing list of things I can imagine doing with him. Or maybe not even that. The ever-growing list of things I don't want to imagine doing without him.

"Let's do prom."

I look up from my puddle and realize he's been looking at it, too, but his gaze meets mine once he feels my eyes. His arms are still on his knees but he's smiling now.

"What?"

"Well, fake prom," he clarifies. "Let's do it."

"What even is fake prom?"

"It's the prom we make for ourselves. The prom I make for you." The sun drenches his perfect skin. "Syd, we don't need a real tomorrow to do the things you want to do. We can just do them. You can just say them and we'll do them. Okay? So let's do it."

When I'm watching and not answering for a second too long, he takes a potato skin from his plate, slides off his pool chair, and gets on one knee with the cutest, cheekiest smirk ever. "Fake prom with me?"

I almost tell him he's not getting it—that that wasn't the point of what I was saying at all. But I can never look away when he really wants me to see him, or see myself, or whatever this is right now. So, of course, I take his potato skin. I take it like it's a bouquet of roses, and I'd take it home and try just as hard to preserve it, if that mattered

Sydney

at all. If 10:15 wouldn't erase it and everything else, anyway.

I tell him I'll do fake prom with him, and he tells me we'll do it tomorrow, and what he really means is that we'll do it once it's today again, but I don't correct him or keep trying to talk about all the differences, because I'm floating in the right now—in the good part about forever. The part where it's him, and me, and potato skins—and nothing else exists in the world.

September 24, Take Twenty: 9:11 a.m.

Marcus

I gotta crush fake prom for her.

If we're gonna make September 24 work forever, I want her to love every second of it. I want it to really grow on her like it's grown on me. It's good to know what's coming. It's good to know that anything bad won't last. Maybe it'll never be her actual prom, but who needs real prom when I'm about to crush fake prom?

I started planning it all out in my head from the minute we talked about it yesterday. I've got a suit at home I can wear, and there's this flower shop right by the ferry where I can get her a corsage (shoutout to Google for expanding my vocabulary). I made a reservation this morning at this Michelin Star sushi restaurant in Fidi called Umi Prime. The wait list is so long that people sell their spots like they're season tickets to the Knicks, but I dropped Mom's name and they told me they'd make room. I never do that, by the way. Name-drop to cut lines and stuff. But I've got fifteen hours and fourteen minutes to pull off fake prom, and I figure whoever's spot we took has been a bunch of times already and gets to go a bunch more times after us.

Marcus

See? Being stuck is kind of fire.

For now, we're at some dress shop in Midtown East. Syd's in the dressing room, which is basically just a nook with a curtain, and I'm waiting for her in the main area on this big, round, futon-looking thing. This is the pinkest, laciest, frilliest place I've ever been. Like Barbie threw up inside a cupcake.

I take another bite of my sausage, egg, and cheese croissant with no cheese.

On another big, round, futon-looking thing, there's this group of women and one who keeps coming out of a dressing room in a different wedding dress. They scream every time, and hug, and cry, and tell her how much they hate her perfect shoulders, and thin arms, and perky boobs? They hate everything that she's made of but they sure do love her. I think it's pretty cool, though. I mean, they're doing this once-in-a-lifetime thing together, on a Thursday morning when they otherwise probably would have been working, or volunteering, or doing some other typical thing that kept them apart. But now they get to do this once-in-a-lifetime thing a million times in a lifetime. I'm happy for them.

One of the women who works here—in this pink dress with a gold name tag—stops by with a tray stacked with prefilled champagne glasses. She smiles. "Would you like one?"

I'm not sure she thinks I'm old enough, but she probably thinks I'm rich enough. I glanced at one of the price tags on these dresses before Syd went in the back, and the one I grabbed was over a thousand dollars.

Marcus

I take a glass and tell her, "Thanks."

"Of course!" she says. "If you need anything, just let me know."

I eat my sandwich with one hand and hold my champagne with the other.

Once Syd gets finished doing whatever she's doing back there, we're gonna split up. She'll go back to her place and I'll go back to mine, so we can both get ready for tonight. Not that I'm gonna use that much time, but of course she can have as much time as she needs. Well, not needs, but wants. She doesn't need any time, if you ask me. She always looks great.

Oh, wow. This is my first time sipping champagne, but it's pretty much just a rocket ship of bubbles straight to your nose. Got it.

I sniff and wag my head.

"Okay," Sydney says. I'm midsneeze but look up once I finish. I didn't even know she came out. "Before you say anything," she goes on, "I've been in a crosstown relationship with this dress for months and it took me fifteen minutes of wearing it before I was even willing to come out and show it to you because this is a big deal, okay? This is like . . . showing you baby pictures or how I eat Oreos—"

Now I gotta know how she eats Oreos.

"—and the verdict is, I love it," she says. "I would make this dress my entire personality. I would sleep in it and even learn how to iron so I could keep it perfect. So if you hate it, it doesn't even matter, okay?" She stares at me and takes a deep breath like she's terrified. "But you do like it, right?"

I'm not a big clothes guy. Mom watches *Project Runway*, and the

Marcus

way the judges will have more ways of describing a hemline than words I've ever spoken in my life blows my mind. So I can't say all that much about this dress. I mean, it's black. It's long—I can't even see her feet anymore. The cloth is like . . . shiny and dull at the same time, if that makes sense. But it probably doesn't, and it definitely doesn't matter. The only thing that really matters about this dress is that it looks absolutely incredible on her.

"I love it." I don't mean to sound so shocked.

She smiles like a little kid who's won something. And when she turns to look at herself in the nearest full-length mirror, I know for a fact that I'm already killing fake prom.

September 24, Take Twenty: 5:07 p.m. (and everything that happens after it)

Marcus

Here's the thing. Sydney and I have only kissed once.

It was that day outside Bounce House, before I knew she'd been stuck, too, and now all this time has passed, you know? Well, not in everyone else's reality, but in ours, it has. I thought I lost her for a day, realized I didn't, told her what I did to Austin, and she didn't even run. If I'm being honest, I really wanted to kiss her then. But it's like in ball when you have a pass lane and then you hesitate and it's gone. I missed my opening. I've missed it a bunch of other times, too.

Now we've gotten so used to *not* kissing, maybe we can't go back. Especially because it's not like she doesn't remember we already did. She knows what happened that day just like I do, and maybe I've taken so long now that she thinks I'm not interested. Or maybe *she's* not interested, and I'm not missing my pass lane so much as she's playing man-to-man. The problem is that I *think* about it. A lot. Like when she laughs so hard that it makes me laugh, too. Or when she's nervous to say something

Marcus

so she does it all at once and wraps it up in a thousand extra words that never had to be there in the first place. Or when my alarm goes off at 10:14 p.m. each night and we hold hands and wait.

It sticks with you differently, I guess. When you kiss a girl at a party versus when you kiss one you could really lo—

Like. My bad. One you could really *like*. A lot.

Anyway. I can't not think about all that when Syd walks out of the elevator and into her lobby. I know I already saw her in this dress, but it's different now. She put her hair up and there's something different about her eye makeup. Plus, she's got these shoes on that make her taller, and I can't really see them because her dress is so long, but it makes it so that the bottom is hovering like a millimeter off the ground, and if someone told me she was floating, I'd believe them.

"You're unreal." I stare as she walks over. But then I catch myself. "I mean, you *look* unreal. That dress is great. Seriously, Syd."

She smiles and twirls, then reaches out and runs her fingers down my lapel. That's right. I'm suited up. Was too busy worshipping her to even remember. It's weird wearing something different, but for fake prom, I will.

Accept. Adapt.

"You look really good, too," she says. "Is there a Brooks Brothers somewhere that doesn't realize they've loaned you a suit?"

"Nah, but I'm sure they'd be honored," I answer, and she laughs. "I already owned this. Only pull it out when I'm trying to be impressive, though." Which reminds me, I've got this duffel on the floor next to me. I lean over, unzip it, and pull out a plastic box stuffed

Marcus

with flowers. "This is for you." I open the box and take out her corsage. Guy at the shop said all I have to do is slide her wrist through the band. "I thought it'd go pretty good with your dress."

I set the box down in one of the chairs in her lobby, and she watches me as I slide the corsage onto her wrist. Easy, just like dude at the shop promised it'd be. Good thing, too, because her doorman is watching like I'm a pigeon trying to swim.

She holds it close after I put it on, stroking the petals. It's a few pink roses but the ribbon is black. It'd been white, but the guy said he could change it for me because I told him about the dress. "Marcus." She sounds sad when she looks at me. "I didn't get you a boutonniere."

What the what? "I don't even know what that is," I promise.

She laughs again. Man, I could listen to that sound forever.

I *can* listen to that sound forever.

Wow.

"Dance tonight?" her doorman asks. Gray hair and a gray mustache in the standard doorman uniform: white collared shirt, black slacks, black tie. Native New Yorker, for sure—I can tell by his swag. Plus the accent.

"Yes," she tells him, and strikes a pose. "You like my dress?"

"A princess, like always." He says it like a dad would. Or the way I imagine a dad would. And she smiles back like she's both used to it and grateful.

"Thanks, Wally," she says.

"What time should I be expecting you back?" he asks, still

lingering behind the desk while I zip that plastic box back into my duffel. "You know nothing good happens on those streets after dark."

I can tell it's a warning he's given her before, probably anytime she's heading out at night instead of heading in. I like that there's someone here noticing when she comes back okay.

"Don't worry," she tells him. "I'll be home at 10:15."

Umi Prime's lighting is kind of like being outside with sunglasses on. Like you can see everything, but the color's off. Warmer looking. Yellower.

"I didn't even have to chew that one," Syd says, holding her chopsticks in one hand and covering her mouth with the other while she swallows. "It basically just evaporated."

She's talking about the sashimi they just put on our table. Two bite-size pieces for thirty-five bucks. This place is all small plates, our waiter explained when we sat down. Emphasis on the *small*.

It's good, though. Worth that Michelin Star it got.

"Butter," I say, setting down my fork. I'm in awe. "Melts like butter."

"*Yes*," she agrees. "It didn't evaporate, it melted. It liquefied and was gone."

It's good she's here. Trying this fancy food. Wondering how they do it. Maybe we could do something like this once a week. Go to some big-deal restaurant. Let her taste everything on the menu.

Marcus

Learn about the flavors and the spices and all that stuff. I bet she'd really like that.

"How was that for you guys?" our waiter asks, reappearing tableside, glancing at me for the okay before he takes away our empty plate. He does that every time. I guess he wants to be sure I don't want to lick it first. I nod and that's when he takes it off the table.

"It was so good," Syd tells him, like he's the one back there making this stuff. It's cute.

"Awesome," he says. "What's next?"

Syd looks at me across the table and I tell her, like I do every time, "Whatever you want."

She smiles and looks back at the menu. Clean print on cardstock. She asks him, "Can we let you know in, like, five minutes?"

"Of course," he tells her. "Another Shirley Temple in the meantime?"

"Yes, please," she says.

He turns to me. "How about you, sir? Another Arnold Palmer?"

"I'm good for now, but thanks."

"Great. I'll go grab that Shirley Temple, then."

He turns and walks back through the restaurant, fast even though it doesn't look like he's rushing—all the staff here moves like that. They navigate around each other like they've been choreographed. This place is pretty big, and there are a ton of tables even though they could fit a lot more, and I guess you kind of do need to move like you've got somewhere to be when people are paying these kinds of prices for a bite of food.

"You have any idea who Shirley Temple and Arnold Palmer are?" I ask. Just out of curiosity.

She thinks about it, resting her elbows on the table and her chin in her hands. "No. Do you?"

"Nope," I answer. "But I wonder if they had beef."

She smiles. "Maybe they didn't even know each other."

"Two of the biggest drinks ever made?" I say, and her face twists at *ever made*, but I'm standing by that. "They had to at least know *of* each other. Shirley probably sitting there throwin' hands when someone asks for an Arnold Palmer. Arnold probably getting in his feelings when people start ordering Shirley Temples."

She keeps eye contact better than anyone I've ever met, when she wants to. She giggles. "Now all I can picture is, like . . . *Freddy vs. Jason*, except with people dressed like glassware."

"A hundred percent chance I'd watch that."

"You know, speaking of famous people"—she juts her chin a little—"the guy from *CSI: NY* is three tables over."

"What guy?"

"You know. The guy. Not like the main guy, but the other guy."

"Oh, right, that guy."

We're busy checking out his table when a hand claps me on the shoulder. No way the spare guy on *CSI: NY* has security watching out for people like us. I turn to see who it is.

No, not security. Some dude in a chef coat and slacks, all black. About Mr. Felix's age probably, graying a little bit over his ears. He's holding a Shirley Temple and he sets it on the table and smiles.

Marcus

"Marcus Burke? I heard you were dining with us tonight. It's a pleasure to have you. I'm Alex Sato, chef-owner at Umi Prime."

I shake his hand. Never met him in my life and didn't plan this at all but it's dope that he's here because Syd is gonna love it.

"Good to meet you," I tell him. "Thanks for coming over—the food is great. This is Sydney Michaels. She's a great cook. Born chef."

"I'm . . ." She kicks me under the table and I chuckle. I can tell she's nervous, but she shouldn't be. Syd's the kind of girl who can do anything. I know it. ". . . barely an amateur." She shakes his hand probably a little too hard, but she's excited and he doesn't seem to mind. "This food is amazing. It's witchcraft—you're like, a Sanderson sister. Thank you so much."

"Wow." He grins. "If someone ever put that in an official review, I'd frame it."

Sydney scratches her forehead, the same way she does with me when she feels like she's talking too much. "Sorry, I—"

"No, I mean it." Alex laughs. "Couldn't be happier that you two are enjoying yourselves. We'd love to have you back." Alex raises his eyebrows at me. "Your mom, too, of course is welcome." He turns back to Syd. "And since you're the next big thing in culinary, maybe we can take you in the back, show you around a little bit? We're hosting a few events for the rest of the weekend, but how about next week? You can work it out with the host on your way out—I'll let him know. Sound good?"

I've never seen someone light up and dim out like Syd does right now. She's probably caught up thinking about next week now, how we could have come back and looked around the kitchen and gotten her a selfie with Alex . . . like that could have been the best night of her life. But there are *a million things better than that,* a million things we can only do *because* there's no next week.

"That'd be great." I speak up since she still hasn't. "We'll do that. Thanks a lot." Alex shakes my hand again. "We'll see you."

"Great. We're looking forward to having you back."

He leaves us at our table and starts to head over to the *CSI* guy. I'm sure he has a list of people that he hits up every night—the ones with reservations who he ought to say hello to. It's a weird list to know I'm on.

"You can still get a tour of this place," I tell Sydney, but she's busy watching him go. "No problem. I'll call back in the morning."

I need her to smile again. I'm supposed to be killing fake prom.

"Hey." I nudge her knee with mine.

She nods, but I can tell she's not really listening. And when she looks at me, those big eyes with their different makeup tonight are officially somewhere else.

"Do you ever think about 'two'?" she asks.

"Too what?"

"Like, the number. The order number we get every time we go to Dunkin'. The reason why we met to begin with."

That's not the reason we met to begin with. Maybe it's *how* we met, but it's not why. We met because how could there be a her, and a me, and never an us?

But I don't want to get into all that right now, just like I didn't

Marcus

want to get into it yesterday. I push her glass a little closer. "You're not gonna drink that?"

"I feel like it can't be that random, right?" She takes the glass but just swirls the ice. "Like there has to be *something* about two that matters, wouldn't you think? I've been racking my brain lately, but there's nothing I can think of that has anything to do with it. I mean . . . except . . ."

As much as I don't want to talk about this—and kill the whole vibe? *Come on*—I can't let her stop there. "Except what?"

She slides her tongue along her teeth like she isn't sure it's worth saying. But she will say it. She always does. "There are two of us, just you and me who realize what's going on." She squints a little. "But . . . it wouldn't be something like that, would it?"

She asks like she really believes I'll know. Yeah, right. I haven't had a good answer for anything since I walked off that beach and Aus didn't.

"Why aren't you drinking your drink?" I ask.

"Who cares about the drink?"

"I mean, you ordered it."

She doesn't stop looking at me, but she finally brings the straw to her lips and sucks.

I know she wants me to say something—about two or some other weird thing I might have noticed—but I've got nothin'. Not because I'm stumped; I just don't care. I don't want *her* to care, either. When did she start caring?

"You wanna get the shrimp next?" I ask.

Marcus

But she sets the glass on the table and watches it instead of me. "I think I'm full."

She isn't, though. All we do is eat. All the time. Every plate at this place is like a bite and a half. She could sit here for hours and still be hungry.

"Do you wanna go?" She pushes back from the table. "I kind of want to go, if that's okay."

She's sliding past chairs on her way back to the main doors before I even know what's happening. But I swear, it feels like we're magnetized. That's how bad I need to follow her.

"Uh, check?" I hold up a hand as our waiter walks by.

He charges me on the iPad he's been using to place our orders. Tells me how we haven't tried the Korean fried duck wings or bao buns yet. I pretend like that's on purpose and say we have a show to catch. I don't really know why I care so much about this guy—who won't even remember me in the morning—not finding out that fake prom may be imploding. Pride, I guess.

"Thanks, again." I grab my duffel off the floor and jog outside.

There's a tour-group-looking pack coming from the left, a husky getting walked on the right. He almost tries to say hello but his owner tugs him back. Beautiful dog, but I can't hang out right now.

Syd is straight ahead, sitting on the curb.

I cut across the flow of foot traffic. She's found a big enough gap between two parallel-parked cars. Her legs are kicked in front of her so I finally see her shoes. A bunch of straps and kind of skin toned.

"Come on, you're gonna mess up your dress," I tell her.

Marcus

She doesn't jump or turn around, and in a way, that's kind of nice—that she just knows it's me. "Doesn't really matter, though, does it." It's not a question, the way she says it.

"Matters to me," I tell her.

It takes her a second, but she stands back up after that, lets me help her. She brushes off her dress and says, "This isn't like you."

"What's not like me?"

"This weird avoidance thing you're doing when all I want is to talk about . . ." She gazes around us at this block packed with people who have no idea how many nights they've been here. ". . . *this*. About what's actually happening, and why, and how we make it stop. Why we get the same number at Dunkin' every day. Why we're the only ones who realize it. I mean, do you really think we can do this forever?" She whispers like it was always too scary to say out loud. "That pain we feel every night—that's not normal pain. It's a *tidal wave*. And it just makes me wonder . . . can our bodies even handle this? What if it kills us one day? Sometimes I . . ."

I'll always love looking at Syd, but it's hard right now. I don't want to see her anxious like this and think about how maybe the truth is that at the end of every night, while she stares at me and I stare at her, she's never been happy to do it all over again. She's been scared every time.

Nah. Not possible. *There's no chance*. The way she laughs? How hearing it feels like someone's pumping sunshine straight into my veins?

"Sometimes you what?" I ask.

"Sometimes I feel like maybe we *are* dead."

"*We're not dead.*" Heaven would never have pain like this and hell wouldn't feel so good. "If it *does* kill us one day—if it kills us one day, then we'll find each other in the next life. Bodies may change, but souls never do. They just find each other and do it again."

She shakes her head. "We don't know that's true."

I do. But I can't handle talking about Aus right now, how he was never wrong. My throat's already on fire. My chest's already tight.

"Syd . . . all I'm trying to do is kill fake prom." I shift my duffel on my shoulder and rub my head—to wipe the sweat off my palm and try to push something halfway worth saying into my brain. "That's all I wanted. *Want.* I want this to be the best night you've ever had. It was that guy's offer, right? That chef guy? That's what got you thinking about all this? Because how can you come see his kitchen next week if we can't even make it past 10:15? But I'm telling you, Syd, I can get you in that kitchen. I'll call them again in the morning, I'll figure it out. Just . . . please don't let that kill the night." A bus flies by behind her and whips pieces of her hair into her face so I can't see it anymore. But I hope that dimple between her eyebrows is gone, the one that's only there when she's having the kinds of thoughts that hurt. "I'm really, really trying. I'm trying so hard to make this good for you."

She tucks those pieces of hair back where they belong. "But *why?*"

"*Why?*" It's like trying to answer why I breathe. "Because if a day goes by when I haven't made you happy, I don't even know what I woke up for."

Marcus

"Marcus..." She drops her neck, and I can't tell if it's good or bad. I don't care. Maybe I didn't know how much she's been thinking about everything, and maybe she didn't know how bad I wanted to kill fake prom. But she can't go another minute not knowing that making her smile has turned into my favorite thing to do.

She takes a deep breath and looks at me again.

"Stay here, okay?" she says. "I'll be back."

She leaves me on the curb and hangs a right on Chambers Street.

I slide my hands into my pockets while I wait. I have no idea where she's going, but at least it's not the way she left the restaurant. Like she was walking *away from me* instead of just walking somewhere else.

I get caught up watching the people across the street. The ones walking or laughing or busy on their phones. The ones with strollers or backpacks. One time, Aus said, *You ever think about how every person you see on the street is going somewhere different?*

"Okay," Syd says, and her voice doesn't make me jump, either. When I turn to her, she's biting the plastic off a pack of stickers. "You're right. It's prom night and all I've done is eat and walk out on the bill." With the corner of the pack still in her teeth, and a good yank, she gets the stickers open and then she starts sticking them on my lapel. "And I'm sure you *would* call this restaurant in the morning and figure out some way that they'd let me into that kitchen. But don't, okay? It doesn't matter. We can talk about all this stuff later—the stuck stuff, I mean. Tonight, it's just prom. I'm sorry I forgot that. And that I haven't been pulling my weight." She stops sticking me with stickers and studies her work. I tuck my chin so I can see it, too. Glitter stars all over, like I'm some kind of genius first grader. "You like it? It's your boutonniere."

I still don't know what a boutonniere is but no way it's this.

I tell her, "Best boutonniere I ever got."

🌹🌹🌹

I hail us a cab to Midtown and we grab fries and milkshakes at Five Guys before we walk to the dog park. I help her hop the fence and we go back to our bench where we sit and talk about everything and nothing. My duffel is on the ground and she finally nudges it with her foot and asks, "Who are we robbing tonight?"

"Just here to steal hearts, that's all," I answer.

She was about to have another fry, but she laughs so hard she has to wipe her eyes.

"No, but really." I hop up and set my milkshake down where I'd been sitting. I put the duffel on our bench, unzip it, and pull out my portable speaker. "Can't have a fake prom without music, right?"

She smiles. "Why are you so good at this? Are you just out here throwing every girl a fake prom?"

I scroll my phone for the playlist I made. Some fast stuff, some slow stuff. I figured variety was key. "Nah. Fake birthdays, yeah. But not fake proms."

I press play and set the speaker on the bench. I slide my phone back into my pocket.

She has another fry. "At least you're well rehearsed."

"Practice makes perfect."

She chews and looks out across the asphalt, where Mr. Parker will be waiting for us tomorrow. "Tonight is perfect," she softly says.

Man, that feels good. To know she's not overthinking anymore. To know that we can have the kind of moment we had outside Umi Prime and snap out of it so we're right back where we're supposed to be.

"Well, we can fake-prom again whenever you want," I tell her. "Just say the word."

But she shakes her head. "It's more special this way. Once."

When a slow song comes on, I ask if she wants to dance. She takes my hand, and we fall into this two-step that's easy enough while I spin her every once in a while and even dip her now and then. She squeals a little each time like she's on a roller coaster, and maybe we kind of are these days. Some twists and turns and drops, but we always end up back where we started.

Please let another slow song come on . . .

Ah, dope. One does.

We keep on dancing, and she accidentally steps on my foot a couple of times, but I don't mind. It's better than me stepping on hers.

"What are the Sonics?" she gently asks.

At first it kind of shakes me. I don't think she can tell, though.

It takes me a second to realize that she's reading the side of my duffel.

"The school mascot for the team I used to play for," I tell her.

"Basketball team."

"Yeah."

Marcus

"How long ago did you play?"

I think about it even though I don't have to. It's pretty much the answer to everything. There's stuff that happened before, and stuff that happened after, with a giant brick wall separating the two. "A month."

She nods. And there's something about her voice—just as quiet as it needs to be—when she asks, "You used to play with Austin?"

Her cheek's against my chest where she stuck all those stickers, and I loved it there a minute ago but I need it there now because I don't want her to see how fast it turns sometimes. How these tears hit my eyes like someone just came by and blew in them. I really wasn't trying to talk about Aus tonight. "Yeah."

We're quiet for a second. I act like I'm clearing my throat so it's not so obvious what I'm really doing—sniffing back these tears before one falls on her head. And then she says, "I think you should play again. Maybe not with the team, but . . . in general. Even a little bit. You know?"

Yeah, I know. I know Coach says he'll have me back anytime, even though I haven't practiced with the team in weeks. I know Mom says she misses the sound of me dribbling all over the house, except really all she ever used to say about it was, *If you break anything, I'll murder you.* I do miss basketball. Of course I do. It just feels easier to miss it than to play it.

To keep Syd feeling good, though, I tell her, "Maybe I will."

Then the music stops. My alarm is going off.

"Welp." I take a deep breath. Another day in the life.

Marcus

I start to pull away so we can hold hands like normal, but she won't let me go. She squeezes me around my waist and presses her cheek harder against my chest. I hug her close and, just in case she needs to hear it, I tell her, "I'm here."

She looks up at me. Maybe it's the fact that we don't have any light, but it's almost like her eyes are wet, too. That kills me, you know? If there's even a chance that she's already upset again. She never used to get upset.

"Syd, what's up?"

"Just . . ." She rubs her forehead. "Thank you. For doing all this, and showing me we can have all this, and for being such a good thing because you are. I never realized it could be this way, you know? That things could be this happy and also be sad at the same time. That life can be both, you know what I mean?"

I do. I'm not sure if the sad part for her is that the night is about to end, or that we're about to feel like we're on fire, or the fact that everything is always gonna have a little bit of Sebastian on it. I just hope that the sad part isn't that we're stuck. Because that really is the best thing we have.

"But you are happy, right? I mean . . . the happy is there?"

She stares into my eyes and I stare into hers, like we've been doing together for days now while we wait for it all to start over. But tonight, I'm looking for even a hint of what I saw outside Umi Prime—her fears about how bad it hurts and if we can really take it, if we can even survive it.

And then she takes my cheeks in her hands and kisses me.

Marcus

Oh man. It's the Mets sweeping the World Series. It's that choir scene at the end of *Sister Act 2*. It's everything.

Then it's screeching tires.

Headlights.

Pain.

September 24, Take Twenty-One: 9:34 a.m.

Sydney

"Are you ready now?" I ask, ripping a corner off my sausage, egg, and cheese croissant sans sausage or egg. I'm not very hungry this morning, so I toss that piece to a pigeon. "To talk about it?"

I finally just blurt it because, otherwise, I'll never say anything. Otherwise, we'll keep sitting here while Marcus laughs his perfect laugh and keeps telling me about this episode of *Family Guy* he saw once. Forever. Literally *forever*.

We're in the dog park again with our daily Dunkin' sandwiches, and our receipts stamped with a giant number two, right where we were when the tires started screeching last night. Right where we were while he twirled and dipped me and then let me kiss him—as easy and flawless as the first time. And yes, I would love to dance here with him again while committing a trespassing misdemeanor under the starlight. But not today. Tomorrow.

Marcus glances at me, back in his standard It's Today uniform: slacks, and a white button-down, and that black hoodie. It's not that I care—he'd be cute in anything. But it's starting to get kind of trippy. Like I really am the only one who notices what's going on.

Sydney

"Make sure none of the dogs get that." He means the sandwich crumbs I've started tossing off to the side. Then he raises his eyebrows. "Talk about what?"

"Like . . ." I glance at Dixon, circling his feet, and Dixon's dad, who's gonna wave any second, and then back at Marcus. ". . . how this is our twenty-first time doing this? We said we were gonna get through last night and then talk about it."

"Get through it?" Marcus softly repeats. His tongue pokes a bulge through his cheek, and he stares straight ahead like now he's rethinking everything.

"Not *get through it*." I tuck my leg under me and shake his knee. "That was stupid—that's not what I meant. It was *amazing*, it's just that . . . you didn't want to talk about this at the pool, and you didn't want to talk about it last night—which was fair. But we said we would today."

He frowns like he doesn't remember agreeing to that, or remember my examples, or remember me having such a good memory. I toss more of my sandwich to the birds. He finished his a few minutes ago and the trash sits crumpled up between us.

"There has to be a reason why you and I are the only ones who can do anything real on this day." I wave at Mr. Parker when he starts waving first, and I nudge Marcus so he will, too; because he's too busy peering at the ground to notice. "What if that's because there's something we're *supposed* to be doing? Something bigger than crashing rooftop pools and paying too much for food—"

"I agree, Syd." He finishes waving to Mr. Parker and turns to me.

Sydney

"Forget about the croissants at Dunkin', let's go get croissants in Paris. Forget rooftop pools, let's go to Jamaica—"

"I don't mean that kind of stuff—"

"Then what kind of stuff? We can seriously do whatever you want—"

"I want to do the kind of stuff that might get us unstuck!"

I feel like I'm losing my mind—like I'm asking him to ingest lighter fluid or hack Google. Like I'm trying to get him to talk about something *that wild*, and it can't be like that. Not when it comes to talking about this or when it comes to talking about anything else. Because we're all each other has.

"Nothing I do is gonna start the world turning." He says it as if it's the simplest fact in the universe. "I'm not big enough to change the world."

He changed mine. "You don't know that."

"Yeah, I do." He chuckles about it, but not like anything is actually funny. "We can't fix something that's meant to be broken. The best we can do is accept it and adapt. Okay?" He rubs my knee like he really wants it to be okay. "You want to go back to the Battery today?"

"Not today."

"We can find a cooking class. That meat loaf was fire, Syd. I still say you would have liked it if you just tried it."

"I don't want to go to a cooking class."

He leans forward on his knees and drops his neck, rubbing it with his hands. "What can I do?" he asks, peering at me over his shoulder. The way he says it, it's almost like he feels it, too: how bad it is that

Sydney

we're in such different places right now. I can't tell if he's asking, *What can I do to fix the world?* or *What can I do to make you happy?* or just *What can I do so that you'll stop?*

"I want to go to the beach in Long Island. The one where it happened."

I started thinking about it when we were dancing last night and he told me about his duffel. I saw how much it hurt. And I felt that twist again, deep inside, that this can't be forever. That this is *supposed* to get fixed. That we weren't meant to find each other just to hold on tight right where we are but because the good stuff is *finally* starting. Maybe we just have to fight for it.

His smile disappears, wiped clean like the spill in a Bounty commercial, and I'm sitting here with the sticky paper towel.

"What?" he answers.

"I feel like there's something big, about you and me, that needs to get done. And the way you look when you even mention that night . . . it crushes you. But it doesn't have to. Maybe you just need to know that, and maybe I just need to help you. Maybe it's that kind of stuff, you know? The stuff we're scared of that's gonna get us out of this thing."

In the senselessness of all this, that makes sense to me as a possibility, at least. Just saying it starts to melt the lump that's been swimming in my stomach, that's been trying to talk to him about this for days.

His eyebrows weave together as he watches straight ahead. The paper bag his sandwich came in is crumpled up between us. At some point, every morning, he absentmindedly grabs it and starts pushing it from one palm to the other. I've never told him that he does it, but I always notice. I've decided it'll be the way I'll know if Marcus has ever been replaced by some evil AI and I'm officially the only one left in this world. I'll just crumple up some paper and see what he does.

"So maybe we should start by going back to that beach," I push.

"Why would I ever go back to the place where my best friend died?" He's doing it again. Asking a question like that's not the real question. The real question this time is, *Did you get your brain removed?*

"I just told you why."

He looks down at his hands, cracking his knuckles. I rip more of my sandwich and fling it to the birds. I know it's the most masochistic thing I can do—that pigeons aren't birds so much as they're fearless bots—and I've already summoned, like, twenty of them with my crumbs. Pecking around, and jutting their necks, and being gross. But I'm too annoyed to stop.

His voice is low when he speaks again. And he's still too busy looking at nothing to look at me. "When you wake up every day at 7:01, does it still hurt?"

I frown. "No . . ."

He nods, like he really is glad to hear it. "Every day, I wake up in this sweat. My skin's wet, my sheets are drenched. And you know why?" He hangs his head for a second, like he's embarrassed, or something. I want to cut in and tell him, *Stop. No.* Because he isn't allowed to be embarrassed. Not in front of me. Never in front of me.

But I don't cut in because that's the thing about momentum when you're saying stuff you don't want to. Once it's gone, so's everything.

He lifts his head and keeps going. "Because the first morning this day ever happened, I was waking up from a nightmare. The worst one I've ever had. It was so real . . . about that night, that beach." His voice barely catches and he clears his throat to cover it up. "That sat with me, you know? Heavy. It weighed me down that whole morning until I ran into you. And I don't know why I ran into you, but you're not gonna convince me it wasn't supposed to happen just like this. So maybe that means every day for the rest of my life, I'm gonna wake up from that same nightmare. But I'd do that to stick with you."

I can't look at him right now, so I peer across the blacktop at Mr. Parker instead and the way he smiles while the dogs play. I try to ignore the shards that have suddenly emerged in my chest, and how they pierce something deep every time I breathe. I can't imagine, on top of everything else—no new movies, or music, and the pain we feel every night at 10:15—that he also has to feel that dream again every morning.

"You can't do that for me." I shake my head, chew the inside of my cheek, keep tearing at this stupid sandwich. "You can't give up, and stay stuck, and say screw you to Jacq waiting on FAM, and screw you to your mom waiting to announce her Orangetheory deal, and screw you to the guys at Nina's who actually miss you, and screw you to the entire world."

"Why not?" he mutters, but it's just another one of those questions he doesn't mean.

"Because it's ridiculous—" I answer, anyway.

"Says who?"

"Says me!" I finally turn back to him, and anyone who couldn't hear us would have no idea he's not okay. His body is so lax, his elbows resting on his knees.

Up until the point when I started talking about tomorrow, Marcus has *always* stayed with me. Showing up is one thing, it's a *big* thing—physically being there with someone else. But *staying* . . . that's the part where he doesn't take his phone out and start texting other people, and he doesn't sit there looking at me when he's obviously daydreaming about something else, and it never feels like I'm keeping him from somewhere he'd rather be. Over the past twenty-one days, he's spoiled me into realizing that staying in every single moment, with the person that you're with, is the hardest, most valiant thing that someone can do.

But right now, he's nowhere near this conversation. He's in Queens. He's on the moon. That's what hurts the most. That's why I keep going.

"I am not staying stuck," I snap. "I'm not gonna pretend like this is normal. Or worse, like this is some kind of gift. I don't want to know you for the *same day*—again and again. *I want to know you every day.* Except for right now, if I'm being honest. Because the way you're acting about this makes me want to shove my head in a garbage disposal."

He nods to himself, frowning. "Well take that, times it by a million, and that's how I feel about going back to the beach."

Sydney

Then he stands up like he's gonna stretch, but he doesn't stretch. He looks at me, finally. While he stands in the swarm of what's likely to be every pigeon on the West Side, he tells me, "You know what? Maybe you were onto something when you spent that day with Jacq. Maybe as long as we're stuck with each other forever, a few days apart wouldn't be so bad."

I stare at him. "Are you on glue? What are you talking about?"

He barely smiles, not like he means it but like he wants me to believe that he does. "Remember my number, okay?"

So maybe this *is* some AI hologram. Maybe this is the moment I've been prepping for, and it's a good thing I have my foolproof way of identifying the fake Marcus because—

He grabs his balled-up trash and tosses it in the air like he's about to take a shot, but it just goes straight up and he catches it with his other hand. He does it again and again as he walks away.

—because otherwise how would I know that's very much the real Marcus who needs a break from me right now?

The birds crowd around my feet, and I tell myself I'm gonna be okay. That if I can face whatever that otherworldly pain is that takes me every night, I can face this, too. It's not so bad. It's not *as* bad.

No, it is.

At least at night, the pain is fast. I'm here and then I'm not and then it's gone. But this—the way it's slow? And lasts?

God.

This is so much worse.

September 24, Take Twenty-One: 11:04 a.m.

Marcus

There are nineteen steps in the Union Square subway station from the level where you pay down to the platform where the L pulls in. I've never straight-up counted, but I can hear the sound in my head, easy. Me and Aus, our feet running up them 'cause we were late for school or Mr. Felix, or our feet running down them trying to catch the next train as the doors started to close. *Thunk, thunk, thunk, thunk, thunk*—nineteen times. I'd bet the apartment on it.

I haven't been on the subway since he died. I can't get myself to do it. Nothing bad happened here, but we took these trains all over the city. We took the L *every day*—sometimes three or four times. We always waited for it next to the same chipped column toward the end of the platform so we could hop in one of the cars near the back. They're usually the emptiest.

I can't tell you why I came here. It's clearly not because I have any intentions of getting on a train. I'm just sitting on one of these nineteen steps, up against the rail, ugly-crying like a damn fool. I've never been like this in my whole life, not even on the night when everything happened. I mean, I've cried before, yeah. But it was always like the way I was with Mr. Felix a few weeks ago. Jaw tight. Deep breaths and stuff. Not this. I have no idea what this is. Huddled underground and crying too hard to see straight.

That's the good thing about New Yorkers. We see you but we don't actually look. Enough to step around you but not much more than that. You mind your business, I'll mind mine. So doing all this right here, it's really not all too different from being locked in my bedroom. Noisier, yeah. But that's about it.

I grip my head and try to slow it down, make it stop. But I can't. Man, what am I doing?

I'm not wrong for not wanting to go back to that beach, by the way. I'm at that beach *all the time*. I close my eyes, I'm at that beach. It gets too quiet, I'm at that beach. Someone talks about a party, or vacation, or swim lessons, I'm at that beach. Getting stuck is the first time I've had a break at all—the first time that beach hasn't been tapping me on the shoulder everywhere I go. Now Syd thinks something's wrong with *me* because I don't want to go back?

That's wild, man. She should know that. She should *get* that.

It's lonely. This whole entire thing, from the second Aus was gone, is so damn lonely. No matter how many people are ever around, they don't fill in the blank, you know what I mean? It's like . . . it's like walking into a store you've never been to before, and they have tennis balls, and soccer balls, and footballs, and baseballs, and dodgeballs, and bouncy balls, and pool balls . . . thousands of them, right? I mean this place has got millions of balls. But you need a basketball. That's it. And they don't have one. They've never even met one. They can't

Marcus

find you one, or make you one, and there's never gonna be another one. They mean well, sure. They toss you all these other balls and say, *Hey, can this work instead?* But they barely know what they're asking because they don't know what you're missing. And you can't explain it, because some stuff you just have to *feel*.

It's lonely like that. Like trying to explain a basketball to someone who's never seen one.

"Hi," someone says. Then, a second later, "Are you okay?"

The voice is close enough to make me look up, and I do a double take when I realize she's talking to me, and then I do a triple take when I think I kind of recognize her.

"Sorry, I didn't want to bother you," she goes on, hiking her bag up on her shoulder. "I just wanted to make sure you didn't need help or anything."

Her bag has a duck on it . . . she's that girl from Dunkin'. The one I bumped into that day and bought her a refill coffee. Weird that I'm running into her here, though. We're forty blocks south.

Next to us, people keep passing on their way up or on their way down. *Thunk, thunk, thunk, thunk, thunk.* Nineteen times each.

"Yeah. I'm okay." It's still hard to breathe. It's still hard to see. For some reason—exhaustion, maybe desperation—I add, "My friend died. Not today or anything. A month ago. That's all." I nod like it's no big deal, so she can keep going wherever she's headed and not worry about me. But then I accidentally add, "He was my best friend."

The way she sits down next to me, she kind of melts. It's so slow that, at first, I didn't even realize it was happening. Her eyes, they're like, *glued* to me. Like I'm the twist ending of a seven-season series.

"I'm so sorry," she whispers.

I can tell she really means it. "Thanks. But yeah, that's it. Just. You know." I really don't want her sticking around just for me.

"My dad . . ." She kind of clears her throat, kind of takes a breath. "He also passed, like, a month ago."

My response sucks. "Really?"

She nods. "I know it's not the same as losing your best friend. But, believe it or not, he kind of *was* my best friend. It's the worst thing that's ever happened to me, and I'm really sorry it's happening to you, too."

Her eyes get glassy with these tears that sit there like warriors. There if she needs them but she hasn't called on them yet. Instead, she stays where she is, looking at me, and I really hope she doesn't mind how close I'm looking back at her. It's just . . . I've never met a grieving stranger before. With Syd, it's different—it felt like I was meant to know her from the second I met her and we talked about so much stuff before I knew she lost her brother. But that's not what this is. This is just a girl who also happened to be in Dunkin' on September 24, and now she's at 14th Street like a hundred other people, and now I know her dad just died.

"I'm Dana." She offers me her hand.

I shake it. "Marcus. And, for the record, I think it's really cool that your dad was your best friend."

She smiles even though I can tell how hard it is. Did she look like this at Dunkin'? I feel like I would have noticed. Like there ought to be a radar for this kind of thing. *Beep—beep—beep. This person's going through hell.*

"You waiting for a train?" she asks.

I nod. Feels like less of a lie than saying yes out loud. "You?"

She nods, too. "Is it okay if I wait with you?"

I don't know why, but it makes me miss Syd. "Yeah. Please, do."

So, here's all I find out: She lives in BK, too. She's a sophomore at Fordham getting a degree in psychology. That's what she's on her way home for now—an online class that starts at 12:15 p.m. Her teachers told her she could take all the time she needed after she lost her dad, but once a couple of days had gone by, she just felt like she had to start doing stuff again.

"It's weird, because I don't really remember any of it," she says. "Like, I know I woke up all those days, got dressed all those days, went into Manhattan all those days, but only because it has to be true, you know? Only because, when I check my phone each morning, it's always a new day. But I don't actually . . . like . . . *recall* any of it. Like I've just been moving, you know? But not actually getting anywhere."

"Stuck," I mutter.

"Yeah," she realizes. "Stuck."

My tongue starts clicking. I don't want to sound crazy for asking, but now I've gotta know. "You're not actually, though . . . right? I mean. Tomorrow. It comes?"

She sighs like I'm just talking about the philosophy of it all, and I can tell by how she's sitting there that she's not doing what Syd and I have been doing. "Every time."

I nod and start popping my knuckles. "My friend . . . his name's Austin. He drowned. Up in Long Island, after I dared him to jump in the river during a storm. Huge storm. Thunder made the ground shake." I ball up my hands, dig my nails into my palms. "And I dared him to jump in the river."

She squints. "What night?"

"August twenty-fourth."

She dry-laughs. The way it comes out when nothing's really funny. "That's the night my dad passed."

I blink. "You're lyin'."

She shakes her head. "I wish. Yeah, it was August twenty-fourth. I wasn't home when it happened. I was sleeping at a friend's. I texted him good night, but he didn't text me back. Which was weird for him but I ignored it, and stayed out, and had fun. When I got home in the morning, he was on the floor. They said it was—" She slows herself down, closes her eyes for a second, takes a deep breath. "They said it was a massive heart attack. That he probably didn't suffer very long. *Probably.* It's weird how sometimes that word is more than enough and other times it doesn't mean anything."

She wonders if she could have stopped it, I can tell. Maybe when it comes to staying home that night instead of going out, or sounding the alarms when her dad didn't text her back, or maybe fighting him harder about some huge Mickey D's habit. I don't know what she wishes she could try to do over, and I don't ask because, if she's

Marcus

anything like me, the list is years long. But, for the first time, I feel like I've kind of got a taste for what Mr. Felix means, and Mom means, and Ashe means when they say it's not my fault. Because I mean it heavy when I tell myself it's not hers.

"Yeah," I say. "You're right. *'Probably'* isn't good enough."

"You know what other word I hate?" she goes on, picking at her shoes. "*Died*. It's so conclusive, you know? Like something's over. Forever. I reject that wholeheartedly. So, I say *passed*—because doesn't that sound more transitional? Like it's just a new phase? Like it's just a race and they got to the finish line first. But one day we'll all catch up with each other again."

Wow, that sounds like Aus. Souls and permanence and all that stuff.

"Oh, shoot, my train's here," Dana realizes, and the gush of thick, warm air that smacks my face confirms it. "Are you headed downtown?" She shifts her bag back onto her shoulder.

"Nah," I answer, even though I should be. "But you go ahead. Good luck in your class."

"Thanks." She forces another sad smile before she jogs down the last few steps.

"Hey, Dana—" I start. She stops at the bottom and faces me again. "—you're gonna hop on that train and, in the morning, completely forget that any of this ever happened. But I won't. So, I just wanted to say thank you." I don't have the words—or the time, really—to say for what. But, if I did, I'd tell her that, for a while now, I've been pretty sure that everyone else in the world is okay but me. That

Marcus

people are made of tougher stuff than I am, and I just didn't have it in me. So everything came to a screeching halt because I wasn't strong enough to keep pushing it forward. You know Atlas? That guy who held the world on his shoulders? That's how I started looking at people. Like a bunch of Atlases, getting their coffees, and catching their trains, and holding up their worlds while I just stopped and stared like, *how*? How are you holding up the *world*?

I don't think Dana's holding up the world, though. I think she's barely convinced she's even *in* the real world. But she's not stuck like I am. She's still moving—or, at least, thinks she is—every day. Who knows why. Or how. But it's cool that she is. And I'm happy for her.

That's what I'd tell her if there was time, but there's not.

She probably thinks I'm the needy type, that I'm saying she'll forget me because I want to hear her say she won't. "I'll remember you," she says, and she's so sure about it that, if I didn't have a daily alarm set for 10:14, I really would believe her. "I'll remember Austin, too."

I push out a smile with no teeth and salute her with two fingers. It feels better than I thought it would, hearing his name come out of her mouth all because I put it there.

"Same thing goes for me with your dad. He's a real lucky guy to call you a best friend."

That's when one of those warriors she held back drips straight from her eye to the ground. Quick, like a bullet. I didn't mean to make her cry, but she smiles, so at least she doesn't hate me for it.

She jogs to join the crowd waiting for people to get off the train so that they can get on. Union Square is a busy stop all day, and watching the horde of people mixing and passing each other is kind of like watching live-action poetry. I've seen it too many times to count, but it looks different right now. Like my New York blinders are lifting, and I notice what people are wearing, and what they actually look like, and maybe they're more like me than I thought. Worlds are heavy. Maybe I'm not the only one who feels it.

I wait for a few more downtown trains to come. I let the thick, hot air smack me upside the head. Eventually, I follow it. Down to the platform, into the crowd, and onto the L.

September 24, Take Twenty-One: 4:07 p.m.

Marcus

I walk down 4th Street for the hundredth time. Syd's number stares back at me on my phone. I should call her. We should talk about this morning, or maybe about this whole thing, or maybe just try and talk to each other at all. But I put my phone away.

I don't know what to say.

September 24, Take Twenty-One: 8:17 p.m.

Marcus

I sit on the step outside Joe's Deli. I mean, why should the beach have anything to do with us getting unstuck, anyway? I'm supposed to go back up there just *in case* it gets us moving forward again? I'm still not convinced staying in this day is the worst thing. Nothing bad happens this day. We can practically live like millionaires. We're not hurting anybody. It's not like anyone misses us. Staying just means that we finally get to *know* what happens next. How things turn out. No more messed-up surprises. No more making mistakes that can haunt us forever. And that ache—that thing at my core that throbs like a heartbeat—it doesn't have to go away. It can stay right where it is, right where it belongs.

I did kind of want to see that next *Fast & Furious*, though.

September 24, Take Twenty-One: 10:14 p.m.

Marcus

There's my alarm. I turn it off.

I'm still sitting outside Joe's. Got a sandwich, though. Pastrami. Thinnest cut in the city.

Well, we've just about done another day without each other. A little space so we can each do our own thing for a minute. Got to clear my head. Take some Me Time. Eat good. And look at that, it was fine. Time flew. That wasn't a big deal at all. Maybe I'll do it again tomorrow.

Yeah, right.

Who am I kidding?

I can't do forever without her.

September 24, Take Twenty-Two: 7:01 a.m.

Sydney

I turn off my alarm and groan.

I hate this.

There should be emergency inventions for purchase after you've had a fight with a boy you really like. Like an EpiPen or fast-acting Pepto. Except it stops your mind from spinning out of control, rethinking every millisecond about how it could have gone differently while you yo-yo back and forth between blaming him for everything and hating yourself for being fully out of pocket.

Ugh, I hate this so much.

Since CVS doesn't carry emergency interventions, I spent yesterday at the Empire State Building. I have no idea why. I'd never even been before. But it was something Marcus and I had never done, and it was far enough away from anywhere we'd ever been, and I thought that might make it easier not to think about him. It didn't, but I stayed, anyway. I stayed so long that three different tourists asked me if I was a guide. I stayed so long that the sun set and the city went from a skyline to just a bunch of lights in the darkness. I stayed so long that that's where I was when the tires started screeching, and

Sydney

the headlights started beaming, and it all started hurting even more than the day already had.

Think, Syd.

I *do* think he should go back to that beach. Even if we weren't stuck, I think he deserves to see it again, and not remember it forever as this place that haunts his dreams but take it in for what it is: a place where a terrible thing happened, but *he* isn't that terrible thing.

I believe that. And that isn't gonna change. Ever.

So why does this still feel so awful?

Because he doesn't have to be ready right now.

I know that's the answer. I knew it yesterday, too, when I brought it up. He doesn't have to be okay enough to do this today, or the next today, or the today after that, just because I'm getting anxious. *Especially* not because I'm getting anxious, and that's what I should have said but didn't. That was the phrase that was missing during that entire, miserable conversation. *When you're ready.* Because I was thinking about him a little bit but I was mainly thinking about us. About the us that *I* want.

Maybe that's what I need to call and say. I've been almost calling him ever since he walked away. At the Empire State Building, I typed his number into my phone and stared at it for so long that some nosy six-year-old finally told me, *You press the green button.* Yeah, thanks, Peewee. I'm sure it's really easy to just press the green button when your pastimes consist of tracing the alphabet and you have no idea what it's like to really lo—

Like.

Really, *really* like someone.

Sydney

Maybe us not talking yesterday was allowed. Like, maybe we can just classify that as the acceptable cool-off period and call it a wash. But now, I'm scared we may be creeping into the danger zone of the Let's Not Speak to Each Other timeframe. The kind of thing that has people trying to remember twenty years later what really went wrong in the first place.

I type his number into my phone. I have that annoying little kid's voice in my head as I stare. *You press the green button.* I bet he's an only child with two parents who've taught him he's brave. I bet he isn't nervous to raise his hand in class, or get an answer wrong, or fall off a bike. I bet they let him stay home alone when the doors are locked and they're just running next door to borrow cinnamon from a neighbor. I bet they're already teaching him that the world is scary, but he can't live his life afraid.

I toss my phone to the other side of my mattress and decide to take a shower instead.

I'm a nighttime showerer—it used to be the last thing I did every day before I got in bed, so I haven't taken a shower since this whole thing started because I wake up every morning in the same freshly cleansed body that I woke up in the first day. But I miss how it feels to have the water hit my skin, and to be lathered in suds, and the way my bodywash smells. So, I go to my bathroom and turn the water on "hot" for the first time in three weeks.

My throat gets tight while I stand there, rubbing my loofah across my shoulders. There's a knot that's sliding into the middle of my trachea, the kind that can squeeze itself so tight that it disappears,

Sydney

or unravel into uncontrollable tears. Maybe it has something to do with Marcus, or maybe it's more to do with how simply I'd accepted that, as long as I was here, showers would be, too. That I would always take another one tomorrow.

Stupid tomorrow.

I finish rinsing off my suds and step out. I wrap myself in a towel and walk back to my room. I sit on the side of my bed and try to decide what I'm gonna wear. Not to be fully pathetic, but it doesn't feel like it matters the same way if I'm not gonna see Marcus. Maybe I can give myself a break today. Maybe I can just throw on leggings and a T-shirt—

My phone starts vibrating on the other side of my bed.

I lean over to grab it and freeze midreach. It's Marcus's number.

You press the green button.

"Hello?" I cringe. In part because I'm not sure what I'm about to be hit with, and in part because I know for a fact that I just sounded way too excited.

"Hey," he says. "Can you come downstairs?"

I frown and speed-scroll through my mind for any pop culture references he could be making. Usually, it's easy to figure out, when he calls and leads with anything but *hello*. But this isn't pizza, and it's not one of those hateful Verizon texts—"Is that some jingle I haven't heard of?"

"What?"

"What?"

"No, that was a real question," he says. "I'm asking if you can come downstairs."

Sydney

"Come downstairs where?"

"In your building."

"You're at my apartment?"

"Only if you'll come down," he says. "Otherwise, this never happened."

"No." I hop off my bed. "It happened. It's happening." I start digging through my drawers for something to throw on. "I'm coming."

Well, looks like it's a T-shirt and leggings either way, at least for now. There's no way I'm gonna make him wait any longer than absolutely necessary.

I grab my keys and run into the hallway. I jam the button for the elevator a few times, because I'm good at convincing myself that it helps, and then bounce while I wait. I would take the stairs but I'm on the sixteenth floor, and Bas told me when I was little there's a woman who eats cats who lives in the stairwell. He was joking, obviously. Probably. Most likely.

I hug myself and wait until there's a ding and the door slides open. I hop inside and oh.

Oh no.

Mrs. Ellersby is coming.

She's been ninety my entire life. Her husband is in the nursing home on 96th and she goes to visit him every weekend. They've lived in the apartment down the hall since 1972. She's the *sweetest*, okay? She talks to me every time she sees me and single-handedly made me really care when we were learning about the Cold War in school, but she's just. So. Slow. Like she could be walking as fast as she can,

Sydney

and you could close your eyes for five whole seconds and open them again, and not even be fully sure if she's moved.

But I press the button to hold the elevator because I could never just leave Mrs. Ellersby.

"Hi, Mrs. Ellersby," I call through the open doors.

She shuffles toward me with her cane and her little white dog named Olive. "Good morning, dear," she says. "Such a pretty day to be here, don't you think?"

Mrs. Ellersby says every day is a pretty day to be here. I didn't always get it, but you know what? She's right.

"It is pretty."

"I hope it holds up for when I see My Daniel this weekend. He loves sitting outside in that garden, you know."

Mr. Ellersby is never just Daniel, always My Daniel when she talks about him. It's kind of the best thing I've ever heard, to be honest. I hope someone makes my first name *My* one day.

"You know, maybe you should go see him today." I force myself to swallow now that my throat's gone dry. "Since it is so nice. Just in case you can't this weekend, or something."

"Oh, sweetie, I can't go today. Today is Thursday."

"I know, I just thought—"

"I go on weekends."

"I know, but maybe—"

"My Daniel might hardly recognize me if I showed up on a Thursday." She laughs, this happy giggle that always leaves her a little out of breath.

I wait another twenty minutes for Mrs. Ellersby to make it to the elevator—okay, more like thirty seconds, *but still*—and jam the lobby button the second she's inside.

"Are you alright, Mrs. Ellersby?" I ask once the doors open again, because I kind of want to leave her in the dust versus accompany her to the main entrance. "It's just that I'm meeting someone and—"

"Oh, you go right on ahead, sweetheart. I'm just fine."

I rush around the corner toward the front of my lobby and there he is. Marcus. Sitting on the cushioned bench by the windows that face the street.

"Hi, Wally," I say to my doorman as I rush over to Marcus instead.

"'Morning, angel." Then, a moment later, "Well, hey there, Mrs. Ellersby."

Marcus had been looking out the window but he looks up when he hears my voice. For a second, I just stand there, looking back. I was so excited to hear from him that I never stopped to wonder if I *should* be. If this is a good thing, or if it's about to be really, really bad.

Olive trots past me on her retractable leash and goes right over to his feet, twitching her little butt and pressing her nose against his leg. He smiles as he bends over to rub her, and when I reach where he's sitting, I bend down and pet her, too.

"Well, I would have grabbed a nicer hoodie if I knew I was meeting you this morning," he tells Olive. A joke, because he's still in the same one he's worn every morning.

"I'm so sorry about that," Mrs. Ellersby says, catching up at the

Sydney

same rate that the continents are shifting apart from each other. "She never runs off."

"Ah, don't worry about it," Marcus says, giving her one last pat. "Probably just smells the bacon in my socks."

Mrs. Ellersby giggles and says, "Nice boy," maybe to compliment Marcus, or maybe to reassure me, or maybe just to decide for herself. She keeps shuffling toward the door, and for the next few seconds, Marcus and I both pretend like we aren't *not speaking*, we're just waiting for her to leave.

I should probably be the first to say something. I'm the one who started everything yesterday, and he's the one who came all the way to my apartment this morning in spite of it.

So, yes. Okay. Me first.

"Dog whisperer," I say.

Ugh. Maybe not that.

"Good news for you," Marcus says. "They're the best judge of character. You know, Nelson Mandela used to walk around and packs of dogs would follow him. Jump fences just to go where he was going."

He doesn't crack a smile as he says it, just like he didn't crack a smile when he said that peaches grow fur because they have testosterone in them, or that clouds weigh more than a million tons. One true, one false. So, this time, I don't even know.

I'd make a joke back but I can't right now. That's how it would go if things were normal.

"Look, yesterday, I was completely—" I start, but he cuts me off.

"Hold on," he says, standing up like I already am. "I don't want to

Sydney

talk about yesterday yet. I want to talk about us." He steps in front of me and his eyes stare into mine, and even though my heart is in my stomach, I've never felt safer in my life. "I've been thinking about this since we split up and here's the thing. Something happened when we met. We don't know what, or why, but you're right—it was huge. *Big enough to stop the world.* Now we're here together, and maybe it *is* because of each other. But if that's the theory—and I'm willing to buy that theory because it's yours—we have to act like it. You know what I mean? We need to be on the same side. We need to treat each other like what we're thinking, and what we're feeling, and who we are is a solid fifty percent of this whole equation. And I guess I just want . . . I want to know if we're gonna do this together. Even when we're not on the same page, and we need a day apart, or a few days apart, or whatever it may be. I'm cool with all that if, baseline, we agree that we're doing this together. I mean for real. Like we're sticking together not because we have to if we don't wanna be stuck here all alone. But because we want to. And that's what I wanted to say. That I really do want to do this together, but I can't be the only one."

I stare up at this guy I met in a Dunkin' that I was never supposed to be in, with all his cracks, and fractures, and flaws. He isn't perfect at all. And I'm even worse. But he's absolutely, undeniably, time-stoppingly perfect for me.

I wrap my arms around his neck and hop into his arms. I kiss him like I'm a girl in a movie, the kind everyone wants to be. The one who almost lost hope the second before she shouldn't have. And then suddenly has enough to pass along to the rest of us.

I kiss him like we're that special, like he's that life-changing, like it's time to roll the credits.

Until Wally clears his throat and I remember:

Real life can't just fade to black.

I smile at Wally in this way that says, *Please don't tell my parents*, and he folds his arms and peers down his nose at me in a way that answers, *I better not see another boy here until you're thirty-five*. And even though it doesn't matter—because of the whole days-on-repeat thing—I take Marcus's hand and bring him outside with me instead.

"Together," I promise, pushing my hair behind my ear. I want him to hear it. To see me say it. "Seriously. You and me—that's the biggest reason why I want out, why I'm thinking about tomorrow so much. Because I want to do it with you."

His mouth twists. Not like he doesn't believe *me*, but like maybe he doesn't believe *it*. That words like those could be meant for him. "You really think we can get out of this?"

I hug myself and glance over my shoulder to make sure that Wally isn't watching Marcus from the door with a bat. "I've been having these . . . *feelings*," I admit, and it feels good to finally say it, that it's not just this gnawing inside me anymore. "I know that's ridiculous. But they're like . . . ideas for how we get out of this, except bigger than just ideas. They feel like that tickle you get in your brain when you know there was something you wanted to say but you forgot. Except it's in my gut, like—" I start to point to the spot, somewhere beneath my breastbone and above my stomach, but it's a location that's too deep to reach, so I don't try. "I know that doesn't make sense."

Sydney

Marcus sits on the ledge that wraps around my building. He gazes up at me, squinting against the sun. "And you think we actually *should*?" he asks. "Get out of this day, I mean."

There's something about the way he asks that wasn't there yesterday. Maybe he was never being lazy, or chill about being stuck. Maybe he's been thinking about it just as much as I've been. That's what his eyes say, and the way his fingers keep pulling at each other.

I sink onto the ledge next to him. "Tell me what you think," I say, because something tells me that he never really has.

"You know, the first time I woke up and it was the same day again, I did think that maybe I'd, you know." The word he's looking for is *died*. I nod so he doesn't have to say it. "So I pricked myself on purpose. Nothing bad. Just nicked my finger with a safety pin. It bled, so I knew that whatever this was, it was real. Blood makes everything real." He holds his hand palm-up on my knee so I can really see it. "But the next day? All gone. No scar. Nothing. We don't get hurt here, Syd. If we do, it's gone at 10:15. We're safe, you know?"

I tuck my ankle behind his and he brushes his foot against mine like they were always meant to cross. "You're right. It is safe here." Two kids run past, racing to the end of the block, screaming and laughing and thrilled. "And if we ever get unstuck, I have no idea what would come next. Probably some bad stuff." I take a deep breath at the same moment that Marcus pushes one out. "But ever since I met you . . . I just feel like there's gonna be at least one good thing that's next. Because *we're* what's next. And that's enough for me."

Sydney

Our feet keep rubbing. "Mom does deserve to announce that Orangetheory deal." He says it mostly to himself.

"She really does," I agree.

We're quiet for a second before he nods and says, "I trust you."

It's the best thing anyone's ever told me.

"I am gonna miss our days, though, if we do get unstuck." He watches the people in front of us, walking north and south. "Dunkin' and dog parks? More than enough for me."

"Let's do it one more time, then," I say. "Let's do all the stuff we love about being stuck, and then try to get unstuck tomorrow." I frown. We've really gotta stop calling it that. "Or the next today. You know what I mean."

He offers me his fist. I bang it with mine. "Down," he agrees.

"By the way," I add. "There's absolutely no guarantee that we'll figure this out anytime soon. So let that be stated on the record: I take no responsibility for failed attempts."

"Nah, you can't go planning the revolt and denying all culpability at the same time."

I laugh as he pulls me in, as he goes on about how I'm either about that rogue life or I'm not.

"Okay, okay," I finally say. "I take all the credit and all the blame."

He lets me go, and as I run my hands down my hair to flatten it, he smirks and says it again:

"I trust you."

September 24, Take Twenty-Two: Our last today (sort of)

Sydney

Marcus is right. We do have good todays.

The way it's always in the low seventies and the moon is always full. The way it always ends and the way it always starts. Even the pain . . . it sucks but at least I know it. It's a part of me now, like my fingernails and my skin, and I don't think I really know anymore who I am without it. Or that I'm even capable of being the person I was before it. But I think that that's okay—I hope it is. Maybe things aren't meant to be the same forever. No matter how good or bad they are, or something in between.

In a way, it feels like our Possible Last Today should be *huge*. Like setting off fireworks from the crown of the Statue of Liberty, or kissing in front of the entire world on the *TODAY* show, or making it onto a digital billboard in Times Square. The kind of major plan that you don't just come up with off the top of your head.

Marcus smiles. "I'm not tryin' to do all that," he says.

Here's what we do instead:

Sydney

We go to the dog park and see if Dixon will *sit* if I say the word *fish*. (Of course, he does, and Marcus is devastated.)

We go to CVS and buy Oreos and cream cheese so he can see the way I eat them. (Twist apart the cookie, lick off the cream, break the chocolate pieces in half, and dip each bite in a jug of Philadelphia. Again, he's devastated.)

I make him try a slice with olives and extra green peppers from my favorite pizzeria on 96th and Broadway. (He gags like he's chugging bile.)

We lay a blanket in the grass at Morningside Park and take a nap so we can remember what it feels like to sleep. (So good. Especially next to him.)

We officially declare Dunkin' "Our Spot" and go there for dinner to order the same sandwiches that brought us together in the first place. (Accompanied, yet again, by receipts with order number two.)

And when the end of the day comes, we're holding each other like always, until the universe makes us stop.

September 24, Take Twenty-Three: 10:07 a.m.

Sydney

Marcus called this morning and said he wanted to go to Long Island.

I gave my speech about how it's okay for him to have boundaries, and understandable for him to have triggers, after all he's been through. That a month is practically a second when you can't even see straight anymore, and I should have acknowledged that. I said, *Whether it's six months, or six years, or never, we can go when you're ready.*

When you're ready.

I said that part a lot.

But still. He said he wanted to go.

We've made no commitments as to what Long Island will entail once we get there. We might hop off this train and hop right back on the next one heading to Manhattan. If we do, that's okay. Whatever happens. We've taken the pressure off. Kept the big part quiet. That maybe this could unstick us. Maybe, today, we get off this merry-go-round.

For now, we're on the Long Island Rail Road, pushed back in our seats as far as they'll go because there's no one behind us.

Sydney

"Little kids who stare are the creepiest," I whisper, leaning into him. There's a blond-haired girl facing our way, probably about the same age as press-the-green-button boy. She's been watching us since we pulled out of Penn Station twenty minutes ago and has blinked maybe twice the whole time.

I glance at him to be sure that he's looking where I'm looking. He is. He twists his mouth after a second. "Eh, I could take her."

I laugh but not while I'm looking at her. In case she's part ghost or something. The last thing we need right now is a curse. Or another one.

"I bet she has one of those canopy beds," I tell him. "The ones with the netting all down the sides. I bet she has the kind of mom who curls her hair for her *before* bed so she wakes up looking like her hair does that naturally. I bet her parents think it's cute when she tells them their cat can understand her, but it's actually true because I bet she's telepathic."

I check on him again, and Marcus is smiling to himself, gazing at the girl as she gazes back at us, like I'm telling him historical facts while he studies art in a museum. The times we've tried to play I Bet together, he's sucked at it. Royally. Zero imagination or ability to suspend disbelief. But he listens whenever I do it.

"I ran into the girl from Dunkin'," he airily tells me, like listening to me was enough to make him drift to another land. "The day you and me took a break. Remember the one whose coffee I knocked over?"

"Duck bag?"

Sydney

"Yeah!" He chuckles. "I noticed that, too. That's how I recognized her, to be honest."

I'm intrigued, but I'm not sure why. Maybe just because something different happened. We don't spend a lot of time bumping into people by surprise these days. "Where'd you see her?"

"Down in the subway," he tells me. "Union Square." He pulls his gaze from the little girl and shifts it out the window instead. "It was kind of wild, Syd. We started talking and she told me that her dad di—*passed*. A month ago. The exact day that Aus did."

My heart speeds up. Maybe she's part of this. Maybe she *matters*. God, I hope he asked. "Is she stuck, too?"

"Yeah," he says, but when I bolt up straighter, he turns to me, shakes his head, walks it back. "No, no, not like us. She said she gets it, though. How it feels. How she's moving every day but she's not really going anywhere. She's a psych major at Fordham. Lives in BK. She was out the night her dad died—*passed*. Sorry, she says she doesn't like the word 'died.' Like it's super conclusive when it shouldn't be, and 'passed' is like . . . I'm not gonna say it as well. It's like movement, though. From one place to another. Like they're still around, they're just not here. I kind of like that. Aus thinks like that. Anyway." He smiles at me. "Weird we ran into each other, huh? Her name's Dana."

He says it all like he's never heard of punctuation before; it's just this thought-blob that comes out and is broken up by his need to occasionally breathe. And now it kind of hovers there, between him and me, like a fog.

Sydney

"What are you thinking?" he asks.

A lot. But I start with, "I kind of like 'passed,' too."

He squeezes my knee before he goes back to gazing out the window. "I'll make a conscious effort, then."

I settle back into my seat. I remember the things I bet about her that very first morning in Dunkin'. Not all of it, but the gist of it. That she was an artist and had a name that ended in an *ee* sound. That the same dad who's gone gave her some gorgeous apartment that she paints in every afternoon.

"Is she okay?" I ask, and Marcus raises his eyebrows when he turns back to me. "Dana. You said her dad . . . *passed*. Is she okay, though?"

"Not yet." He shifts in his seat and turns to face me a little more. "But you know what, Syd?" He says it with this whiff of hopefulness, a glimmer in his eye that almost tickles. "It kind of made me realize something. I think I sort of felt like no one could really get what this whole thing is like. Not even you, entirely, because you lost a brother and I lost my best friend, and neither of us knew the other person's person, you know? But what hit me yesterday is that . . . it's not just us. It doesn't have to be just us. Maybe this grief stuff is everywhere. Maybe this train is dripping in it—maybe that little girl, even. Maybe she's not staring because she wants to drink our blood but because she's seen blood, you know? I don't mean that in a bad way—I don't mean it like there's just a whole bunch of messed-up people everywhere trying like hell to keep it together. I just mean it like . . . well. Maybe there *is* a whole bunch of messed-up people out there trying like hell to keep it together. And we're not so alone after all."

It feels taboo. Like something we're not supposed to mess with or talk about. I think it's supposed to stay close when you're talking about death, within the network of those affected but not ripple much further than that. It's not meant to be me correcting new acquaintances when they call me an only child or admitting to Mr. Wilson that sometimes the hardest thing for me about his class isn't the coefficients but the fact that he was Bas's favorite teacher of all time. So that's why it's shocking to me that Marcus could do this with a stranger. And that she could do it back. Because if we were supposed to talk about it—if it was actually okay—how come nobody ever does?

"How do we even find them?" I ask. "The people like us," I clarify.

He rests his head on his seat. "I think maybe we just have to . . . say it. That's all I did yesterday. All I said was my friend died—*passed*—and just that quick, she was right there with me."

I gnaw my lip. It just sounds so risky. What happens if I say it and the person crosses their pointer fingers and backs away slowly? Or, worse—I say it and they don't even care?

But I nod because I hear him and I think that's the most important part.

"You know . . ." I rest my head on my seat now, too. "I actually played I Bet with Dana the day I met you. I think the whole reason I still play it at all is because it's a way of giving people the lives I hope they have. Like . . . stuff that's almost too good to be true, but if it *can* be true for them, then maybe it can be for all of us."

He presses his lips together and stretches out his left arm to make room for me underneath it. I scoot closer and rest my head on his shoulder.

Maybe that's the biggest thing. Maybe that's why I don't want to risk telling strangers about my truth. I don't want it to hurt when I find out theirs.

September 24, Take Twenty-Three: 6:06 p.m.

Sydney

Long Island is kind of great.

I've never been here before, so I wasn't sure what to expect. There's this cute "downtown" with some local shops that all smell like potpourri or some kind of herbal essence. There's this incense place owned by a woman who doubles as a fortune teller and a flower shop with twinkle lights in the front window. This one guy has a storefront where he sells his "art" for thousands of dollars. Modernist stuff that I don't get at all, like a giant red dot on paper.

We went to this mom-and-pop Italian restaurant. We had so much pasta, and meatballs, and garlic bread that it was actually ungodly. But the old Italian lady who was half the ownership decided she liked us a lot, Marcus especially, and kept bringing by more, kept saying, *Just try it*. So, we tried it. We tried all of it. And when the bill came, they hadn't even charged for half.

Now I'm so full, I can barely breathe.

"You wanna go to the beach?" Marcus asks. He isn't looking at me when he does. His hands are in his pockets and he's checking

Sydney

both ways at this intersection outside the restaurant, like he's making sure it's safe before we cross.

I don't think he's offering to go to the beach because he feels like it's what I want. I think I could be back in Manhattan, or at the Empire State Building, or on Mars, and he'd still be thinking about going. That's how it sounds when it comes out, at least.

So that's why I tell him, "Okay."

September 24, Take Twenty-Three: 8:31 p.m.

Sydney

We've been staring at the water for almost two hours and I still can't believe how beautiful it is.

Walking here only took about thirty minutes. Marcus glanced at it on Google Maps but never actually turned on the navigation. This fancy little neighborhood is like something out of a limited series. Stone houses with giant windows tucked behind just enough trees that the people inside can probably see us, even though we'll never see them. Marcus points out the one his mom had rented that night; I really think it's the prettiest one of all.

The road is so steep, my toes slide to the tips of my shoes as we walk down it. I have no idea how these people get out of here when it snows—and *it snows*—but I keep that, and a hundred other things I've wondered since we got here, to myself.

There are these wooden steps at the end of the road that lead to the sand. It has to be at least two stories down. They're dark brown and really steep. I can't imagine navigating them in the pouring rain, and drunk. That had to make it so much harder. Or so much easier.

The sand is rocky, riddled with broken seashells and probably other things that can cut you. I wouldn't want to walk that far on it barefoot, but it's okay with my shoes on and sitting in my jeans. I wonder how long this beach has been here. If people made it or it's supposed to exist.

Another question I keep to myself.

Marcus has been next to me since we sat down—before that, he was leading the way and I just followed. He walked slowly, his hands twitching in his pockets, while he stared at the water and let it pull him closer. He stood for a while, and eventually, he sat. So I sat, too.

There's a constant drone of nothingness, the soft waves like a static you can turn down but never off. The sun turned the sky pink and then disappeared into the water, and now it's this full moon that's so bright I can barely look at it.

Marcus's breathing isn't louder than the waves, but I feel it more. I focus on it so that I know when it's the steady, effortless breaths of a distracted mind. When it's the long, conscious breaths of someone trying to calm down. When it's the choppy, jagged breaths of a person trying to survive. Those are the ones that slice me like knives, that bring tears to my eyes. It isn't fair. I want to touch him, but I don't think I should. I want to say something, but there's nothing to say.

It's strange being in a place that's an unmarked grave. People come here all the time, I'm sure, and they have no idea what happened that night. Or they do, because they read it in the paper, but it's a fleeting thought; a story that starts with, *Hey, did you hear?* and then the waves carry it away.

Sydney

Maybe that's how it should be. When you lose your world, it stops for you. But it can't be that way for everyone.

I didn't know Austin, but I do all I can to remember the things that Marcus has told me about him. The Sixty Minutes game. Their tuna fish and *Grey's Anatomy* nights and the years they shared a bedroom. The two of them cleaning the kitchen at Nina's. The two of them playing basketball for the Sonics. The way he would talk about souls, how they find each other in every life, and the way that gave me this warm glimmer of hope. It's strange. Marcus never sat me down with the intention of making sure that I know who Austin was. But he's still there *all the time.* He's still become this tiny part of me because he's such a big part of Marcus. And I realize that I miss him, too. I know it can't compare, not at all, but I miss the idea of knowing him one day. I miss the now-impossible fantasy of me and Marcus, and Jacq and Austin, living happily ever after. For a second, I feel like I'm sinking, thinking about the Austin I'll never meet, and all the other Austins I'll never meet. All these amazing people who I'll never know. But maybe, somehow, we know them through each other. Maybe we're never really gone as long as someone we love is still here.

I keep that to myself, too.

"I think I'm gonna get in for a little bit," I say, just so he doesn't think that I'm leaving.

I start to stand but he grabs my wrist. "No."

I turn to him. I didn't even know he could move that fast, latch on to me quicker than a striking cobra. But even in the dark, his eyes shine like marbles, and they're scared.

The water is the scariest part. It hits me then. Of course it is.

"I'll be okay," I promise.

"Syd, for real, don't go in there."

"I'll be okay." I say it firmly this time because it isn't just a promise, it's a fact. "Nothing's gonna happen to me."

His fingers loosen enough for me to slide my wrist free.

I stand up and take off my shoes, feeling the broken shells that I swore I wouldn't walk on press against the bottom of my feet. I slide out of my jeans, and I pause before I make a decision about my shirt. But it's the only one I have with me, and if I keep it on, I'll be wet the rest of the night.

I take a deep breath and can't look at him as I take it off.

I walk toward the water. Slow enough to avoid cutting my feet and as slow as I believe that Austin deserves. I imagine that picture from Instagram, with his freckles and that little gap between his teeth, as the water brushes my ankles for the first time.

It's freezing. It's so cold it burns, but I keep going. When it reaches my shoulders, I tread water while the waves lift me and drop me, lift me and drop me—gently, the way you'd toss a baby. There's a glare on the surface of the water from the moon, and in this moment, I can't explain how, but I feel something watching me. Something strong and safe. Maybe it's Austin, maybe it's Bas, or maybe it's bigger than both of them, but it's here.

I turn back to face the shore. I'm only a couple of yards from the beach, but Marcus is standing up now, watching me on alert, his hands in fists by his side like he's ready to dive in at a moment's notice.

"Do you want to come in?" I ask.

"I don't know."

"Okay," I assure him. "You don't have to. I'll be back soon."

He watches me and I watch him. Then I turn away and stare as far across the water as I can. I hope there's something out there. Something beautiful.

I hear his steps in the waves. I'm not sure how long it's been since I asked him to join me. I face him as he gets close, and when he stops in front of me, his cheeks are wet and so are his eyes. I hate that he has to know this pain. I hate that I can't wash it all off him and feed it to the sea.

I wipe my thumbs across his eyes. I start to smile because it's hard not to when I'm looking at him. "You're okay," I promise. "I'm okay. We're okay."

I pull him in and squeeze him around the neck, and as my arms hold him and our legs start to tangle, I realize he's left his shirt and his pants on the shore. He's only still wearing his boxers.

I don't let go and I close my eyes as I keep whispering my promises. He's okay, I'm okay, we're okay. He's okay, I'm okay, we're okay.

"Yeah," he whispers back. "We are."

September 24, Take Twenty-Three: 10:12 p.m.

Sydney

We sit on the sand, drying off and waiting. We have our clothes back on and we still haven't said much. The water gently roars, friendly until it gets hungry.

"Thanks for coming up here with me," he says.

The waves bob, hypnotizing me a little more every second. "I think I'm in love with you" is all I can say back.

Next to me, he chuckles, and from the corner of my eye, he drops his neck. He hasn't laughed—cracked a smile, even—in hours. Good sign or maybe awful.

"It hits better if you say, 'I know,'" he answers.

Now I smile. He's such a jerk sometimes. "Alright, well, maybe I'll never say it again."

He laughs and ends it with a sigh, the kind that empties out his whole lungs. He rocks his shoulder into mine. "I love you, too."

His alarm goes off, but neither of us moves.

After a second, he asks, "What are you thinking?"

This has to be different. It *feels* that way, all over my body. Like we've done what we're supposed to. Like *we* aren't stuck anymore, so we *can't* be stuck anymore.

"I think maybe we did it," I whisper.

"You're not gonna make me say your number just in case?" Marcus asks, lips curled to one side.

No, I don't have to. My number is in his phone, and his is in mine, and this time it's gonna stay that way.

I know it.

I—

No.

Screeching tires.

No . . .

Headlights.

No!

Pain.

And then white.

September 24, Take Twenty-Four: 7:01 a.m.

Marcus

Okay, so we're still stuck.

But . . .

I pat my chest, pat my sheets.

Whoa.

Dry.

I don't feel that nightmare anymore. That heart-racing, survived-getting-flattened-by-a-semi-but-kind-of-wish-I-didn't thing. I stretch my arms over my head and let them drop. I forgot what it felt like to wake up like I used to.

It has to be because of yesterday. Right? The beach wasn't what I remembered at all. In my head, it was so much darker . . . *black*. With waves high enough to touch the trees. It felt like I was swimming for days just to get from one end to the other. But that beach isn't even a quarter mile long.

It's wild how your mind breaks when your heart breaks, too. I bet this is what Dana was talking about, how she does the days but she doesn't remember them. It's the weirdest thing—feeling like you can't trust yourself. I didn't realize how off I'd been about that place, and that's really why I wanted to stay so long last night. So I could tattoo it on my mind and give my broken brain the extra time it needed to let it all sink in. I gotta remember the truth, at the very least, forever. I gotta do it for Aus. Maybe also for me.

My phone vibrates. Syd.

I settle in and smile. Here's her text:

> Hi! I'm running for city commissioner. I believe in free parking everywhere, shorter school days, and no forceful consumption of asparagus. Can I count on your vote?

I laugh. Asparagus?? I write back:

> Is it 1 or 2 to unsubscribe

A few seconds later, my phone vibrates again:

> Great job failing at democracy. Fine. Can I count on you for something else?

This response, I really mean:

> Anything.

Marcus

It takes her a little bit to write back. I know Syd, though. She's sitting there smiling about it, trying to decide whether to talk trash or appreciate me. I'm good with either, coming from her.

My phone buzzes. No trash. No emojis. A real question:

> Let me try to unstick us again?

September 24, Takes Twenty-Four through Twenty-Seven

Marcus

She tries dozens of ways to get us unstuck.

She has this one idea that we need to go back to the crosswalk we were in when it first happened and actually kiss this time. Hell, I'm down—I'll kiss her anytime I can. But it doesn't work.

Neither does volunteering at the library—*Because maybe we're supposed to be using this time to help other people.*

Neither does walking backward for a whole afternoon—*Because maybe we have to reverse ourselves to right the universe.*

Neither does wishing over fortune cookies—*Because who are we to say those cookies aren't magic?*

Neither does taking the train to Westchester where it's dark enough to look for shooting stars—*Because we know those are magic.*

She crams a bunch of potential fixes into each day. Nothing works.

She still gets those feelings she told me about—the ones that make her feel like she's really onto something. Every time, she's sure she's right until she's wrong. I don't mind—it's not like I'm busy. But it's wearing on her, I can tell. And I hate that. She's not some dummy just because she can't figure out how to beat the universe. Who beats the universe?

"Do you think we're actually living, or are we just alive?" she asks.

We're on a bench in Central Park, and we just got finished combing *The Times*—*Because maybe we're supposed to stop something from happening, and how else will we know what happens today if we don't read the paper?*

"Tell me the difference," I say.

"Like, I feel like . . ." She folds up her side of the paper and her skin glows under this streetlamp. "I feel like alive is what a houseplant is. It eats plant food, drinks water, exists. But living is a *risk*. The good kind. Where it's worth it because stuff could go wrong, stuff could go *crazy*, but that's why you do it in the first place. Because maybe it won't be bad. Maybe it'll be great. And living . . . I feel like living is finding out."

She's looking at me in the way that kills me, when she wants me to have answers that I don't. Maybe since these days started, we have just been alive. But that's a big deal, too—at least, I think so—when there are times it hurts like hell just to do that much.

"Hey, why don't we take a break tomorrow?" I suggest.

"A break?"

"Yeah. And do something fun. Clear your head some—maybe it'll help. I mean, unless you fixed it today. Which you could have. For sure."

She nods but doesn't answer, and I don't say anything else, either.

Marcus

My alarm goes off.

I take her hand, just in case. Actually, not even. I take her hand because I know we're gonna get yanked apart, like always.

"Chicago," she says.

"What about it?"

"Let's go tomorrow."

"It's on Broadway?" I ask.

"Not the play, the city."

"You want to go to Illinois?"

"Just the Chicago part." She raises her eyebrows. "Come?"

I shrug. "Of course."

And then the tires start to screech.

September 24, Take Twenty-Eight: 2:22 p.m. (Chicago time)

Marcus

In the morning, Syd told me that Wellesley Culinary Institute is in Chicago. It's the school where Gigi went, and Syd said she's always wanted to see it.

"That's a good enough reason for me," I told her.

We were starved when we landed—we didn't have time to make our normal pit stop if we were gonna catch our flight—and Syd's eyes went huge when she spotted the Dunkin' in O'Hare. She ran over to it, and at first, I figured she was just hungry, because same, but then I saw it on her face. The same thing that'd been there for days now. She ordered her sandwich and I let six people go ahead of me before I ordered mine.

We both still got order number two.

I threw my receipt away with one hand and wrapped my free arm around her neck. I kissed the side of her head. I said, "I thought we were taking a break today."

"We are. I'm just hungry." She dropped her untouched sandwich into the trash.

Marcus

I didn't say anything about it—just did the same. "Alright, well, let's get you some food."

🌹🌹🌹

Now we're rolling out of The Little Pink Cow, stuffed. It's some big-deal restaurant around here that Syd knew all about. She'd been dying to go, so I said let's do it. They've won awards and stuff. Been on TV. Expensive, but I only look at price tags out of habit these days.

We stand outside the restaurant and she stretches her arms over her head like she could take a nap. But, instead, she says, "Ready to hit up Wellesley?"

We're on Michigan Ave, that's what our Uber driver told us when he found out we'd never been here before. It's kind of like 5th Ave in New York—a bunch of fancy stores and packed with people who probably have to be here, or tourists.

"Yep," I tell her. "You know where we're headed? Can we walk?"

She's swiping on her phone and looking at the street signs to figure out which way we're pointed. "It's a forty-minute walk."

"So Uber?" I take out my phone so I can call one.

"Or we bike?" she offers. She shows me her screen. "There's a stand two blocks over—I think they use something called Divvy Bikes here? It looks like all we have to do is download the app."

It's nice in Chicago today, too. Warm enough. Sunny. I nod. "Down."

We start walking, close enough that I could hold her hand. I don't, but I would.

Marcus

"It's slower here," she says, and it really is. No one's honking in the street. No one's speedwalking past.

"Yeah." I slide my hands into my pockets. "Are we strolling right now?"

She smiles. "Moseying."

"Sauntering."

She thinks for a second, running out of synonyms. "Skipping to my lou?" She starts skipping backward ahead of me.

I chuckle. "Maybe that's what you're doing, but that's not what I'm doing."

She starts walking next to me again. "Probably better that way. I bet tall people suck at skipping."

"Hey, can we watch the hate speech?"

Quietly, she adds, "I bet you're not flexible, either."

I grab her and pull her into me, and she laughs and stays close like it's what she wanted me to do all along. "Look, I've got feelings, alright? I'm not gonna let you be talking to me all crazy." I tighten my arm around her shoulders. "That's why I'm not voting you for commissioner."

"What can I do—" She's almost laughing too hard to talk, and it's the first time I've seen her like this in a while, ever since she's been trying to get us unstuck. "What can I do to win your vote?"

She squirms free, catching her breath. She watches me in the middle of the sidewalk. She *has* to know she's got me sprung. I bet I look like I'm drunk when I'm looking at her. When she told me she loved me at the beach, I almost didn't worry about saying it back.

Because of course I love her. It feels like I've always loved her. I can't remember how it ever was to *not* love her.

So, yeah, she has my vote. She has everything about me.

But, to her, I say, "Maybe some sensitivity training."

"That's not fair." She pouts. "Real politicians only have to say 'thoughts and prayers.'"

"Yeah, well." We start walking again and turn the corner. "I wouldn't vote for them, either."

We reach the bike rack and I take out my phone to download this Divvy Bikes thing, make the rental. Then she says, "Get two."

I look at her. "Get *what*?"

"Two. Bikes."

I squint. *"No."*

"You just agreed it's slower here!"

"Yeah, slow like someone's not gonna shank you for getting in the way on the sidewalk. But not slow like a bus can't still crush you."

"We'll take the sidewalks." She takes my hands, squeezes them. "I bet they don't even care here. Look how much space there is—there's barely anything to hit." She's begging now. "Please? I can do it. And if I can't, and I break my ankle, whatever. 10:15 and *poof!* All better. This is our free day, remember?"

She did do pretty well the last time we practiced. Made it around Morningside Park twice. Besides, I can tell by her face that I'm not gonna talk her out of it. I don't really want her riding on the back of my bike, anyway, in the kind of mood she'll be in if I insist this is a bad idea. She'll probably spend the whole time smacking the back of

Marcus

my head until we both end up broken on the side of the road, waiting for my alarm to go off.

"Fine. But follow me and I'll navigate," I say, so she's not trying to steer one-handed.

She grins. "Thanks, Dad."

I smirk and go back to renting these bikes. "Yeah, sure. And quit talking back."

September 24, Take Twenty-Eight: 3:07 p.m. (Chicago Time)

Marcus

She killed it. I couldn't be prouder. Expertly avoided an old lady in the crosswalk and now we're both here, all in one piece.

This campus is pretty cool. The buildings are real modern. Metal looking and built in all these unconventional shapes, like spheres and arches. Even the benches aren't normal benches. They're this smooth stone with rounded edges, carved to be something you can sit on.

We head down the brick walkway that winds through all this green grass. It's cut so perfectly, it looks fake. It could be, actually. Maybe it has to be in Chicago. I'm pretty sure it gets cold as Antarctica in the winter.

Anyway, we're headed to admissions and, according to the digitized welcome sign at the front of campus, it's this round-looking building straight ahead.

"You wanna come in?" Syd asks.

"I'll wait out here." I plop down on one of those stone benches.

Marcus

"Okay. Don't talk to strangers."

"You were a stranger."

"Yeah and look how that turned out." Then she disappears inside.

I start to reach for my phone in my pocket but catch myself. Habit, even all these redo days later. It's silenced so it's not buzzing nonstop with people trying to figure out where I'm at. I can handle it when I'm going in with a purpose, like to open up maps or rent a couple bikes. But if I'm not pulling out my phone for a reason, I know I'm not gonna be able to avoid that home screen and see those red bubbles next to my messages and phone icons. The day Syd hung out with Jacq, and I stayed in bed, I actually did look at some of those messages. I still wish I hadn't. I still hate how it feels knowing those words are on my phone every day, that people are worrying about me like that all the time. Mom sent me at least fifteen texts. Threatening me. Caps-lock screaming at me. Questioning me. And finally, the last one, the one that kills me the most because I can hear her saying it. This strain in her voice. The tears in her eyes. All it said was:

> Baby please

So yeah, I don't need to take my phone out. I bend over and run my fingers through the grass instead.

"Huh," I mumble to myself. "Real."

"Okay!" Syd says when she comes back out. "I got a welcome pamphlet." She holds it out as proof. "The woman told me that we're

Marcus

welcome to walk around campus, if we'd like. There's actually a food museum on west campus. This is east campus. Oh! And there's this baking class with seats in it for visitors. The next one starts at four and all we have to do is show these two tickets she gave me." She pulls them out of her pocket. "Would you wanna do that? Maybe they'll let us taste test."

I'm still full. But I'm sure a place like this bakes some ridiculous cakes. So, I stand up and slap my hands on my stomach. "Let's do it."

September 24, Take Twenty-Eight: 4:19 p.m. (Chicago Time)

Marcus

You ever seen someone who's in New York City for the first time? It's something, man. They look around with eyes twice as big as anybody else's. They point at all the stuff they've heard about but never seen up close. You can tell they're a little bit scared of this big new place but, more than anything, they're excited. They *want* it. Their whole life flashes in front of them. A life that—for at least a few minutes—feels like it always belonged right here.

Seeing Syd watch those Wellesley kids bake their éclairs from scratch—mixing stuff, and talking technique, and laughing with their professor while we watch from the sidelines?

It's like that.

September 24, Take Twenty-Eight: 8:55 p.m. (Chicago Time)

Marcus

"You love it here," I tell Syd, staring at the sky.

At first, she doesn't say anything and we go quiet again like we have been. There's no one else out here, and campus might be closed, but we haven't been kicked out yet. So, we've just been lying in the grass. Chillin'.

"Yeah," she finally says, like it kind of freaks her out to say it out loud. "Do you?"

"To be honest? I don't think I'm a Chicago kind of guy."

No shade to Chicago, or anything. I know I only saw a little bit of it today, but it's not really for me. Seems like the kind of place a lot of people drive to get around. And that deep-dish pizza thing? Yeah, I'm not doing that.

I turn my head in the lawn to face her, and the second I do, she does, too. "I'd visit, though," I promise.

I think she smiles. It's hard to tell between the blades of grass and the darkness. "I knew you wouldn't love it," she says. "You're one of *those* New Yorkers."

"The right kind?"

I can hear it for sure now, the smile on her lips as she rolls her head back to face the sky. "You'll never leave. You'll never even want to—the thought won't even cross your mind. Nothing will ever *come close* to the city, as far as you're concerned, and—if it does—it's a threat and has to be annihilated immediately."

"Hey, you gotta lower your voice before someone puts a hit out on Chicago and the feds start looking at me."

She laughs. It's the only sound for miles. That's another thing about this place. It's too quiet for me.

"You don't spend a bunch of time thinking about that, though. Do you?" I squint, trying to see her better in the dark. Her chest rises and falls each time she breathes, smooth enough to convince me she's made out of water. "I mean . . . I can't see myself ever leaving New York, but that doesn't mean anything. You know?"

"I don't think about it regularly," she says. She plucks a blade of grass and then plucks another. "Just sometimes. Like when I imagine what it'd be like to get out of this day."

"I told you how it'd be. I'd just visit, that's all."

"Like, I'd probably have this super-crappy studio apartment"—she goes on like she didn't even hear me—"with, like, one window. And just a microwave, not even an oven. Because that's all I could afford. And if you did visit, we'd have to squeeze past each other just to walk around. We'd probably never be there. Just to sleep, you know? Because it'd be that miserable." She lets out a sigh and her chest sinks with it. "Except it wouldn't be."

Marcus

"It wouldn't be at all."

She rolls over to face me, her hair in this pile sitting above her head.

I roll all the way over, too. "What would your parents say if you just told them, straight up, this is what you want?"

She makes her voice low. I guess it's supposed to be some impression of her dad. "'You're cut off, but I'm sure Burger King is hiring.'"

She laughs, but it's not that funny to me. "What if my mom and I helped?"

She rolls her eyes. "Shut up."

"No, tell me. For real. What if?"

Her eyes are unbelievable under this moon. A color I've never even seen before. Purple is the best way I can describe it, but that doesn't do it justice. Maybe, if I stare long enough, I'll think of something better.

"You're not doing that," she whispers.

"Why?" I get it—it's a good thing that she's hesitating. For her—because it's dangerous to trust favors, no matter who they're from. And for me—because it's dangerous when people accept them too easily, even when it's someone you love.

I wait for her to say something like that. Like she could never let us do that for her, or she hasn't been hanging on to me through all this just because we've got money now. But what she ends up saying is "Because what if my parents are right?"

She rolls onto her back and keeps talking.

"My parents don't believe in me because I've never given them a reason to. I can't do math. I couldn't play tennis. I'm mediocre, at best, when it comes to just about everything. And for some reason I"—her voice trips and she wipes her eyes like there's just something in them, that's all—"I really did believe I could get us out of this. Like those feelings I've been having meant I was gonna figure it out. Jacq would get FAM. Mrs. Ellersby would get to see her husband at the nursing home. You and I could see the new *Fast & Furious* together. But I'll probably never get us out of this. And I'd probably suck at being a chef, too."

I scoot closer and pull her in, her back against my front. Her quiet sobs press on my chest even while I hold her still. I didn't realize it before, but it hits me now—that, from the moment I met her, I swore she didn't need me. Even if she needs me so we can get to tomorrow, that's just a technicality—*hey, this guy's stuck, too, bring him with you.* Maybe that's why I tried so hard to give her good todays. I knew that this girl was amazing, but I was just a bunch of baggage, and if all I could give her were good laughs and company and sunny days forever, I'd do that with everything I had.

She needs to know she sounds ridiculous right now—so ridiculous that I'm glad she's not looking at me because it's killing me to keep a straight face. Maybe that's what I'm good for. Making sure she knows now and always that everything she just said is the wrongest she'll ever be.

"I bet you're getting us out of this day any minute now. Watch," I tell her. "And when you do, I bet you're gonna put everything you've got into being a great chef one day. I bet you're gonna push for it even when you're scared, or it gets hard, or when it drags you to some runner-up city like Chicago. I bet you'll conquer this town. And once you're here—or wherever you go—it won't matter, because I bet you're gonna make the kind of food one day that makes another girl somewhere believe she can do it, too. I bet you're gonna change lives, Syd. You've already changed mine. I bet you've given your parents, and your friends, and anyone you've ever met a thousand reasons to believe in you, just like you've given me."

For a few seconds, nothing happens. Then she whispers, "Thank you."

"Anytime." I really, really mean it.

She pulls out of my arms and rolls over to face me. She reaches out and wipes my cheek. I'm not sure what was on it, or how she saw it in this light, but her touch does what it always does—gets me spinning so fast that everything else is a blur.

"I do have another idea," she admits. "To get us unstuck."

Great. "I'll do whatever you think we should. And I'll start thinking, too. I haven't been, to be honest, but I'll start. I don't wanna be deadweight in all this. I'm not gonna be some anchor slowing you down anymore."

She stares at me with those better-than-purple eyes and promises, "You're never weighing me down."

I nudge her. "What's your new idea? I'll do anything."

"What if we do the days we were supposed to do originally?"

Except for that.

My heart speeds up like I'm doing warm-ups, except I haven't moved. "What do you mean?"

Marcus

"Like . . ." She bites her lip. "What if I never go to Dunkin', and I go to school like I was supposed to, and take that precalc test like I was supposed to, and you finally go to picture day and get photographed in this outfit you won't quit wearing?" She tugs my collared shirt. "What if we did the days we would have done if we'd never met?"

She's so clearheaded about it. Like she's been sitting on it for days and was just waiting for the invitation to spit it out. "You've been thinking about this?" I ask.

"It just feels like it's worth a try. Because maybe . . . maybe if we want tomorrow to get here, we have to face today first."

I meant it when I said I'd do anything. I would have tried blood pacts. I would've taken a hot-air balloon as high up as it would go or spin counterclockwise until I threw up. But I wasn't expecting her to say this. Just do the day I should've done all along.

The day I didn't do the first time because I didn't want to.

I still don't want to.

"Okay," I agree.

"We won't get our hopes up or anything."

"Nope."

"We'll just try it. On today again. Yeah?" That's what she's been calling our fake tomorrows lately. Today again.

"Cool," I say.

We shake on it.

She presses up against me and I wrap my arms around her. She fits like I'm never supposed to let her go. Then she kisses me and sends me to the stars.

Marcus

It's like that, really. Kissing her, I mean. Like something I've never felt before. I even *hear* things. Not music, exactly, but like . . .

Screeching tires.

Wait, what? My alarm didn't even go off—

Headlights.

Oh, right.

Pain.

Time zones.

Anddd we're gone.

September 24, Take Twenty-Nine: The day she should have had

Sydney

My alarm blares on my phone at 7:01 a.m., and I grab it from my nightstand and turn it off. I squeeze my eyes shut, rub my head. We haven't been yanked away from each other without expecting it in weeks and it's as disorienting as being knocked out cold. I was supposed to be looking into his eyes and holding my breath because it hurts a little less if I exhale—as hard as I can—the second after the screeching tires start . . .

My phone vibrates. Marcus.

> **Central time**

Oh.
Oh.
I write back:

> **Your beef with Chicago multiplies**

And then more:

> But the plan still stands? Try the days we would have had today?

I chew my lip while I wait for him to answer. Those three dots show up, then disappear, then show up, then disappear. I swear, it's been forever, but the timestamp says it's been a minute.

> Plan stands.

I was expecting an essay with how long he'd been typing, but maybe my phone was just being funny.

I put my feet on the floor and my quiet room stares back. It's just another one of my unfounded *How to Get Unstuck* ideas, but my shoulders are heavy and I'm not sure why. Maybe because it's *so similar*. The way it is now and the way it was that first morning. The way I sat here, ready to cry. Tired of being the dumbest one in this family. Dreading another conversation with my parents about how it's basically genetically impossible for me to be such a mathematical disaster. Desperate for a way out. Not just from this test, but from this apartment, from this cycle, from the destiny of being a constant disappointment.

So much of that hasn't changed. But I have.

I take a shower because the last one was so nice, and once I finish, I go to my closet and pick out the same outfit I wore the first time I did this day. Skater dress, tights, oversized cardigan. I lean into my mirror and draw on my eyeliner, dust on my eye shadow, paint on my mascara. I comb through my hair and then look at what I've done. It's eerie, how easy it might be to believe that I'm back at that first day all over again, that all this has just been some long dream.

I grab my phone off my bed and there's another message from Marcus, twenty-one minutes old. He's probably already in that same old picture-day outfit, cute as ever. He's probably sending me some perfectly ridiculous joke because we haven't done that yet today.

But it's just a white heart.

I send one back and slide my phone into my bag before I sling it over my shoulder. No Dunkin' today, so I'm gonna grab a banana from the kitchen—

I stop.

I stop at Sebastian's room.

At some point, when the days started repeating themselves, I stopped starting my mornings with him. I told myself I didn't have to because, technically, I already had. But that wasn't actually the reason. The real reason was because I didn't want to be in this room where I'd pretended not to listen when he and Max talked about the girls they wanted to ask out. Or where he and I would debate what movie to watch later. Or where I'd tell him that I didn't think I could be a doctor and he whispered that he wasn't sure he wanted to go to Corinthia. I didn't realize it until I got stuck—how much Bas and I always talked about what was next. Whether it was coming in the next five minutes or the next five years. It hurt too bad, I think, to walk in here and say, *Nothing*. That there is no next. Not now and maybe never again.

But I can't pretend like I'm living this day the way it would've gone the first time if I don't stop and talk to Bas.

I go into his room and drop my backpack on the floor. I sit on the side of his bed, stuffing my fingertips under my thighs.

"Hey," I say out loud, my voice all alone. "I'm sorry for ghosting the past few days. Or over and over again on this day. Time doesn't move anymore—at least, not beyond the hours of 7 a.m. and 10:15 at night. I'm trapped here—even though Marcus doesn't like when I call it that. Marcus . . . he's the guy I mentioned to you the last time I was in here." My knees start to bounce. Not on purpose, but I don't try to stop them. "It *does* feel like being trapped. You know why?" Words I've never thought before reach my lips. It happens that way, now and then. A warm spell that only this room can cast. "Because the therapist, he asked me once, what I thought about the afterlife. And even though Mom and Dad would throw a bunch of science in my face if I ever told them, I still believe in it. I *actually believed* I was gonna see you again one day." I pick at the sewn pattern on his comforter. "And I remember that was, like . . . the first session that made me feel a little better, until it made me feel a million times worse. Because it hit me how many years, and *decades* might pass until that day would finally come. When I'd see you again, I mean. And waiting all that time felt *impossible*. But now I'd gladly wait it—I'd do *anything* to wait it—if the days would just start moving again."

The realization swallows me like a wet blanket.

Sydney

"I'm trying to get us unstuck." I sniff back the tears. "I keep getting these ideas that feel really right at the time but then they never actually fix anything. And this is my latest master plan—doing what I should have done on this day all along. Which means failing Wilson's test. You'd think that wouldn't seem so miserable now that the entire world is running on repeat, but . . . I just really want to get something right. Finally."

I swallow through the ache of talking to someone who will never talk back. I don't think anything will ever hurt like knowing his voice without hearing his answer. But today, I feel something again. In that place that's buried so deep that it could be in my stomach, or maybe behind it. In a part of me that I don't think even has a name, or—if it does—I'm not doctor enough to know it. But it's there, I'm not imagining it, and all of a sudden, there's an answer, bigger than the ones I've felt the days before. Something that feels like Bas but feels like me, too. Something strong yet soft, unidentified but full of love. It twists through me like colorful smoke, and it tells me:

You will.

🌷 🌷 🌷

"Want a cupcake?" Jacq asks, holding it out to me.

I just reached our corner in the science wing, where we meet in the morning, at lunch, and at the end of the day. The halls are filling up but they're not packed yet; they will be in the next fifteen minutes.

"Yes." I take it from her, peeling the crinkled paper from the sides.

Sydney

It's chocolate with white icing and rainbow sprinkles. Which I would have known without unwrapping it and taking a giant bite, because those are the only kind of cupcake Jacq and I ever want to eat. "Why?" I ask as I chew.

She takes a bite of hers, too. "I figure we should celebrate today in case there's nothing to celebrate tomorrow."

I frown. "Jacq, there's gonna be beaucoup to celebrate tomorrow."

Tomorrow. Please, please, tomorrow.

"You're gonna get the best news from FAM," I go on. "Your mom is gonna make the most decadent asparagus-centered celebratory dinner—"

Jacq laughs and fake-cries at the same time. "My insides . . ." she groans, and I laugh, too.

"—and it's gonna be the beginning of everything that comes next. Cheers, okay?" I hold out my cupcake and she holds hers out, too. We tap them, the edges of our icing mushing together.

"Cheers, and other forms of manifesting," Jacq agrees.

"I actually need to get to class early for this precalc test, but let's do something after school, okay? I have an idea."

"It's too late to photoshop me into a kayak and send it to the admissions team."

"Is it?" As I back away, our classmates start to pass between us. "Plan B, then."

"Your quick thinking is my eighth-favorite attribute!" she calls before we're too far apart for me to hear her. Jacq has spent our whole lives giving my traits arbitrary rankings on the scale of What Makes

Syd Great. Nothing has ever been the number-one thing. That's the joke.

I've missed that joke.

I turn around before I collide with someone and risk dropping my cupcake. Slipping through the crowd is muscle memory, as much a part of my weekday routine as *America's Next Big Chef*. Everyone looks the same—of course they do—but I still say "Hey" more enthusiastically than I should. People look at me funny. Like there's nothing to be so excited about. It just feels like it's been so long since I walked these halls and really noticed the faces I was smiling at.

I peek into Mr. Wilson's classroom through the little window in the door. *Please let me be the first one here.*

Oh, good. I am.

"Hi, Mr. Wilson." I poke my head inside the room. "Sorry to just swing by like this. I wanted to see if you maybe had a second to talk?"

He's humming to himself and writing on his dry-erase board, but he stops and faces me with big eyes and a bigger smile now that he knows I'm here. "Hello, Sydney! Of course, I have time to talk. What a lovely surprise."

I smile back. I can't not. Mr. Wilson is like the prototype of what the 1950s said a teacher should be. Glasses. Khakis. Sweater-vest over a button-down *constantly*, even that June when the school didn't have AC. His hair is white and I'm pretty sure, according to the law, he could have retired at least ten years ago. But he's so happy here, doing what he loves, that I wouldn't be surprised if he was teaching *my* kids math one day.

Sydney

I walk into his classroom and leave the door mostly closed behind me. Mr. Wilson is capping his marker and setting it on his desk. "Quite the delicious breakfast you have there," he says, and not in the sarcastic way that Mom would use right before reminding me how easy it is to get diabetes.

I slide into a desk at the front of the class, the one right in front of his. It's not my usual seat. Normally, I'm three rows back, to the right. "It's chocolate with vanilla icing and sprinkles."

"One of my absolute favorites," he says, sitting behind his desk. "Although, I'm a big fan of buttercream, too. Is that a celebratory cupcake or just coincidental?"

"Anticipatory. You know Jacqueline Nelson? She took your class two years ago. She finds out tomorrow if she got into the Film Academy of Manhattan."

He grins. "Well, how about that? That does deserve cupcakes! She's a bright girl. They'd be lucky to have her."

"She's the best," I agree, breaking off a crumb and putting it in my mouth. But I'm kind of anxious now that I'm here, and I need to say what I told myself that I would on my walk to school.

"And you?" Mr. Wilson asks, eyebrows raised as he peels off his glasses. He starts cleaning them with the little piece of cloth he keeps in one of his desk drawers. "Everything alright?"

He waits patiently, while the hallway sounds get louder and the clock on his desk ticks every time a second passes.

"I promise you I'm not stupid." But my voice breaks as I say it.

Mr. Wilson frowns and slides his glasses back onto his face.

"Now, you know I don't tolerate that kind of language."

"I know." We're not supposed to say *dumb* or *idiot*, either. "I'm sorry. But I just want you to know that I'm not trying to be bad at your class. It's not that I don't care. I actually do care, a lot. And I watch your YouTubes. Which are so cool, by the way. No other teacher makes YouTubes for us. But the thing is . . . I don't know if you know this, but . . ." I take a deep breath and I push out the words. "You were my brother's favorite teacher."

At some point, my gaze drifted away from his and to my shoes instead.

"Sorry." I pull my head up. "Sebastian Michaels. He was in your class, like, ten years ago—"

"I absolutely know who your brother is." He says it with a firmness I wasn't ready for, and I feel the fragile parts of me start to fracture under the force of his words. "He was remarkable. It was an absolute honor to know him and to teach him."

I know it's just the kind of thing that people are supposed to say about the ones who aren't here anymore. But I really think Mr. Wilson means it because, with Bas, it really is true.

I sniff and keep picking at my cupcake, but at this point I'm just making crumbs that are never actually reaching my mouth. "When he di—*passed*. When he passed away, we got the card from the school that all the teachers signed, and it was really nice. But then you also sent those flowers, and all his tests that he took in your class . . . and my parents really appreciated that. They both cried when they realized what it was. They didn't cry about much when we lost him. But they did cry about that, and I'm not sure how they ever thanked you, or if they ever did, but it really meant a lot."

"I've held all of you very close to my heart for a very long time."

I take a deep breath and try to feel it down to my toes. "Ever since it happened, it's felt like I'm not supposed to talk about it. That people would think I'm just making excuses or I should have moved on by now. But the truth is that Sebastian was always the one who explained stuff to me. He made everything make sense, and he just knew how to make me get it. When he passed away, everything got harder. And sometimes I feel like it's supposed to stay harder. Because if there *is* someone else who can make me understand... or even if I just figure out a way to understand on my own... does that mean I just don't need him anymore—"

"Vanessa," Mr. Wilson says, looking past me at the classroom door. "Would you mind waiting in the hallway until the bell rings this morning? I'm just wrapping something up with Ms. Michaels. Thank you. And would you mind asking others to do the same?"

Behind me, the door softly closes. It's a good reminder, though. That I should wrap this up. I'm rambling, anyway.

"Sorry, I didn't come in here planning to have a whole existential conversation." I push my hair behind my ear. "I guess I just wanted you to know that if I do bomb this test this morning, it's not for lack of trying. It's really no disrespect."

Mr. Wilson leans forward, folding his arms on the surface of his desk. "It's a very good question, though. The question of need. Perhaps we don't always need the people we've once had. We grow and become

Sydney

sufficient in other ways, not unlike a child who once was carried and now knows how to walk. But just because one no longer needs the gentle care of a parent, let's say, that doesn't mean we no longer want it. And want . . . I've always believed wanting is even more powerful than needing. Because it's a choice we make for ourselves."

His stare is so strong and I think he knows it, because right when I'm worried I might cry, he clasps his hands into a fist and glances down at that instead.

"Sydney, I feel so deeply for you and your family and all you've lost. And I don't, in any way, claim to be an expert on how we carry on in spite of tragedy. But what I would like to tell you—and I think about it often, even today—is that I lost my older sister when I was right around your age. It was a car accident. I was in the car, too. I survived and she didn't. We were very close. She had something special about her, just like your brother. Just like you, for that matter. When I tell you my heart was broken, that hardly does it justice. But you know what else was true, while my heart sat in pieces?" He takes a shallow breath and then gently declares, "It kept beating."

He lifts his stare from his fisted hands and back to me. For the first time, I notice how deep his wrinkles are, and that his blue eyes have a slight milkiness to them.

The warning bell rings.

"Thank you," he says. "For trusting me with such a big part of who you are, and for allowing me to trust you with a piece of myself as well. If you're willing, I would be very happy to help you better understand this class."

Sydney

I nod. "I would really like that."

He smiles. It doesn't look the same, though. It'll never look the same. "Very good."

He stands up and walks to the back of the class. The doorknob clicks and my classmates walk in, laughing, and debating, and saying "Hey" to Mr. Wilson. I get up so that Ben Sanders can have the seat he usually does, and I head to mine by the window.

I make it a rule not to play I Bet with people I could actually know, so I've never done it with Mr. Wilson. But, if I had, I probably would have bet that he loved math his whole life. I would have bet that he went to some small liberal arts school where you can major in guitar and that was where he met his wife who was probably completely adorable and just as giddy about number jokes as he is. I probably would have bet that he had a white picket fence somewhere in White Plains, and two sons and one daughter, and they all went off and got married and gave him grandchildren who he's obsessed with. I probably would have bet that he gets them model planes for Christmas, and that the gold band he wears on his ring finger has never once been taken off.

I still hope most of that is true, but I also get now that there's more. That the lines on his face have depth, that he's not just this flat thing on a page.

When Marcus and I were on the train to Long Island, and he was telling me about that conversation with Dana, and how much it made him realize—he was right, I think.

Maybe grief really is everywhere.

Sydney

🌹🌹🌹

I cannot believe how much money Jacq and I just spent. Fully unacceptable if tomorrow's actually coming this time. Because we have *bags full* of essential oils, and incense, and sage. I wanna burn stuff for FAM again, but not asparagus and math homework. I wanna do it for real. I wanna try. I wanna call in spirits, and the universe, and anything else that's good, and I want to trust it to take us where we're meant to go.

"I can't believe good vibes cost us over three hundred dollars," Jacq says, eyeing our receipt. "And that *you* just convinced *me* that that's completely fine."

"You've gotta spend money to make money," I tell her. "Your Oscars will pay for it."

We're on 58th and 7th, because Yelp said there was this holistic healing shop that was unmatched, so we came straight here after school let out.

"I like this era on you," Jacq says, dropping the receipt back into one of her bags. "Endless and abundant power. Fearlessly wielding emergency credit cards for the greater good."

I bring my hands to prayer position in front of my chest, the arms of my bags sliding down my wrists. "Namaste."

We round the corner to start heading up 58th Street.

"Whoa," Jacq slows down. "You think someone got hit?"

There's this huge crowd, which in other towns might mean a major celebrity or politician had been spotted. But we're generally unfazed by that kind of stuff. We're much more likely to gather in large numbers due to emergency.

Sydney

I push up on tiptoes and crane my neck, but I can't get a good view.

Jacq nudges a guy who looks a little older than us, one who's standing around like he knows what's going on. "Hey," she says, and juts her chin in the same direction everyone's facing. "What's up? Accident?"

"Nah," he says. "Tryouts for some gig, or something. My girl's about it. Made me stop."

"Who's your girl?" Jacq asks.

"Babe!" he calls, this deep bark that's capable of cutting through everything else. Then he tells us, "Cutie in the pink dress."

Jacq peers through the crowd, sees her when I don't yet, and says, "Got her. Thanks!"

She takes my elbow and drags me that way while I laugh and insist, "What, are you scratching filmmaker to be a model now?"

"As sure as I am that I could absolutely pull off that double threat, what if it's not that kind of tryout?"

"What does it matter what kind of tryout it is?"

"You're gonna have me walking down the street with a thousand different essential oils and in the same breath tell me to just ignore the giant crowd that happens to be here on the same day that we happen to be? On this day where we're manifesting?" She tugs me along. "Come on."

The closer we get to where she's taking me, I realize there's a crowd but there's also a line. It goes to the end of the block, and then turns up Broadway. Jacq stops in front of a girl in a pink dress.

276

Sydney

"Hey!" she says. "I just met your boyfriend and he says you know what's going on?"

"I was wondering why he was calling me," she says, like he's annoying. "I was about to lose it if he was ready to go already. I swear, he's barely patient enough to wait at a crosswalk." But she smiles at the end and we smile back.

"I'm Jacq," Jacq says, and flicks her wrist, presenting me next.

"I'm Sydney."

"I'm Dee. Sorry, I don't actually hate my boyfriend."

"Secret's safe with us," Jacq says. Then she nods to the front of the line. "So . . ."

"Oh, right, sorry." Dee leans in close, so we do, too. "Do you guys know who Gigi Goodall is?"

My stomach jumps. "Is that rhetorical?"

Dee smiles. "Have you been on her Insta today? She's in town for a few days with a pop-up in Midtown, but, like, an hour ago she dropped a story saying she has a big announcement, especially if you're a senior in high school who loves to cook." Dee curtsies like that's her to a tee. "Here, you wanna see?" She pulls up IG on her phone and holds it so the three of us can look at once. "Rumor is she's announcing an apprenticeship and this is the line to apply."

I stare at her phone, at Gigi's full face on screen, the one I met IRL just a few weeks ago. She's saying something I can't hear, but the stickers she added are plenty. A flashing, hot-pink one that says, *Big News!!* Another neon-yellow one that's blinking on and off, telling people where to be: 58th and Broadway at 3:15.

Sydney

Exactly where we are. Seven minutes early.

This was it—*this* was the reason she told me to watch her page for an announcement coming soon. It wasn't coming tomorrow, it was coming today, and I just never checked. Something inside me—the part that always counted the amount of leaves on a clover or used to hide in Genevieve's reading books about girls with magic—sputters awake after its yearslong coma.

"This . . ." Jacq slowly starts, and I can hear the smile on her lips as she goes on. ". . . is un. Real."

Dee smiles as she slides her phone into her purse. "Do you cook?"

"Not even slightly. But she does," Jacq says, bumping me with her hip.

"Actually?" Dee's excited like she's never met someone else like her. "Me too. Nothing, like, professional, obviously. But I feel like Gigi doesn't care about that, you know? Like, it's not nepotism with her. Seriously, if I could do one thing forever, it'd be food."

"Oh, *a hundred percent*," I insist, and my excitement pours out of me, too. I guess I've never met someone else like me, either. "All the flavors, and the colors, and the styles . . . it's edible art. And the way she knows food doesn't have to be fancy to be amazing. Like, it can be so delicious, and require so much technique, without alienating half of the population because it's unpronounceable."

"*Exactly!*" Dee insists. "Food is just love. And love is for everyone."

Food is just love. And love is for everyone. I've never heard it like that before. But it makes my skin tingle.

Sydney

"So, you're applying," Dee concludes. "I mean . . ." She glances from me back to Jacq like it's the most obvious thing in the world. "You literally have to."

I glance at the line—at least twenty more people have gotten behind Dee since Jacq and I started talking to her. It's unbelievable. Not that the line is growing—that part is completely believable—but that this moment has happened so many times and today is my first day being a part of it. That I've been so busy being stuck that I missed Gigi's announcement all the days she made it.

And the wildest part? I don't even regret it.

Because that's the reason I got to do that cooking class. That's the reason I got to try all those different foods. That's the reason I got to see Gigi's pop-up with my own eyes and eat all her incredible recipes. That's the reason I got to go to Wellesley and lie in the grass with Marcus while he looked into my eyes and believed in me.

"Syd," Jacq says, twisting me toward her so it's just the two of us. "I know this is pretty much sacrilegious to how you were raised, but I really think we should deal with your parents later, and you should give this a shot. There's *no way* we just stumbled upon a chance for you to learn from your idol on accident—"

"I'm gonna do it," I tell her. Not hesitantly. Not nervously. I'm as sure about this line as Marcus was about me back in Chicago.

Jacq blinks because she doesn't know this Syd. The one who wouldn't walk away. The one who's lived this day nearly thirty times before. She had no idea how much could change since yesterday, and neither did I.

Sydney

But she smiles. And I can tell—thank God—that she likes it.

🌹🌹🌹

In Jacq's bathroom, we conduct our ritual, but this time we include my dreams, too. We want FAM, and internships with the coolest studios, and a mentorship with Ava DuVernay. We want Gigi's apprenticeship, and a passing grade in precalc, and parents who will forgive me for what I'm not. We want to matter in every room we walk into and leave people feeling better than we found them. We want to be happy—and anytime we're not, remember that we will be again.

When her dad gets home, he says it smells like a Yankee Candle shop blew up in here.

I feel like that means we did it right.

🌹🌹🌹

"So, you can submit a written application with a short essay or you can submit a video application. No prompt. Just 'tell me about yourself.' Which is *so* Gigi but also ridiculously harder than a specific question. But it's okay because Jacq is such a phenomenon when it comes to storytelling and making videos . . . I have to show you what she sent to FAM one day. It's actually ridiculous."

I lie on my bed, on top of my comforter, with one knee bent and my other leg crossed over it. I watch my foot as it bobs.

"You know I could also just talk to Gigi for you," Marcus offers.

"I don't want you to. I want to get it myself. Don't you think I can?" I'm just messing with him, though. I know he does.

Sydney

"Of course I do," he says, anyway. "If anything, I'll probably hurt your chances. She'll probably be like, 'If she's so great, what's she hangin' out with you for?'"

I roll onto my side and bring my pillow with me, hugging it to my chest. I stayed at Jacq's for asparagus dinner—it actually wasn't that bad: quiche—and got home a couple of hours ago. It's dark. I'm trying not to watch the clock, and it's easier tonight than it's ever been. I know 10:15 is probably close, but I'm happy right here and want it to stay that way for as long as possible. "Tell me about your day." I settle in, ready to hear all about it. "We've been talking about mine forever."

"Yours was way more exciting than mine. Just school. Nothing special."

"Did you do the goody-goody head tilt in your picture?" I smile.

"Did I do it? I practically invented it."

I squeeze my pillow, wishing it was him. "Even if we're still stuck, I'm glad we did this today."

"You know, Syd," he says. "I'm glad we did this, too. I think you really were meant to have this day. I mean, it was everything we've been talking about, and you deserve all of it. Really. And if this wasn't a day that deems you worthy of a tomorrow, I don't know what is."

I've never heard Marcus bet that tomorrow's coming. But of the two of us, for *him* to think we've gotten there . . . it hits different.

I still don't check the time, I just listen to his voice. We make plans for all the September twenty-fourths that will hopefully, once a year, follow this one. We say we'll always go to Dunkin' that day. We'll

Sydney

always order the sandwiches that—put together—make a whole one. We'll make a wish every time we see the number two—whether in an address, or on a clock, or on TV. We'll commemorate it like the rest of the world treats 11:11, except two will just belong to us.

The way I fall asleep is perfect. The kind of sleep I'm only aware of once I'm waking up from it.

And that's when it turns terrible.

Because it's screeching tires.

Blinding headlights—

Forget it.

You know how this goes by now.

September 24, Take Thirty: 7:01 a.m.

Sydney

ARE.
  YOU.
    KIDDING ME????

September 24, Take Thirty: 7:02 a.m.

Marcus

Okay, so I kind of lied.

I've kind of *been* lying.

Not explicitly. Nothing I've said isn't true. Today *is* picture day. They bring in an outdoor setup and a library setup and depending on which one your parents requested in the order form, you either go to take your picture in the morning or the afternoon.

All that's real. And it's a hundred percent the day I could have had. It's the day I *did* have while she had hers. I wanted that to be enough.

I pull out my phone and put in Syd's number. I take a deep breath and start typing before I can decide not to. It's hard getting the words out. It's harder knowing she's probably devastated right now. That she had a day like that and it didn't change a thing.

But I don't want her thinking that because I think it *really did* change something. I meant what I said last night—that day was meant to be hers.

So that's what I'm saying in this message, as best I can. To please try again. One more time. Do everything she did the first time so I can do my part for real. That I never meant not to. That it was just hard.

Every single one of these repeat days, all of this has been so damn hard.

> **But please, Syd? I'm so, so sorry.**

Send.

I lie there for a second, waiting for her to read all my nonsense. Hoping she's willing to stomach it—stomach *me*—just one more time. The dots come and go. She's typing, then she's not. Then she's typing again.

I haven't sweat in this bed since we got back from the beach, but I'm starting to now. It never should have taken all this—I never should have had to watch Syd lose her perfect day.

But I did.

My phone vibrates. It's her. Every time my heart beats, it hurts.

She says:

> **I don't even know what to say**

And then:

> **Don't be sorry. I'M so sorry. For you . . .**

And finally:

> **I had no idea we've been living in the worst day of your life**

September 24, Take Thirty:
The day he should have had

Marcus

I've never been in a church before. I'll probably never be back. Don't know how I could without this moment being all I see. I don't remember getting dressed, or how I got here, or even what this place looks like from the outside. But this part? Standing at the beginning of this aisle, all these empty pews on the left and right while a casket sits lit up and open on the other end? This part is a part of me now. I'll never be able to forget it.

"Excuse me?" a heavy voice says next to me. My instincts are slow but I turn to face him. He's in a black robe with a cross stitched into both sides. "Forgive us, but we're closed this morning for a private funeral."

"Yeah. That's why I'm here."

Maybe it was this hoodie that made him think I was just wandering around—the one I've thrown on top of these same clothes every day for the past thirty todays in case I somehow ended up coming here. I've got Mom's pink sticky note in the front pocket, but I've

Marcus

been messing with it so much, it's just pulp. *I'm sorry I had to leave so early this morning but I'll see you soon. We're gonna be ok. M&M forever* ♡

"Oh, I apologize," he says, handing me a couple of pieces of paper folded and stapled together. "We're letting family in first this morning. Are you family?"

I glance down at what he gave me. There's this big picture of Austin on the front, cheesing like a little kid. He'd be clownin' it if he were here. I can hear him now. *What am I so happy about? I won the lottery and forgot?*

I almost close my fist around it, crush it the way this past month has crushed me. But I look back at the guy waiting on me instead. "He's my brother."

His mouth goes into a tight line. "I'm deeply sorry for what you're going through."

Then he walks off somewhere else.

The aisle is long and it feels steep, even though I can't tell if I'm facing uphill or down. One step is like climbing and the next one's like falling. The pews are too far apart to hold on to, and this little program that Dude at the Door handed me—it's worthless.

So, I just hold myself up. One step at a time.

When I reach the casket, and Aus is lying inside with his eyes closed, in this blue-and-white striped button-down I've never seen before, it just seems impossible. All of this. How anything like this could even happen. How a person can just go. How *my* person can just go.

I try to breathe.

Marcus

I don't know what I was expecting this to be like, or what I thought I was gonna see. What I do see, though, isn't my best friend. I know that for sure. On some level, that kills me. Because if this is the last time I'm ever gonna see him, and this isn't even him, what now?

But it also, for a second, makes this whole thing feel a little different. Because if this isn't Aus, maybe what we bury won't be him, either. Maybe he isn't really gone, not completely.

I sniff hard and wipe my cheeks on my sleeve. Even though I know I'm not looking at Austin, I can't take my eyes off him.

"I'm sorry I took so long." My empty hand is in a fist and I bang it on repeat against my thigh. "You shouldn't have had to wait on me like this. But something about not coming here, not finishing things . . . it meant it wasn't final, you know what I mean? Like it wasn't time to figure out what's next. Because I really don't know, man." I shake my head. "I have no idea what comes after this.

"But I don't want you worrying about that, okay?" I sniff and clear my throat. "I'm gonna figure it out, I promise. I'm gonna get myself back together."

I slide my tongue along my back teeth, trying to fight how big these tears could be if I let them come. I missed talking to him. It hurts so bad, but now that I've started, I don't want to stop.

"You got some good people to meet now. Alright?" I sniff again. "You got, um, this dude named Sebastian Michaels. Real smart. Went to Corinthia, was gonna be a doctor. He has this, um, unbelievable sister who has kind of saved me the past few weeks. So. Let him know that, okay? That he's got a really special sister.

Marcus

"And, um, I'm not sure this other guy's name but he's got a daughter named Dana—she, uh, gets an oat milk latte from Dunkin', and she goes to Fordham for psychology, and she has this bag that has, like . . . a duck on it. Say hey to him, too, because if he's anything like her, he's a real cool dude.

"And, you know"—my voice is so broken that there's hardly any left—"I'll be around for your mom and mine. Bet. I'm gonna make sure they're good. And um, yeah. I miss you, man. I know we don't really talk like this, but . . . I love you. No cap. We'll do it up even bigger the next time around, right? In the next life, you and me all over again."

I've gotta walk away now. My body can't take it anymore. I turn around and drag myself to a pew on the right. I sit down in the corner. And then I hunch over and cry.

🌹 🌹 🌹

I recognize Ashe's fingernails on my back. She always keeps them longer than Mom does. I'm not sure how much time it's been since I got here, and I don't lift my head, but I slide my arms around her waist and squeeze. Her thick, curly hair grazes my cheek. She smells like Ice Breakers because she pops them like an addict. It's wild how normal some things can still seem in the middle of a storm.

I've gotta stop, though, get myself together. She and Aus were obsessed with each other. No one was about to tell him anything about his mom. She loved him so much—it was the clearest thing I've ever seen.

Marcus

So I've gotta stop crying. For her. She lost her son.

She lost her sun.

When I look at her, she's as pretty as she's always been, but the rims of her eyes are red. From her perspective, we saw each other two days ago. She slept at our place and we turned on a movie, but none of us were really watching. You know what's tough? Finding stuff to watch after someone passes away. Happy people are hard to watch. Sad people are hard to watch. Funny people are hard to watch because it feels like you shouldn't be laughing. And all that stuff where someone's passing is just a plot point? That stuff's impossible.

I don't even remember what we ended up picking.

There are a couple more people here now. Not many. Ashe had said she only wanted family and close friends here. We've been saying we'll do something bigger in a few months, something happier where more people can come. Not sure how likely that is, but sometimes it feels nice to talk about.

"I'm sorry," I tell Ashe. I never have before. Not really. The night it all happened, when I was losing it, I remember crying into her shoulder and saying how sorry I was while I tried to sober up. But I don't think that counts.

"No," she says, running a thumb under my eye. It comes out easy for her, like I'm a baby who just tried to stick my finger in an outlet.

"Yeah," I insist, holding her gaze because she deserves it. "I never should have said we should get in that water. I never should have done that to either one of you. I didn't mean to take him from you—Ashe, I swear to God, I never thought anything like this could be real—but I'm gonna do everything I can, I promise. My whole life is gonna be about trying to make this even a little bit better for you..."

"No," she says again, and she takes my face in her hands. Her tears are a steady stream, but her voice doesn't shake, and that's because Ashe doesn't shake. Not when rent was due and we didn't have it. Not when she was on her thirtieth job interview and still nothing. Ashe is always solid. At least, in front of me. "No, because you see, sweetheart, you've already done everything. You're the only person in the world who loves Aus like I do. You showed him that every single day. You're showing him that right now. So, no, Marc, you've done *everything*. There's nothing left to do.

"You are not. Allowed. To blame yourself for this. Okay? I am his mother. I knew you were both drinking that night. I didn't pay attention to what you were doing or where you were going..."

"What—"

"...and I can't even explain it, but I had this pit in my stomach just after ten o'clock that night, right when it was happening. I felt something and I ignored it..."

I squint. *Was it* right after ten o'clock? Like...

10:15?

"...and it was the biggest mistake of my life."

"Stop." I frown. I shake my head. No way. *She's* not allowed. She's not allowed to think that, or to say that. *"You're perfect*, Ashe. In *every way*, and you can't... *you* can't think you had anything to do with any of this. Okay? *Please*. Aus would hate that. Aus would kill me if I let that happen."

Marcus

I don't know when I did it, but somehow my hands are holding her face now, her tears tracing my fingers.

"He would kill *me* if I let that happen to you, too," Ashe whispers.

She pulls me back against her and it hits me that she's right. I know how she feels. She can't let this be my fault any more than I can let it be hers, and maybe that's the best thing I can do for her right now. Forgive myself so she doesn't hurt the way I will if she doesn't do the same.

"You know I McDreamy you always, right?" She says it while our chins are still stuffed into each other's shoulders.

God, that hits me. This phrase Mom and Ashe coined back when *Grey's Anatomy* was life. When the main girl kept choosing this one doctor—McDreamy—no matter what. Like he was water. Like he was air. It's the biggest way you can choose someone, as far as they're concerned—to McDreamy them.

I close my eyes and tell her, "I'll always McDreamy you, Ashe."

Behind us, Mom wraps her arms around our shoulders. I don't see her, but I'd know that woman anywhere. She squeezes us in the tight way that only she does, and I hear her kiss Ashe's head right before she kisses mine.

Then she whispers in my ear, "I hope this is the worst thing we'll ever have to do. But I promise you, even if there's more, we'll do it together."

We will, that's the thing. Even if Syd and I don't get unstuck—even if we never do—I'll be here every today that comes next. Just like they've been. Like I always should have been. Going through hell but going through it together.

Marcus

Man, they deserve a tomorrow, though. So does Syd.

And for the first time since everything stopped, a part of me sort of feels like I deserve one, too.

🌹🌹🌹

"Javi," I say, as the bell over the door at Nina's jingles behind me. "How's it going, man?" He's swamped already. It's just about 12:45 and the lunchtime rush is what it always is.

"Hey, what's up, man?" he calls to me in between making change for the woman at the front of the line. "Felix is in the back. I'll catch up with you in a bit."

"Cool, thanks."

I called before I came, just in case I was running late and Mr. Felix left before I had the chance to get here. When I talked to Javi on the phone, he said he'd just heard from Mr. Felix. He was on his way in.

Ask him to wait for me? I said.

You got it, man, Javi said back.

I jog down the short hallway to the room with the small desk where he prints the paystubs. I've been rushing since I left the church and everyone else headed to the cemetery. It's upstate somewhere. Some place I'm convinced I'll never go. Not because I'm scared of it, or avoiding it, or it hurts too bad. That's just not where Aus really is. So I don't really see the point in me being there, either.

I push through the door, breathing hard, and Mr. Felix is sitting behind his desk with his reading glasses slid down to the tip of his nose. He hates those things but also can't read without them. Says they make him look like Mother Goose.

He slides them off, face stone straight. "What're you runnin' from?" he asks, real serious about it. There was a time I could tell him the cops were trailing me and he'd hate me for it, but he'd still help me hide. I really hope that time hasn't passed.

I shake my head, catch my breath. "Runnin' to, sir," I correct. "I just didn't want to miss you. I was hoping we could talk. If you have a minute."

He pushes back in his desk chair and folds his arms over his stomach. "It's been a while."

"I know." I take a step closer and pull the rolled-up program out from the back pocket of these dress pants. I hand it to him and step back to where I was. "The funeral was today."

Mr. Felix doesn't say anything. He just runs his hand down his mouth and slowly flips through the pages.

I clear my throat. "You can keep that one. That's kind of why I came by. I wanted to make sure you had it."

"I'll be damned, son," he whispers to himself. With his hand still on his mouth, he asks, "You've been doing alright?"

"For a long time, no. But today, I am."

He rolls the program back up the way I had it, and he stands up and walks around the desk. He leans against it and crosses his ankles. He taps the tube of papers against the hand that's not holding it. "You know," he says, with the same stern stare he always has. "We tried not to take it too personally when we didn't see you anymore after we heard the news."

Marcus

"We or you?" I swallow hard and add, "Sir." I stuff my hands in the front of my sweatshirt so he can't see me wringing them out. "Because if I should say sorry to everyone, I will. But I really want to say it to you. The last thing I wanted was to disrespect you. Ever. I just . . . I really just didn't know what to do."

"You're not supposed to know what to do when something like this happens, son." He leaves the program on the desk as he walks over to me. "People three times your age don't know what to do when this happens to them." He grips my shoulders. "But you know what you don't do? Hey—" He smacks his fingers against my cheek when I don't answer. "You know what you don't do?"

"What don't you do, sir?"

He's back to gripping my shoulders like he's gonna squeeze this truth into me even if it means dislocating my arms. "You don't try to do it alone."

He hugs me. I hug him back. It's different than it was when I was in this office before. Different in a million ways. The first time I was here, I was lonelier than I've ever been before in my life. When Mr. Felix hugged me then, it didn't matter—it didn't change anything. It was like being on the phone with someone who's on the other side of the world. Just because you can hear them doesn't mean they're close.

I really think that's why I avoided this day for so long. I couldn't imagine doing it while I was so damn lonely. But you know what? It's almost like going to that funeral helped me realize I'm *not* lonely. Or, at least I don't have to be. Those people there today, *they* get it. Mr. Felix, here, right now? I really think he gets it, too.

Marcus

"Can I come back?" I ask. "Clean the kitchen at night? Not for the money—I don't even want you to pay me. I just want to be around again. If that's okay."

"I'll tell you what," Mr. Felix says, and I really hope whatever comes next is a term I can abide by. I need this. I need it bad. "If the guys in the kitchen say it's good with them, then it's good with me."

I chuckle and he rubs my head, letting me go. Those guys aren't about to tell me no.

"Rules stay the same," he says, walking around his desk and having a seat. "Show me you did your homework or you're not getting in."

"Yes, sir."

He nods. "I'll see you tomorrow, then."

I sure hope so.

"Yes, sir."

🌷🌷🌷

I got a hoop to myself at the court two blocks from the apartment. Talk about a miracle.

Came straight here from Nina's, didn't even change. I haven't balled in two months, but I melt back into it like I never stopped. It feels good to move again, to hold a basketball, to take some shots. There's something missing, something huge—don't get me wrong. The way Aus and I used to play one-on-one on this court was like we were playing for all future smack-talking rights. I miss it more than I could even try to say. But something about being out here again makes him feel closer, not further away.

"That doesn't look so hard."

I smile as I rebound for myself and take another shot before turning to see her. Her fingers laced through the metal fence. Squinting as she watches me because the sun is setting in her direction. Jeans. Chucks. Long-sleeved top. She's so pretty, man, I can't take it.

"Why do people get paid so much to do that?" Syd goes on.

"Blessed," I answer, laying it up. I catch the ball as it falls through the hoop. "Come on. Let me see you shoot."

She walks onto the court and I pass her the ball when I'm sure she's close enough to catch it.

"You got here okay?" I texted her when I first got to the court to let her know where I was. She wrote back right away and asked if she could come, too. Told her she didn't even have to ask.

"Punched two old ladies who tried to mess with me at Forty-Second Street." She does this cute little hop when she takes her shot. It bounces off the rim and I jog out to get it for her. "But other than that, smooth sailing."

"Can't trust old people, man." I pick up the ball. "They be smugglin' stuff in those walkers, too."

I roll the ball to her while I walk back to where she is. She waits for me to get close. Then softly, she asks, "How was it today?"

"Awful," I tell her. "And it felt really good."

Her eyes hurt deep. "I'm so sorry for you," she says. "But I'm *so happy* for you, Marcus."

"I wasn't trying not to tell you what this day really was. I should've, but I think . . . I think I just never wanted you to look at me like I'm the kind of guy who'd miss his best friend's funeral."

She picks up the ball at her feet. "I'd like looking at you no matter what."

I wipe the smile off my face with the back of my hand. "Tell me your day stayed good?" That's the only missing piece right now. "Tell me you did everything like you did the day before."

"Identically," she promises. "Except for this part." She bounces the ball with both hands. "You think you'd be as good at teaching me how to play basketball as you were at teaching me how to ride a bike?"

"You mean am I good at everything? Yes."

She laughs. Don't get me wrong, I love that sound. But, right now, she's laughing a little harder than seems fair. "Yeah, *okay* . . ." She pushes the ball into my chest. "Prove yourself."

I start easy, of course. Take her right up to the hoop and have her stand off to the side. I make sure she can see that red rectangle on the backboard. I tell her to aim for it—try and hit it, and the ball should go in every time.

"There's a whole box to aim at?" she asks. "Okay, I was joking when I first asked why people get paid so much to do this, but now it's kind of a real question."

"Syd, you've been out here two minutes. Don't make me make you take that back, alright? Now, aim for the rectangle."

She smiles and bites back whatever she might have said in response. She shoots, hits the rectangle, and scores.

I catch the ball as it falls through the hoop. "Nice. Two points."

Marcus

Easiest shot in the game. But she still looks at me like I'm something special. And when she does, it's almost enough to make me believe that I am.

We play a long, fake game of one-on-one while the stars come out and streetlights turn on. I let her take shots she shouldn't be open for and foul her over and over because I can't resist hugging her from behind. I shoot left-handed to give her a better chance and don't call traveling. I mean, her whole game plan is traveling. I'm not about to break that habit in one practice.

We laugh so hard. I'm exhausted but I want to keep going until we can't anymore. Let the universe decide it's over, not us.

We call time-out so Syd can have some of my water, and I take some free throws while she walks over to my pile of stuff.

"Hey," she calls.

"Yeah?" I answer as I take my next shot. But she doesn't say anything, so I look at her. "Yeah?" I frown. "What's the matter?"

She's on her knees next to my sweatshirt and my water bottle. She's got her phone in her hand. She's staring at me. "It's 10:37."

I guess that is kind of late. "You gotta get out of here?"

She squints at me like I forgot her Dunkin' order. *"Marcus."* She blinks. "It's *10:37 . . .*"

Oh.

OH.

"Hold up . . ." I grab my phone from my pocket and check, too. I guess I missed my alarm because we were messing around so much.

"It's 10:37 and we're still here!" She runs into me, leaps onto me, hugs

me so tight I hope she never lets go. I hold her while her legs are wrapped around my waist. "You have to meet Jacq tomorrow. She's gonna be obsessed with you. You can help us shoot my video app for Gigi. And we can pick out prom colors, like, real ones—" She laughs into my face, that beautiful smile and those beautiful eyes. "Do you promise not to hate me for all the annoying stuff I'm gonna make you do?"

To be honest, I've never really let myself think about it. I was always ready to do unending todays with Syd, but I never once imagined a real tomorrow. The closest I ever got was while we were in Chicago, and I saw how bad she wanted Wellesley, and I knew how bad I wanted her to have it. But even then. That would be a year away. It's wild how sometimes that's easier to think about.

But Syd's gonna be great at tomorrows, I can tell. They're never gonna feel the same again. They're gonna be something I lie awake thinking about. Something I can't wait for.

That smile hasn't left her lips, and the best thing that could ever happen would be if it never does. "Okay, that wasn't rhetorical, and I actually need you to reassure me now because I'm kind of freaking out."

"You're not gonna annoy me," I promise. "And I can't wait to meet Jacq tomorrow."

She squeals, takes my face in her hands, and then kisses me like it's our last day instead of the beginning of so many more. I don't want to sound like that guy right now—the one who gets the girl and a dance sequence while the credits roll—but I know for a fact that the luckiest thing that's ever happened for me was meeting Sydney Michaels.

And if I never had, I'd spend the rest of my life trying to.

September 25: Tomorrow

My alarm is so loud, I can hear it behind my eyeballs.

I grab my phone off my nightstand and turn it off. I'm the kind of sleepy that if I don't sit up right now, I'll pass out again before I even officially wake up, and I can't sleep in. Zero chances I'm letting that happen. Not on the day we've been waiting for.

I prop myself up on my pillows and open Instagram. I go straight to Gigi's page and slow-scroll like the biggest fangirl. The link in her bio has all the deets about the apprenticeship and I read it *a hundred* times after I crawled into bed last night. Legit. I could recite those words like Beyoncé lyrics at this point. I know I'm being moderately and/or extremely obsessive. If I get this apprenticeship, and Gigi ever finds out how many times I stalked her page, she'll probably have a pretty valid case for pursuing a restraining order.

But I haven't been excited in forever. Not like this. I didn't even know how much that feeling could change me until it wasn't there.

I open my messages and type:

> Happy first day of the rest of our livessss

I drop my phone on my mattress and roll off my bed. For some reason, I kind of feel like a shower even though I took one last night. I tap my phone so the home screen lights up. 7:05.

I have time.

When I get back to my room—wrapped in my towel and decidedly wearing my black pinafore dress from Zara today because it makes me feel unstoppable and cute at the same time—I have a text back on my phone. I smile as I sit on my bed and read the response.

> Meet me at 55th and 8th before school today?

I write back instantly.

> Yes ♥

I do want to get to school, like, ten minutes early again so I can talk to Mr. Wilson about tutoring, so I start getting ready a little faster than usual. Gigi wants an apprentice with at least a 3.5 GPA. So, not failing precalc is kind of ideal.

When I'm finished getting dressed, I pack my bag and send an update text as I sling it onto my shoulder.

> On my way

Before I go, I poke my head into my brother's room. "Hey, Bas. I can't really hang this morning; I'm trying to get some extra help in math from Mr. Wilson. I promise I'll update you on everything soon, especially because yesterday had some *major* developments." I rap my knuckles on his doorframe and bite back my smile. "Wish me luck, okay?"

I pull the door back to just as closed as I found it, and grab my keys on my way out of the apartment.

My phone starts vibrating in my hand on 55th and 8th.

I almost don't answer it because I'll be across the street—and we'll be together—in just another twenty seconds, according to the countdown on the crosswalk signal. We'll get to have this day—a day I'm already so convinced is gonna be so big and so *good*—in no time.

But I answer my phone, anyway, because *this is what excited feels like*. That thing I stopped feeling and never knew I could miss. That thing that makes twenty seconds, even *two* seconds, this intolerable amount of time to try to contain yourself.

"Hi! I'm about to cross Eighth with the rest of New York." There are a hundred people on this street corner.

"I. GOT. IN!!!!" she screams.

I scream, too, but so many people are muting out life with their headphones right now that no one even notices.

"JACQ! I freaking *knew* it!" I insist, stepping into the street and looking uptown for a break in the traffic. Because now these seconds really *are* taking too long. "You're about to be the best thing that's ever happened for FAM. You're gonna be there for three weeks and already have a building named after you—"

"*Hey, hey, hey, hey!!*"

A man's voice yells, and I jump backward just in time to avoid getting clocked by him and his bike, zooming uptown with so much speed, it whips my hair across my face. My heart stops.

Okay, so I do need to wait for these next couple of seconds.

He's in a business suit and already five blocks down. Jacq's going on in my ear and I'll be back to freaking out with her in a second, but right now, I'm just trying to catch my breath.

It's unreal how fast a bike can get you around this city.

One day, I really am gonna learn how to ride one.

September 25: Tomorrow

Marcus

Whoa, that girl almost got *rocked*.

She looks like she's okay, though. Just a little shaken up. Probably new around here if she's wandering into bike lanes like that.

Glad she's okay, though. I once saw a guy get hit by a bike so hard in Tribeca that he flipped in the air. Broke his nose. At least, I assume he did, with that kind of blood everywhere.

She's way too pretty for that. Not that only unpretty people should be getting hit by bikes, or that I should be the one deciding who is and who isn't. I'm just saying, she's a pretty girl.

Maybe I should tell her. I mean, why not? If I can get through yesterday, surely I can—

The light changes and I lose her just that quick now that everyone's crossing at once. She was headed east. I'm headed west.

Oh, well. That's how you know things like that aren't meant to be.

I open the door to Dunkin' and pull up to the back of the line. I've got another twenty minutes before school and this line will move quick. It always does.

I slide in my AirPods to kill the time.

When it's my turn, I pop one out. "Jenessa! How you feelin'?" But she just looks at me like I'm a mess and I can't help but smile about it. "That's alright. I still think you're gonna remember me one of these days. But hey, can I get a sausage, egg, and cheese croissant—"

I trip up because the "without cheese" part is instinctive, but I'm not sure I mean it this morning. Which is wild because that's been my order for years. But something about cheese doesn't sound so bad today.

"That's it," I finish.

Jenessa blinks at me like she wants to say, *Then what was that big ol' pause for?* "So that's all you want?"

"That's all I want."

"No Munchkins?"

"Nope. No Munchkins."

She types into her iPad and I hand over a ten-dollar bill. She gives me back my change and a receipt.

I glance at it as I head to wait somewhere in the back, so I know my number when it's called.

Order thirty.

Part Four:

Them

October 30, One Year Later

When tomorrow came, they didn't know what they were missing. They didn't know there'd been a magic so great that it'd stopped time just to bring them together. They didn't know they'd ever loved each other, or known each other, or had each other.

Without him but because of him, Sydney Michaels committed to her senior year, earned a B in precalculus, and applied to Wellesley Culinary Institute. They were thrilled to hear of her apprenticeship with Gigi Goodall—she was among their most esteemed alumni, after all. So, she told her parents *yes* after they had told her *no* and found a babysitting job in Chicago and the loans to cover the rest.

And, without her but because of her, Marcus Burke rejoined his high school's basketball team and rebuilt his family at Nina's. And when he made a very unexpected, last-minute decision to apply to a college in Chicago—a city that would never be New York but was calling to him, nonetheless—his mother hugged him and told him, *Go.*

Sydney and Marcus moved forward.

They were happy.

They were better.

Until they weren't.

They say when you love someone, you're not alright when they're not alright. Perhaps that holds true when you've never even met.

Or, at least, you don't know you did.

Because on October 30, on a particularly discouraging and overwhelming day, Sydney wandered into a Dunkin' right off Michigan Avenue.

Marcus came in two people behind her.

She ordered her sausage, egg, and cheese without the sausage or egg.

He ordered his without the cheese.

They waited on opposite sides of Dunkin', drowning in their thoughts while they fought to stay afloat. Too distracted to look up, to notice each other or anyone else.

Just like it was the first time the universe intervened, the day Sydney's brother had passed, and their order number was four.

And the way it intervened again, two days after Marcus had lost his best friend, and their order number was three.

And the way it did once more, almost a month later, and their order number was two.

When they bumped into each other this time, it wasn't unlike the times before. Marcus's breath caught in his throat and Sydney lost hers completely. Their jokes were easy, and maybe that's the way it always is with people you once knew. They both had a feeling, deep inside them—where the candles and the Christmas lights hide—that somehow, somewhere, their eyes were always meant to meet.

There are plans for us that are bigger than us. Roles we'll play that we may never realize. Stars we'll create but might never see shine. Maybe that's love in its simplest form—being with someone in their moment of need, even if it is only a moment.

The idea flashed into Sydney's mind just as quickly as it was gone, a shadow that makes you turn but as soon as you look, nothing's there. *Maybe I was meant to be here and so was he*, she thought to herself. At least, that's how it felt for an instant.

Because it was true. Regardless of if, this time, it was for now or forever.

"Order number one?" Marcus asked her, flashing a smile and his receipt between two fingers.

She held her receipt next to his, amused by how perfectly they matched. Then she bit back her own smile and answered, "Order number one."

Credits

ART AND DESIGN
Maithili Joshi
Maeve Norton
Bex Glendining

EDITOR
Tiffany Colón

COPYEDITOR AND PROOFREADERS
Sarah Mondello
Crystal Erickson
Sola Akinlana
Sarah Jacobson

SCHOLASTIC TEAM
Abigail McAden
David Levithan
Abigail Jordan
Seale Ballenger
Janell Harris

THE TOBIAS LITERARY AGENCY
Ann Rose

PART ONE: SYDNEY

"Invisible String" (Taylor Swift)
"Ironic" (Alanis Morissette)
"Issues" (Julia Michaels)
"Imperfect for You" (Ariana Grande)

PART TWO: MARCUS

"I'll Be There for You" (Method Man feat. Mary J. Blige)
"Nothing Even Matters" (Lauryn Hill)
"See You Again" (Wiz Khalifa feat. Charlie Puth)
"If the World Was Ending" (JP Saxe feat. Julia Michaels)

PART THREE: US

"You're All I Need to Get By" (Aretha Franklin)
"Where I Sleep" (Emeli Sandé)
"All My Life" (K-Ci & JoJo)
"Slide" (James Bay)

PART FOUR: THEM

"Lover" (Taylor Swift)